THE ARDIS COLE SERIES

THE Curse OF Senmut

VICKIE BRITTON
LORETTA JACKSON

Rowe Publishing
and Design

Copyright © 2011 by Vickie Britton and Loretta Jackson

ISBN 978-0-9833971-0-6

Published by
Rowe Publishing and Design
1080 15 Road, Stockton, KS 67669

For information about special discounts for bulk purchases, please contact Rowe Publishing and Design at www.rowepublishingdesign.com.

1 3 5 7 9 8 6 4 2

Printed in the United States of America

Rowe Publishing
and Design

To Rose Davis,
a wonderful friend and supporter

The Curse of Senmut

Preface

Historical legends reveal that Queen Hatshepsut did have a scribe named Senmut who was believed to have been her lover. Historical documentation exists that she wanted to erect obelisks of gold. There was also an expedition to Punt during her reign.

The spelling of Egyptian names vary according to the reference used. For consistency, we have chosen the references of American archaeologist James Henry Breasted, Ph.D., *A History of Egypt* (1921), for the spelling of historical character's names.

Chapter 1

The heat of the Egyptian sun beat down relentlessly on the Jeep's canvas roof, heat so stifling that barely a soul stirred in the Valley of the Kings. Beyond the little village of Qurna loomed vast reaches of desert, miles of sand broken only by deep-cut natural cliffs and eroding stone monuments left by the Egyptians centuries ago.

The rush of morning tourists had long since departed leaving the valley empty of life. Ardis felt oppressed by the merciless heat, by the immense solitude, but these conditions would have little effect on Jane Darvin. She would be waiting for Ardis at the newly discovered tomb of Senmut, sipping iced tea from her plastic jug, oblivious to the heat, oblivious to everything but her work.

Jane had not even taken time off last night to meet Ardis' flight from Chicago, but that lack of welcome had not in the least offended her. Ardis had worked as assistant to the famous Egyptologist long enough to know Jane's habits, long enough to understand her total absorption in her work.

Ardis had simply waited, as she had done so often before, for the inevitable contact. By noon her patience had been rewarded by a brief, scribbled message delivered by one of the hotel porters. *Ardis, meet me at site at three o'clock. Important! Enclosed are directions and ID that will get you through security. Jane."*

Important—Ardis pressed down harder on the gas pedal. Locks of ash-blonde hair spilled across her forehead as the Jeep bounced over the rough terrain.

Because of her sister's wedding, Ardis had missed the opening of the tomb. Even though an ocean separated them, she had felt the exhilaration of Jane's moment of triumph. Jane had defied history to prove that this tomb existed—the tomb of Senmut, scribe and architect to Queen Hatshepsut.

"Although two tombs believed to be Senmut's have already been discovered, his mummy has never been found," Jane had written. "The Egyptians often created false tombs to fool their enemies; for if their real tombs were discovered and their mummies destroyed, they believed they would be denied eternal life. I have evidence another tomb exists, and I'm not giving up until I find it, even if it takes me the rest of my life."

The discovery that had only a week ago made international headlines had quickly become a disaster for Dr. Jane. The tomb she had searched for throughout a career that spanned thirty years Jane had found stripped and empty.

Even though Ardis had not been on hand to console Jane, she had shared Jane's bitter disappointment at finding that tomb robbers had gotten to the site first. Nothing of value was left, not even a mummy in the tomb's sarcophagus. This had led scholars to debate whether the site Jane had found was indeed Senmut's final resting place or yet another false tomb.

Ardis had expected Jane to abandon the project, but instead she had remained in Egypt. When Ardis had received Jane's unexpected call, she had lost no time delegating her own work at the Chicago University and catching a flight out.

"I need you here right away. I must have an assistant. One I can trust."

Trust—the sinister implications of the word, like the swelter of the desert, closed around Ardis. She thought of all the questions she should have asked Jane on the phone and wondered why she had left them unspoken.

Only one reason would have compelled Jane Darvin to summon her to Egypt. Jane had discovered something in the empty tomb of great significance. Excitedly, Ardis began to form wild guesses. Jane could have deciphered a message left centuries ago by one of the world's greatest architects, Senmut, that did reveal his final resting place. Or she could have located some hidden chamber. Becoming even more anxious to talk to Jane, Ardis leaned forward as she drove, green eyes squinting against the harsh rays of sun. Ahead, the famous temple of Queen Hatshepsut loomed like a mirage through a wavering haze of light.

Ardis paused to study the map, but her attention was drawn instead to the magnificent temple of Deir el-Bahari. Queen Hatshepsut, the subject of Jane's life-long study, was the only woman who had ever ruled Egypt as a pharaoh. Even in its ruined state, the monument, designed by the queen's master architect, Senmut, seemed gracefully proportioned. The sprawling structure with its slender, almost Grecian-like columns fit naturally into the gigantic cliff and extended into the barren land in such a way that no eye could ignore it. Ardis remembered Jane telling her how centuries ago the armies of Thutmose III, a contender for the throne of Egypt, had smashed most of the statues and had obliterated the queen's name wherever it appeared and replaced it with his own. Once Thutmose had gained power, he had attempted to erase every trace of Queen Hatshepsut's existence.

Deep aversion for Thutmose III—for all people who desecrated graves—stirred in her. It took her a moment or two to shake free of her intense feeling of revulsion and glance again at the map. She should turn left about a mile beyond the monument, then right again. Six miles further, then another sharp turn should place her near the tomb site.

Ardis proceeded slowly, veering from the main route to follow the line of cliffs running south. She could make out only a bare trail through the hard-packed sand, but she could see the recent imprints of wheels. She marveled that Jane, always plagued by fragile health and now in her late fifties, was still physically able to cope with such rugged conditions. Ardis, robust and not yet thirty, was already beginning to feel an overpowering sense of exhaustion. She dreaded the thought of leaving the flimsy shelter of the Jeep. She should have thought to purchase a hat from the hawkers who had swarmed the streets of Luxor.

Ardis turned on the road that forked back toward the sheer cliffs. Ahead of her several guards lounged in the mid-day lull under a drooping shade. One of them strode forward and stood like a wall in front of her vehicle. Amid this desolation, Ardis was glad to see anyone, even a face so unfriendly.

"I have papers," she said, offering them to him.

He said nothing. He merely took his time examining the note Jane had written to her and the card that identified her as an archaeologist.

Ardis became weary of the wait, weary of the piercing rays of sun that bore down on her with increased intensity. "Have you seen Dr. Jane this morning?" When he didn't answer, she asked, growing more impatient. "May I go on through?"

He continued studying the papers, then never having said a word—perhaps he spoke no English—he brusquely motioned her forward. Ardis wondered who had chosen him, and why so many guards would be needed for an empty tomb.

About a fourth mile from the gate, a makeshift building set close beside the jagged, roped-off opening to the tomb. She had expected to find no one here except Jane and maybe a few workers, but she felt unprepared for this total look of desertion. Ardis pushed open the door to the shack and called, "Jane."

Light streamed from gaps in the wood, streaking across a worn desk littered with papers, a filing cabinet, and a cot with a tousled sleeping bag. Electricity from an outside generator supplied energy for the small fans scattered around the room. A huge water can set on a rough-hewn wooden table. Ardis knew Jane would pay no mind to the inconveniences. She had always been content to do without to be close to her work.

Ardis cut across uneven ground toward the excavation site. The gaping hole, roped off at the sides to prevent accidental falls, dropped off into a surprising depth. Weak bulbs suspended from a wire draped from the rafters overhead cast shadows upon carved and painted walls covered with endless hieroglyphics. Row after row of writing intermingled with symbolic pictures of snakes and scarabs.

Once Ardis had reached the bottom, the airless tomb closed around her, making it difficult to breathe. She could see the sarcophagus and two life-sized male figures crudely cut in limestone standing guard on either side. Some grave robber from the past had tried to chip at these also, but had failed in the attempt to break away large sections of the massive stone. The tomb seemed unimpressive, barren. No wonder Jane had sounded so vastly disappointed.

Beyond the sarcophagus, a soft light glowed where Jane had fashioned a work area. Ardis approached slowly. Jane's dark hair, streaked with sun and gray, had slipped loose from its silver clasp and spread across the desk. The glare of light fell across Jane's closed eyes and accentuated her high cheekbones and aquiline nose. Ardis felt a moment of empathy for Jane who rested, one arm supporting her head like a pillow. Jane, like Ardis, rarely slept all night, but caught quick cat-naps during the day and had fallen asleep waiting for her. Ardis touched Jane's shoulder, but Jane did not stir.

The disarray of papers on the desk showed that she had been busy sketching some of the tomb's wall writings. Ardis gathered some of the hastily scribbled hieroglyphics, which had fallen to the floor. As she did, she caught sight of a small, dark object lying close to the familiar red and white thermos of tea near Jane's foot. She recognized the distinctive shape of an obelisk, likely a replica of Queen Hatshepsut's that Jane must have been using in connection with her studies.

She shook Jane lightly. "Jane." With alarm Ardis now noted how gray Jane's skin looked, how a ridge of pale blue had formed along the edges of her mouth.

Ardis felt a stirring of panic. Jane was not asleep, but unconscious. How long had Jane been working in the unbearable heat before coming down into the tomb? Long enough to suffer heat stroke? The airlessness of the tomb, overwork, exhaustion—any one of these conditions might have triggered this collapse.

Ardis grasped one of Jane's hands and felt the slight, rapid flutter of pulse. At least she was still alive! But for how long? Ardis listened to Jane's faint, shallow breathing. All the while Jane remained motionless, with not even a flicker of her eyelids.

Ardis glanced toward the steep ladder whose rungs were placed so far apart. Bright sunlight from far above penetrated the semi-darkness. She must get Jane to the surface at once, to fresh air. But she would never be able to lift Jane up the precarious rungs of the ladder without help.

Ardis clamored back up the ladder. "Is anyone here?" Her frantic call seemed lost in the simmering emptiness. She must drive back to the gate and summon the guards even though that meant wasting precious time.

Before Ardis reached the Jeep, a tall man with straight, black hair and very broad shoulders appeared, halting in the angle of shade from the shack. He paused a moment, then moved quickly through the layers of fiery, desert heat toward her. At first, because of the white, gauzy material of his brussa shirt, she mistook him for one of the locals.

His image became indistinct in the glaring brightness of the sun. As her vision cleared, she could see his strong features, his dark eyes that regarded her with concern.

"Jane," Ardis gasped. "She's in the tomb, unconscious. We must hurry!"

He moved quickly to the entrance. Ardis followed, shakily descending the ladder. The stranger leaned over Jane. When he looked toward Ardis again, her own assessment echoed in his dark eyes.

Ardis' thoughts leaped to the time-consuming ferry ride back across the Nile to Luxor. "We'll never get her to the hospital in time!"

Decisively he lifted Jane. In his powerful arms Jane's thin form appeared weightless. "You go up first so you can help me get her through the entrance."

Above him on the ladder, Ardis looked back. One strong arm supported Jane, pressed her tightly against him, as if she were a small child. He used his free hand to pull them both upward. "Don't try to lift her. Just ease her forward on the ground."

Ardis gripped Jane's shoulders and guided her safely through the jaggedly-cut opening. "Let's take her to the cabin."

He carried Jane into the shack, laid her on the cot, and stepped away. As he gazed down at Jane, a muscle moved in his jaw line, betraying the fear his eyes did not reveal. "I'll go to the gate and call for a helicopter."

Ardis angled the fans on Jane, knelt beside her, and bathed her face with cool water. Nothing she did revived her. Once her eyes fluttered open, large, hazel eyes that soon fell closed again.

Ardis choked back tears. Jane Darvin, her mentor, Jane, the reason Ardis had decided to become an archaeologist, was going to die before the helicopter arrived! And there was nothing she could do to prevent it.

In despair Ardis rose, her gaze locking on the statue that dominated the cluttered shelf above the cot. Jane had called her the day she had received this award from the Cairo Museum—a beautiful replica of the rose-quartz sphinx Ardis had found in the desert so many years ago, the find that had launched her career making her internationally known. The rose-colored statue, its golden base embossed with Jane's name, in the heat and misery of the moment bore the appearance of a gravestone.

Ardis forced her eyes from the sphinx with its serene face of Queen Hatshepsut. Surely Jane's life wouldn't end here, in this stifling shack, with her life's work uncompleted! Dr. Jane Darvin must live! She had so much to do and to give!

Heavy footsteps sounded behind her, and Ardis whirled around. A short, burly Egyptian with a stern, leathery face entered. He looked only at Jane, striding forward and dropping to his knees beside her cot. Ardis could see his wide, thick shoulders, the touches of gray along his temples and at the nape of his thick-set neck.

Hopelessness, rage, and agony seemed to merge in his groan, "Oh, no! Not this!" He gathered Jane into his arms speaking pleadingly as he held her. "Jane, you've got to hear me. You've got to speak to me!"

His muffled voice became almost inaudible. Ardis soon realized he was speaking Arabic, saying some sort of prayer, or perhaps a continuing of his plea for Jane to return to him. Whatever it was, his words finally ended in harsh, broken sobs.

Who was he? Friend? Lover? How little she knew about Jane's personal life. His outpouring of emotion touched Ardis.

•

She found herself offering up inane words that presented no truth or comfort. "She's going to be all right."

He had not once looked toward her. He didn't now. She went on, "It could be heat stroke. Or just sheer exhaustion. Jane has always worked far too hard."

He ceased sobbing, his stony silence even harder to bear. Ignored and feeling a little faint, Ardis filled a glass from the cooler and offered it to him. He shook his head.

Ardis with shaking hands brought the drink up to her own lips. The water was warm and did nothing to soothe her dry, aching throat.

After what seemed like hours, the buzzing of a helicopter, like the cry of an angry hornet, broke through the stillness. The man who had left to summon help was the first to enter the room, others followed. The stocky Egyptian reluctantly released Jane and allowed the two attendants to lift her to a stretcher.

They followed Jane to the helicopter; then the Egyptian climbed in, as if it were his right as lover or husband to do so.

"We'll meet you at the hospital, Ramus," the tall man beside Ardis said.

Confronted by the whirl of blades and sudden rush of hot wind, they moved back toward Ardis' Jeep. Once the helicopter lifted and began its flight to Luxor, the dark-haired man slipped in behind the wheel and leaned over to open the door for Ardis. She climbed in silently beside him. They did not speak until they had passed the main gate.

"I'm Blake Lydon," he said at last. "Jane's assistant."

Assistant? Her gaze momentarily clashed with his, the words Jane had spoken on the phone echoing around her. "I must find an assistant at once. One I can trust." Why had Ardis sent for her when she already had an assistant? The answer struck Ardis with alarming certainty. Jane did not trust Blake Lydon.

Silence hung heavily around them. Thick waves of heat floated across the narrow road, across the buff-colored stones of Queen Hatshepsut's temple. "Jane didn't mention you," she said, trying to drive the suspicion from her voice. "How long have you worked for her?"

He did not answer her question directly. "I've known Dr. Jane or known about her, all my life."

"Everyone knows about her. Who is Ramus?"

"Ramus Montu is a long-time associate of Jane's. He lives at Qurna. He and his nephew Matthammed have been working with us at the tomb." Blake paused, as if trying to find words to convince Ardis of Ramus' qualifications. "Ramus used to teach at the Cairo University. He met Jane there years ago and has been her loyal friend and supporter ever since."

Blake was forced to slow the pace of the Jeep as they drove through the small, sun-baked village of Qurna. Near the ferry he parked the truck where Ardis had been instructed to pick it up, in a compound filled with battered vehicles used by Jane Darvin's crew. They waited in the shade of a palm.

Blake Lydon kept gazing anxiously across the long stretch of the Nile, his almandine eyes, opaque beneath dark brows. After a long time, when he seemed to notice her again, he said, "I arrived at the site just before the tomb was opened. I hadn't seen Jane for some time and her appearance caught me by surprise. She looked so weak, so very weary."

Ardis' heart sank. She wondered if Jane had sent for her because she had a disease that was growing progressively worse. "Has she been seeing a doctor?"

"You know Jane better than to ask. She wouldn't consider taking time away from her work."

An old man wearing a turban sat fishing by the shore near them. Beyond him, on the vast water of the Nile, little fishing boats bobbed tranquilly. The placidness of the scene did nothing to soothe Ardis as she waited for the ferry.

The boat along with the few occupants that ventured out in the hottest part of the day, set a leisurely pace toward Luxor's East Bank. When they reached the landing, they had to wait for a taxi to take them to the hospital, there to be told by the receptionist that Dr. Sirdi would be unable to talk to them for at least an hour.

In an upstairs waiting room, Blake went directly to Ramus, who slumped in a chair and stared down at the faded carpet. "I think I could use a cup of coffee," Blake said to him. "Let's go down to the cafeteria."

When Blake glanced toward her, Ardis declined the unspoken invitation to join them. After the two men left, Ardis went to the nurse's station and began to question the woman there.

"I know nothing," she was told in halting English. "The doctor will talk to you when he is finished with the examination."

Ardis continued her apprehensive waiting. She was soon jolted from her thoughts by a loud voice speaking to the nurse in Arabic. Although she understood little of the rapid exchange, she could make out the name Ramus Montu.

The nurse glanced up and vacantly scanned the room.

"Ramus is downstairs in the cafe," Ardis said.

The man turned with a swirling of his long white jellaba. His alert, black eyes glinted over a hooked nose and narrow tapering chin. He wore a turban with a flowing scarf, very white against extremely black hair.

"You must be Ardis," he said in heavily accented English. "We've all been anxious for you to arrive. I am Matthammed Yusef, Ramus' nephew." His voice lowered. "I came right over the minute I heard. How is Jane?"

"She's with the doctor now. We don't know yet."

Matthammed Yusef stepped closer to the couch and sank down beside her, stretching long, thin legs out in front of him.

He brought his scarf up to wipe the sweat from his glistening skin. "I was afraid this was going to happen," he said, more to himself than to her. For a few minutes he remained in deep dismay, the scarf pressed tightly against his lips. Then he said in a low, ominous voice, "I warned Jane not to disturb the tomb."

Ardis knew since Jane had allowed Matthammed on the site, he had met all of her very high qualifications. He surely couldn't be superstitious, couldn't believe in ancient curses. Ardis regarded him with astonishment.

As if he could read her thoughts, he said, "There is a curse." As he spoke, he drew himself up, feet now flat on the floor. "She didn't tell you about the curse, did she?"

"Jane wouldn't believe in curses."

"It is written in the tomb, 'Death will devour he who disturbs the eternal rest of Senmut.'" The widening of Matthammed's black eyes gave his thin face a look of intense fear. He started to speak to her again, but instead, rose.

Through the glass that separated them from the hallway, they could see Blake and Ramus heading back to the waiting room. Between them walked an elderly man in white. Their hushed voices warned Ardis that the news about Jane was not good.

"Ardis," Blake said, "This is Dr. Sirdi."

"What is causing Jane's condition?" Ardis asked.

"It baffles me," Dr. Sirdi said, "It's not heat stroke. She is suffering from a minor heart condition and her collapse could be related to that. Is she taking any regular medication?"

"Jane's not one to go running to the doctor," Ramus replied. "I don't think she was even seeing a physician."

"Will she recover?" Matthammed burst in.

"We're going to do all we can for her. I have been consulting Dr. Fahmy, a cardiovascular specialist from Cairo."

"Does he know anything about poison?" Matthammed demanded.

"Poison?" Ardis echoed, unable to keep the shock from her voice.

The old doctor, very sincere and patient, glanced at her and explained, "Deadly spiders and scorpions often lurk around the tombs, but there's no sign of an insect or snake bite."

"What about tomb dust?" Matthammed persisted. "What about the curse?"

Dr. Sirdi suppressed a faint, tolerant smile. "I think that can be safely ruled out."

Matthammed's gaze shot to Blake, then back to the doctor.

"She should never have gone into that tomb!" Matthammed's words, edged with panic, grew louder. His frightened gaze settled on Ardis. "I warned her again and again. She should pay attention to the curse. Now look at what's happened!"

"We'll find some logical explanation for Jane's illness," Blake spoke calmly. His gaze rested sympathetically on Ardis. "And a cure."

Matthammed's black eyes snapped with heart-felt conviction. "Jane's going to die!" he moaned. "You know it, Blake! No one can survive such a curse! It is certain to kill her—the curse of Senmut!"

Chapter 2

Ardis didn't leave the hospital until early the next morning. Mixing with the bustling crowd that strolled the Luxor streets increased her deep sadness. She couldn't bring herself to go back to her hotel, so she joined the group of tourists that walked by the row of sphinxes toward the gate of the Temple of Karnak

She quickly bought a ticket and wandered through ruined temples to a large, standing obelisk, one of a pair erected in the 1400's B.C. by Senmut for his queen. She gazed up at the obelisk, which rose like the Washington monument high into the already burning sky. The sight caused her to feel close to Jane and her lifelong mission.

Ardis could hear Dr. Jane's words now."The queen dreamed of sheathing the entire surface of the obelisks with solid gold, a feat that Senmut promised to accomplish for her. What a dream, what a tribute to their great love for each other and for their god, Amon. But Thutmose III began waging war on Queen Hatshepsut before her dream of the golden obelisks could be realized. What you see at Karnak is her unfinished dream, one standing obelisk, one fallen, both half-hidden— obelisks of stone."

No wonder Jane had been obsessively drawn to the study of this enigmatic queen and her forbidden lover, Senmut. Jane was in so many ways exactly like Queen Hatsehpsut, a lady of purpose and mystery. Jealousy and the malicious rumors that always encircle the strong and the great had plagued Queen Hatshepsut. In a like manner, rumors had always surrounded Jane. Rumors of a failed marriage and an abandoned child clouded her past. Whispers of many lovers.

Ardis felt a rush of fear, almost as if some unknown force were communicating with her. Jane's collapse had no natural cause. Someone, perhaps a person very close to her, wanted Jane out of the way—enough even to commit murder.

Jet-lag, long hours at the hospital, and the terrible heat, had perhaps caused irrational thoughts to intrude into her mind. Still, as she glanced again at the towering granite point of the obelisk, she once more was assailed with warning voices. Queen Hatshepsut, before her over-throw, must have felt the same undercurrents of treachery.

Abruptly, Ardis left the Temple of Karnak and returned to the hospital. Ramus stood alone near a window that overlooked a crowded market-place. His broad, slumped shoulders, the aura of exhaustion that hung over him, engaged her pity. She approached him, saying quietly, "Where's Blake?"

"He left with Matthammed. He'll be back soon."

Ramus did not turn toward her. She studied his profile silhouetted in brilliant light. Although he was not over five-foot eight, he seemed gigantic, powerful. His dark, weathered features, dominated by large, heavy-lidded eyes, reminded Jane of the Ramses II statues seen everywhere at Luxor; though Ramus' features seemed, somehow, much more mysterious, much harder than those carved in granite.

Ramus continued to stare out across tops of uneven buildings, a skyline broken with high towers of minarets.

"Matthammed is right," he spoke grimly, "Jane should never have disturbed this tomb of Senmut's."

His words, spoken with the same conviction as Matthammed's, startled her. She would not have thought that Ramus, well-educated and ambitious, would actually believe in the power of some ancient curse.

Ramus recited with voice low and haunting the fabled curse of Tutankhamen, "Death will slay with his wings whoever disturbs the peace of the Pharaoh."

Ardis thought about the endless reports exaggerated by the media, stories about how this "curse" had been inscribed above the doorway, and then later about how it had been written on a clay tablet found within the tomb. "No curse has ever been authenticated."

"Written or unwritten, the curse exists." Ramus' voice became grim and certain. "Less than two weeks after the opening of the burial chamber, Lord Carnarvon died from an infected mosquito bite. Other deaths followed, too many to be a coincidence."

Heavy stillness served to accentuate his words, to give life to his superstition, to place Jane Darvin's name among a long list of cursed victims. Despite the warmth of the room, a chill stole over Ardis.

Ramus faced her. "I've lived in Qurna at the tomb sites most of my life. My father knew all the famous Egyptologists, Howard Carter, James Breasted, Abrahim Khet. He used to talk about Carter's spells of dizziness and his hallucinations, almost the same as those experienced by Abrahim Khet." He paused, then explained, "Abrahim Khet was Nihisi Khet's father. Nihisi, who is a director at the museum at Cairo, raised Blake Lydon. Nihisi's father Abrahim died when he was in his early forties. Even though I was just a child at the time, I still remember his slow, agonizing death. He grew more and more depressed. Finally he couldn't answer a direct question or finish a coherent sentence." He paused solemnly. "I'm so afraid the same thing will happen to Jane!"

Ardis felt her heart sink. "When did you first notice any difference in Jane?"

"Shortly after the tomb was opened. When Blake Lydon arrived, they began sketching the tomb's hieroglyphics. That very day she had a severe spell of faintness." Ramus sighed wearily. "Since then Jane has had continual hallucinations which she confuses with reality. One afternoon she thought she saw a huge, black snake poised to strike. Only nothing was there." He turned abruptly back to the window. "It took me hours to calm her. I tried to get her to see a doctor then, but she refused. You know Jane."

Ardis did know Jane—logical, rational Jane. Her quick, clever mind had never been a breeding ground for illusions.

"Do you actually think there could be something present in the tomb, some mold or poison, that's causing this reaction?"

"The ancient Egyptians were master poison-mixers," Ramus replied. "They often dusted the tombs with compounds that have remained within those airless, stone walls."

"I've read about the practice of burning candles with wicks soaked in arsenic before sealing the tombs. But would that be deadly 3,000 years later, even in this case when the tomb seal had been broken once before?"

"Deep in those chambers deadly vapors would never totally disappear."

"But if it is poison within the tomb," Ardis asked, "why would only Jane be affected by it?"

"Why did so many escape the curse of King Tutankhamen? I don't know all the answers." Ramus, his large, dark eyes filled with tragedy, continued to stare from the window. "I've heard of strophantus poisoning. Strophantus is a plant which was well-known to tomb makers, one that produced symptoms similar to those Jane has—disruption of equilibrium and hallucinations. But it is also known to cause a reduction in heart rate, while Jane's heartbeat has accelerated." He lapsed into a gloomy silence. "They'll never find the cause. Even if they do, I'm afraid they won't be able to help Jane, not any more than they were able to save Abrahim Khet."

Dr. Sirdi spoke from the waiting room doorway, "I've got some good news." His announcement, following so soon after Ramus' doomed predictions, caused light to flow into the darkness of Ardis' thoughts.

Dr. Sirdi's voice expressed his great relief, "Ms. Darvin has regained consciousness." His gaze shifted from Ramus to Ardis. "She has been asking for you."

In response Ramus moved forward, but he was stopped by Dr. Sirdi's next statement. "No, she wants to see Ardis Cole. Alone."

Ramus stood, solid as stone, watching her leave. The doctor stopped outside of Jane's room. "Dr. Darvin is in no immediate danger, but she is extremely weak. A few minutes are all I can allow."

"Do you have any idea what is causing her illness?"

Dr. Sirdi shook his head. "I've come up with nothing definite. But from what I have learned of the lady, it's possible that she is suffering from sheer exhaustion. With her heart problems, she should not have been working under those strenuous conditions."

Dr. Sirdi listened carefully as Ardis confided in him what Ramus had told her about Jane's spells of faintness, the dreams and hallucinations. "Could it be possible that Jane did come into contact with a rare poison?"

"These stories about the tombs persist through the years," Dr. Sirdi replied, " They grow with each telling, but I assure you there is little substance to them." He added, not unkindly, "The type of behavior you are describing, including the delusions, are common symptoms of a complete emotional and physical collapse."

"I find that difficult to believe … about Jane."

"Anyone, given the right circumstances, can suffer a break-down."

Ardis' spirits rose at the sight of Jane's brave smile, white against skin deeply tanned from long hours in the blistering Egyptian sun. "You gave us quite a scare."

"I don't know what came over me," Jane answered in a voice Ardis could barely hear. "One moment I was translating hieroglyphics, the next I found myself here." She gazed around the sterile, white room in dismay, then struggled to lift herself. The effort seemed too much for her. As she fell back, her dark hair fanned out against the pillow.

Ardis' apprehension returned as she drew closer. Jane's arm, connected to the IV line, looked so frail. Ardis compared her with the old Jane, always brimming with life and energy. "You haven't been well for a long time, have you?"

"I haven't been … quite myself." Jane's eyes widened as they stared up at Ardis. In that instant they changed, became a livid, chemical green. Their feverish brilliance gave Jane an expression Ardis had never seen on her face before fear.

"You're going to be all right," Ardis said.

The eyes remained the same. They did not seem rational, yet the words she spoke did. "I sent for you, Ardis, because I know I can count on you. And that is important. I'm not sure who I can trust anymore."

A motion at the door caused Ardis to turn toward the doctor hovering anxiously outside. "I promised Dr. Sirdi I wouldn't …" Ardis started to say, but was stopped by the frantic grip of Jane's lean, brown hand.

"The minute you leave here, you must go to the tomb. Right where I was working, you will find a small stone obelisk.

This obelisk is of great importance. You must go after it right now. At once! And put it somewhere safe!"

Was this request part of another delusion? Questions flooded through Ardis' mind, questions she could not ask Jane because of her condition.

Jane's grip on her wrist tightened urgently. "My entire life's work hinges upon this. You must go alone. Now. Promise me!"

"Of course I will."

A glassy dilation appeared in Jane's pupils and her voice grew high and shrill. "You must waste no time!"

To comfort her, to calm her, Ardis reassured her, "You know I'll do anything you ask."

Jane's hand fell limply to the bed. "Ardis, you have been more to me than you know—student, friend, the child I never had time for." Her voice had become very faint, as if she were drifting beyond Ardis' range.

She stirred once again and said in a more natural way, "We'll talk later." Her eyes fell closed. "Now I can rest—knowing the obelisk will be safe."

Ardis intended to stop by the waiting room to speak with Ramus, but he was gone. In the heat of late afternoon, the street outside the hospital was deserted. Only one person walked close to the bank of the Nile, a solitary figure whose long robes fluttered … She waited impatiently for the ferry. When it finally docked, tourists, led by an exuberant guide, poured out. Only a few locals, laden with sacks and packages, boarded. The rows of empty seats gave her an eerie feeling as the boat began its slow journey to the opposite bank of the Nile.

Upon arrival, Ardis showed the ID Jane had given her and obtained a Jeep from the compound. In the back seat she discovered a flashlight, which she checked to make sure it still worked. She heard the distant barking of dogs as she drove past the village of Qurna and into the barren terrain beyond it. She passed Queen Hatshepsut's temple, Deir el-Bahari. Behind it rose jagged pinnacles of sun-scorched rock.

Ardis soon faced the endless world of sand and emptiness that stretched on and on. The air was so hot that the dunes appeared to undulate. The mental vision of Jane's frantic eyes mingled with the waves of heat and made the scene before her look wasted, bleak, and cruel.

Ardis felt a growing dread of entering Senmut's tomb. The fear she had read in Jane's eyes alerted Ardis to hidden dangers whose source did not lie with the ancient tomb builders.

An unexpected wind whirled, lifting and spinning grains of sand and dust. Gripped by the over-powering solitude, she narrowed her eyes and concentrated on locating the road that would wind back toward the cliffs whose great height broke the flat rim of desert.

Past the pile of limestone rocks, she eased along the rough road that would eventually end at the gate. She showed the ID to the same guard, who this time abruptly gestured her through.

The drive from the gate to the tomb seemed much farther; it seemed to separate her more completely from all human life. The shack where she had waited with Jane for the helicopter looked isolated in the harsh streaks of sunlight.

Her eyes shifted to the dark opening of the tomb and she steeled herself for what lay ahead. The noisy Jeep engine died with the flick of the key leaving an unearthly silence. Ardis remained motionless, scanning the area for some small trace of activity.

She wondered as she remained in the Jeep whether the obelisk was of genuine importance, or whether it just seemed so to Jane because of her illness. Whatever the case, Ardis had given her word to secure the object. Forcing every step, Ardis left the vehicle and moved toward the yawning, black entrance of the tomb.

She stopped to switch on the primitive generator system, grateful for the dim lights that would guide her way downward. Trying to control the pounding of her heart, she stepped on to the ladder and took two cautious steps, then stopped. Her eyes followed the pattern of hieroglyphics and settled upon the curving arch of wall that from her vantage point obscured the burial chamber. Illumination from a dim bulb eerily lit the dark shape of a writhing crocodile, a stake piercing its heart, a warning to those who would enter. In her mind the words echoed, *Death will devour he who disturbs the eternal rest of Senmut.*

The Curse of Senmut. Although Ardis did not consider herself superstitious, she hesitated, assailed by the thought of curses, of centuries-old poisons. With hands sliding along the sides of the ladder, she took one slow step downward, then another.

Ardis had reached the middle of the ladder when the step she was on unexpectedly gave way. As she dropped downward, the ladder supports tore away from the wall. For an instant Ardis felt as if she had been lifted and hurled away by some angry, supernatural force.

Unable to break her fall, Ardis attempted to land on her feet. A mistake. She was jolted by the sudden impact of stone, which brutally wrenched her right ankle as she hit and sprawled backward.

Dim, intermittent bulbs, lit from the generator system near the cabin so far above her, flickered and weakened into a strange, ghostly glow. Her flashlight had bounced away from her, hitting against the rock wall and then going out. She was more concerned about reaching the flashlight than about the stab of pain spreading into the arch of her foot and upward into the muscles of her leg. As Ardis crawled toward the flashlight, the overhead lights extinguished, leaving her engulfed in silence and darkness.

For a moment Ardis felt disoriented by pain and shock. She groped for the flashlight. Blindly she worked with the batteries, the switch. To her relief a weak beam of light appeared, but offered small assistance against such overwhelming blackness.

Testing her injured ankle, Ardis rose and cautiously moved forward. She reprimanded herself for venturing out here alone. She could have broken her leg, could have been stranded in this wretched darkness.

Ardis quickly settled the light on Jane's desk. The thick folder Jane had been working with was still there, and beneath the desk she could see the dim outline of the stone obelisk. In the terrible silence she seemed to see Jane's glowing eyes, hear her saying, "My whole life's work hinges upon this!"

Ardis took another step forward, then froze. A sense of terror crept over her, the feeling that she was not alone in the tomb. She flashed the light around in panic. It shone across a stylized figure cut deeply into the stone wall, the god Queen Hatshepsut worshiped, Amon Re, portrayed with a king's beard and holding a staff.

She focused the beam from the stone god to the empty sarcophagus. She shifted the light across one of the stone figures that towered on either side of the coffin. In the shadowy light the powerful features, the large, hollow eyes of the stone guardian seemed to be watching her.

She must take the obelisk and get out! Focusing only on this mission, she flashed the light beneath the desk. With the beam trained on the obelisk, she reached out; her fingers closing around it in a compulsive grasp.

Bracing herself against Jane's desk, Ardis felt a jolt of pain as she rose and put pressure on her injured foot. The intensity of it, along with the lack of air and the horror of being alone in a dark tomb caused her to feel sick and faint. She hurriedly stuffed the scattered papers in the canvas backpack Jane used as a briefcase. She had just enough space left to slip the obelisk inside. Limping slightly, she hurried toward the entrance.

Ardis strapped the pack to her shoulders and replaced the ladder. From the far recesses of the tomb, a muttering voice sounded, faint, disembodied. It seemed to drift upward, like distant chanting coming from another world. With one hand holding a death-grip on the ladder rung, she played the light behind her. It shifted across the two huge statues, across the stone sarcophagus. Was someone hidden inside that black void?

The sound, wherever it had come from, abruptly ceased. The empty silence of the chamber horrified her. Whoever was in the tomb was purposefully attempting to frighten her. From the time she entered, he had been concealed, watching—he knew she had the obelisk.

Sweat broke out across Ardis' forehead as she pulled herself upward. She reached the great gap between the broken rung and hesitated. Above her was blessed daylight. Desire for freedom renewed her strength. Oblivious to the agony of her throbbing ankle, Ardis stuffed the flashlight into the edge of the backpack. With both hands free she was able to draw herself up to the next level and drag herself from the tomb. Ignoring the pain, she raced toward the Jeep.

The Jeep key—she was certain she had left it in the ignition—was gone. She began frantically searching for it, in the folds of the canvas bag, on the seat, on the floorboards. She must have without thinking removed the key. Perhaps she had dropped it in the tomb. She must either go back and look for it or try to get help from the men at the gate.

The brilliance of sun and the shimmering layers of heat mingled with the form that stood between Jane's shack and the tomb. The strange movement of light and heat gave the tall outline indefinite dimensions like a ghostly apparition.

Blake Lydon. Just as he had on their first meeting, he strode toward her. The sharp light exaggerated the intensity of his dark eyes, etched hard lines around his tensely set lips. For an instant, he reminded her of Ramus whose mysterious features seemed carved of granite.

"What are you doing out here? Are you alone?"

She told him about her fall from the ladder, about the haunting voice she'd heard.

He frowned, seeming even more remote and distant. "Was Ramus at the hospital when you left?"

"I don't know."

He crossed to Jane's cabin, entered and came out, clicking on a flashlight. "Be careful!" Ardis called to him. She walked back to the entrance, thinking about how easily he could have slipped from the tomb while she was looking for her keys. Those muffled words that echoed in her mind might have been his.

Blake soon emerged from the tomb. He stood squarely in front of Ardis, eyes staring at her, not blinking against the sun. "There's no one down there. What you heard was probably a gust of wind drawn in from the opening."

"I heard a voice, words spoken in Arabic."

Blake did not press the subject further. "I found this," he said, producing the Jeep key. "You must have dropped it when you fell."

Blake guided her toward the Jeep. Ardis slipped in under the wheel. "Are you coming with me?"

"No," he replied. "I must stop at Qurna."

Ardis turned the key in the ignition. Blake's words were almost lost in the noise of the engine.

"Things have been happening here that I can't begin to understand," he said. His voice rose, sounded harsh, almost threatening. "You are not to come out here alone. Whenever you are at this tomb site, I must be with you."

In her hotel room Ardis lifted the obelisk from the canvas bag. It, square base attached, was cut from one piece of granite. Intricate writing, deep and sharp against her fingers, covered the twelve inches above the base. Jane must have been comparing these markings with similar ones found in the tomb.

If so, it must not have been original to the tomb, but something Jane had brought in with her. The obelisk appeared to be a replica of the original ones Senmut had erected at the Temple of Karnak. Although Ardis could not determine whether or not it was old, she realized it was of great value. Knowing it would be too risky to keep it with her, Ardis went immediately to the clerk's desk and requested a safety deposit box.

The Nubian clerk, whose nametag read Essa BenSobel, rose politely and led the way into a small room behind the desk. It was filled with rows of boxes of various sizes.

Ardis felt more at ease once the bag containing Jane's recent work and the obelisk was locked behind the firm metal door of number 45.

"I notice you're limping," the clerk said as she started away from the desk.

"It's nothing."

"People often get injured here. Wait." He left the empty lobby and returned some time later with a small package. A kindly smile lit his swarthy features. "Wrap your ankle tightly in this. It will help you walk and ease the pain."

"Thank you."

Ardis returned to her room. She thought of Jane, deathly ill from some unknown cause. She thought of the obelisk now protected by hotel security. Confusion filled her. She did not know why this particular stone object was so valuable; or why Blake, if he had been the one watching her, had made no attempt to take it from her. Neither did she understand why, now, safe behind a locked door, she felt such an overpowering sense of fear—fear that had nothing at all to do with ancient curses or with muffled voices able to span centuries.

Chapter 3

Jane had been transferred to a large hospital in Cairo. Ardis had caught the first morning flight from Luxor to be with her. Ramus, who had accompanied Jane, had evidently been watching from an upstairs window, for he met Ardis at the elevator on the third floor.

"How is Jane? Can I see her?" she asked.

"The doctor is with her now. They still don't know what's wrong with her, but," he added hopefully, "she seems to be steadily improving."

"Is Blake here?"

"Matthammed and he are flying in this afternoon." Ramus ushered her into the small lobby across from the elevator. They sank down on the hard, worn sofa where he must have slept the previous night.

Hospitals the world over, Ardis mused, are drearily alike. This one, with its sterile, impersonal atmosphere could have been located in the United States or anywhere in the world.

Ramus lifted a newspaper from the coffee table. "Have you seen this?" He read aloud, his voice husky with deep undertones of anger. "Lifelong Search for Lost Tomb Uncovers Ancient Curse."

Ardis accepted the paper, titled the *International Reporter* and read the article.

After well over a quarter of a century, archaeologist Jane Darvin has returned to the Valley of the Kings to resume her search for a long-lost tomb.

When a tomb bearing the inscription of Queen Hatshepsut's scribe, Senmut, was discovered, hopes ran high. But the opening of the tomb revealed little but a dark hole in the ground, an empty sarcophagus ... and a withering curse "Death will devour he who disturbs the eternal rest of Senmut."

Did Senmut actually ever rest here? Or is it a decoy Senmut fashioned in an attempt to conceal his true resting place and save his eternal soul from the ravages of Thutmose III? The mummies of Queen Hatshepsut and her lover/scribe Senmut have never been found. During her lifetime, two known tombs were prepared for the Queen. An early tomb with an unfinished sarcophagus of crystalline sandstone was abandoned after Hatshepsut became Pharaoh in her own right. A grander tomb, with a hidden passage which connected the sarcophagus chamber to her temple at Deir el-Bahari, was also discovered empty.

Senmut had at least two tombs built for himself; one, for dignitaries, located in the Valley of the Kings, another, a secret tomb at Deir el-Bahari near the Queen's own. The sarcophagus of this secret tomb was found smashed, and Senmut was never interred in either tomb. It is believed that both Senmut and Hatshepsut had been murdered by Thutmose III and their corpses thrown to the dogs to prevent their entrance to eternal life.

Who was buried in the tomb recently discovered by Jane Darvin bearing Senmut's signature? Nobody knows. This tomb has been violated by grave robbers, past or present. What was found in the tomb, bronze vessels, stone beads, and pottery, all disappointingly humble, have been transported to the Cairo Museum.

For the literally millions spent on this project, funds drained from the Cairo museum's valuable program with the blessing of its director Nihisi Khet, Dr. Jane Darvin uncovered only an ancient curse. And maybe there is some truth to that curse. Yesterday morning Jane Darvin was rushed to the hospital after suffering a nervous breakdown.

Ramus snatched the paper Ardis extended and hurled it angrily down on the table. A picture, of a springy-haired girl with an upturned nose and a saucy smile gazed boldly up at them. The large by-line beneath her photograph identified her as Faye Morris.

She was likely some student who had betrayed Jane's trust. Like Queen Hatshepsut, Jane must have been aware of the shadows surrounding her notoriety—felt the envy, the resentment, even the betrayal, of those closest to her.

Ramus, with deepening hostility, said, "That girl is a nobody! A stupid little nobody! What right has she to belittle Jane's work, to exploit her illness? This—mere child—has no idea how important the discovery of this tomb is to history."

Ramus' worry over Jane had increased his animosity toward the journalist. Ardis, caught up in his indignation, managed to speak calmly. "There's always someone like this journalist, trying to make a name for themselves at another's expense. But why worry about it? This paper is just a gossip rag, not a professional journal. Jane wouldn't give it a second glance."

"The public will believe what they read in black and white. Let the curse fall on her! She has done irreparable damage to Jane's reputation!"

Ardis, growing impatient, searched for the doctor and found him checking charts at the nurses' station. Dr. Fahmy, a man in his early forties with sharp-cut features, spoke English with the clipped preciseness of one who has studied at the best of academies. To Ardis, his bearing seemed curt and professional; and his eyes lacked the spark of kindness, the empathy she had noted in Dr. Sirdi.

"We are still running tests," he replied briskly to her inquiry about Jane. "It is possible we will never know the exact cause of her illness. In the meantime I have prescribed rest and medication to ease her symptoms, and she is improving. Of course," he cautioned with grim pessimism, "this could change at any time. Until we know for certain what we're dealing with, we cannot hope for a complete cure."

Once again, Ardis brought up Ramus' concern that Jane might have come into contact with some rare, poisonous substance within the tomb.

The doctor paused to adjust the notes on his clipboard. "I see no evidence that we're dealing with any kind of poison."

"Aren't there special tests that could be run?"

"Only if you know exactly what kind of toxin is involved. Without that knowledge even extensive testing may prove futile."

His air of dismissal told her that the subject was closed. "May I see Jane?"

He considered her request. "Only for a few minutes. And absolutely no talk of curses or tomb dust or anything else that might upset my patient."

Jane sat up in the bed propped against pillows. She had dark shadows beneath her eyes, and her face, thin and drawn. But Ardis was relieved to see in her alert, restless manner vestiges of the old Jane.

"Did you find the obelisk?" Jane asked anxiously by way of a greeting.

After making certain no one was listening at the door, Ardis stepped closer and replied, "It is in one of the hotel's safety deposit boxes."

"Good." Jane sounded relieved. "I knew I could depend on you to choose the best possible place. What about my papers?"

"They are with the obelisk."

The tense lines of Jane's face still did not relax. "You know, Ardis, we didn't find any items of great value as you would expect to discover in a tomb. But the items we did find failed to arrive at the museum at Cairo. I haven't told anyone about this except you."

"You mean they were stolen? Who could have taken them?"

"Blake, Ramus, Nihisi Khet, Matthammed—they're the only ones who worked with the cataloging and transport of the artifacts … I have always trusted them implicitly."

"Then, who?"

"What's happening here …" Jane started as if she intended to confide something important. "What I believe may be happening is surely impossible. All I can tell you, Ardis, is that this tomb is far more important than anyone knows."

Heeding the doctor's warning not to upset her, Ardis did not pressure her for more information. Nor did she tell Jane of her meeting with Blake at the tomb, or of her suspicion that he, too, might have been searching for the obelisk. "Why does this obelisk have value?"

"The obelisk belongs to me. It didn't come from the tomb; I inherited it from my grandfather." Jane's eyes grew brighter. "In fact, it's this obelisk that first started my search for Senmut's tomb. Rolled up and hidden inside is a rare scroll he entrusted to me, what I call the Senmut Papyrus. I usually keep it under lock and key, but I had taken it to the tomb so I could use it in translating the hieroglyphics. That's why I wouldn't want it to fall into the wrong hands while I'm being … detained here."

Ardis smiled at her choice of words, relieved at Jane's return of spirit, her obvious improvement. "You make it sound as if you were in prison."

"You know what they are saying about me, Ardis. That I'm having some kind of emotional breakdown. I've always thought of myself as a strong woman."

"You are." Jane seemed so lucid now, almost her old self. Ardis had difficulty believing she would ever crack under the pressures of over-work and exhaustion.

"Would you believe I was scheduled to be in Cairo this very weekend?" Changing the subject, Jane lifted the glass of iced tea near her bedside. "The doctor prescribes pills, but this tea is what's curing me. You remember how I always keep a thermos beside me while I work." She took a long drink. "As it is, I've arrived in Cairo much faster than I had planned. So much the better. You know how I dread the time it takes to travel. Now if only I could convince Dr. Fahmy to let me keep my appointments."

Never content to relax, Jane must surely dread the thought of today, the long hours confined in this tiny room, of doctors running endless tests. Although she put up a brave front, Jane hadn't recovered enough to fulfill the day's carefully planned obligations. "Maybe I could see to your business today."

"I have a meeting with the museum director, Nihisi Khet."

The name was becoming familiar to Ardis—first mentioned by Ramus, and then in the article by the journalist, Faye Morris.

"Because the funding for my project comes mostly from his department, Nihisi must approve every detail." A gesture of her thin, brown hand dismissed his importance as she added, "He opposes each of my projects in turn. I've spent years of my life going over the obvious with him, which is what I had scheduled for today." She laughed, but her laughter held some hint of resentment.

"I'll be glad to keep that appointment for you."

"I wouldn't ask you to do that. I'll have Blake deal with him. He's accustomed to Nihisi's inflexible stubbornness. Nihisi all but raised him, you know. As a baby Blake was left—abandoned—at an orphanage here in Cairo. No one knows his parentage. It was thought his mother was some American student. Nihisi took him under his wing, became a foster father to him. When Blake was sixteen, Nihisi sent him away to school in the U.S. where he became a citizen. He only returned to Egypt this year."

So Blake was raised in Egypt by the museum director. No wonder Blake had such pull—enough to have established himself as Jane's assistant.

"Poor dear Blake!" Jane gave a short laugh and again reached for the tea. "I'm so very thirsty. The hospital wanted to deny me this simple pleasure, but the nurse relented at last." She drank in meditative silence. "There is one appointment you *could* keep for me. I was to meet Thomas Garrett at one the Temple Hotel dining room, in walking distance from here." She set the half-full glass back on the stand. "He's a young archaeologist from London. He sounds eager and ambitious—nice—the way I might have sounded before years of tomb dust and hassle. Yes, he sounds very nice."

Nice—a word Ardis had always associated with Mike, her childhood sweetheart, who had just married her kid sister. The last thing she wanted to do was leave the hospital to dine with some *nice* stranger.

"Yes, you can do that for me. I refuse to let everything come to a complete standstill just because I'm chained to this bed. I'll be fine. Ramus is here, and Blake and Matthammed will be arriving shortly, so I won't lack for company." Jane settled back against the pillows, and spoke in a voice reminiscent of her years of teaching, "Your assignment, Ardis, is to go to the Temple Hotel, have a decent meal, and take a break from this miserable hospital."

"Is there anything special you would like me to tell him?"

"Just explain what has detained me. He wanted to tag along to my meeting with Nihisi today. Once you meet Nihisi, you'll understand why. No one ever wants to meet that man alone! Thomas has asked for my assistance in obtaining permission from the Cairo Museum to do some reconstruction work at Karnak. Tell him …" Her voice faltered. "Everything is going to be delayed … for a little while."

When Ardis returned to the waiting room, Ramus was speaking with a tall, slight Egyptian man with fine, handsome features and a straight and rigid bearing.

"Nihisi Khet," Ramus introduced. "This is Ardis Cole."

"Jane speaks very highly of you," Nihisi Khet spoke, the compliment lost in an air of coldness.

Nothing about him inspired affection, although his evident singleness of purpose commanded an almost immediate respect.

Ardis studied him. So this was Nihisi Khet, the museum director, Blake's foster father—the man Jane and everyone else considered all-powerful. She wasn't prepared for the image he projected, his thinness, his cold, intellectual bearing. Despite the fingers of gray that shot through his thick, black hair, he appeared a good deal younger than the fifty-odd years he must be. Deep frown lines cut between his brows, giving him a stern, critical look that wide, brown eyes somehow betrayed.

"Blake will be arriving before long," Ramus said.

"I can't stay." He checked his watch. "I'm going to drop in to see Jane for a moment, then I must return to the museum."

Because of Nihisi Khet's curt, businesslike manner, at first Ardis had believed he cared little for Jane Darvin; yet because she knew them to be lifelong friends, she guessed the opposite were true. He wouldn't be a man to show emotion, but would hide his true feelings behind a formal, unrevealing facade.

"But first, I believe I'll have a word with Dr. Fahmy. I want to make sure Jane is getting the best treatment available." Nihisi Khet started briskly from the room in search of Jane's doctor. As if an after-thought, he stopped, "Have Blake stop by the museum."

"Nihisi Khet is one of the most intelligent men I've ever met," Ramus said as they watched him leave … "He is Jane Darvin's male counterpart. Blake and Nihisi don't always see eye to eye, but I know Blake has always tried hard to follow in his footsteps."

For a moment she pitied the boy Blake must have once been, suspecting, that Nihisi Khet, the man who had raised him, would have had little time for him.

Outside the hospital the streets of Cairo bustled with noise and confusion. Ardis had not bothered to ask Ramus for directions to the Temple Hotel, which Jane had assured her was within easy walking distance from the hospital. Around her the smell of the deep, sluggish Nile mingled in the hot air, heavy with fumes from endless cars, trucks, buses. Ardis was glad for the bright sunlight and the clamor of Cairo, with its strange mixture of modern and ancient, glad, to distance herself for a little while from the strain of long hours spent in the waiting rooms of hospitals.

As Ardis wandered through the crowd, she became aware of the foreign voices surrounding her, of dark men wearing turbans and of women in the long, black dresses that designated them as married. In need of directions, she was glad to catch sight of a slightly heavy, middle-aged man with carefully-styled gray hair and a trim moustache walking in the direction of the hospital. He looked very prosperous, very British.

"Excuse me. Could you direct me to the Temple Hotel?"

The man replied with a pleasant smile. "I'm a newcomer here myself. But I believe if you'll turn right on the next street, it's the huge, limestone building at the end of the block."

"Thank you."

The gentleman nodded courteously. "My pleasure."

Just as the British man had said, the Temple Hotel stood on the corner of a congested street. Ardis could see the towering walls of aged stone, the pale yellow sign bearing the design of the great pyramid at Giza. The huge, air-conditioned lobby seemed dark and chilly compared to the brilliance outside. The booths and tables were half-shielded by rattan screens each decorated with a single, glaringly blue ibis with long legs and beak. Ardis searched the crowd of people and immediately identified the young man she was to meet.

He wore a light jacket, a blue shirt and tie—his best, no doubt, to impress Jane Darvin. Straight brown hair, streaked with gold by the sun, brushed the collar of his jacket. He might have sounded *nice* to Jane on the phone, but Ardis' first impression of him opposed any such belief. In fact, she did not like his cold appraisal, his deep-set, very pale blue eyes, or the slightly arrogant arch of sandy eyebrows.

"Are you Thomas Garrett?"

He rose at once with an almost military politeness. When he was seated, she had formed the impression that he was short, but his rangy form loomed far above hers. Ardis gazed up at his angular features, the rather large nose and the wide mouth with white, slightly protruding teeth. Smiling, he seemed somehow agreeable, in fact, quite attractive.

The large smile disappeared in disappointment when she told him that Jane could not see him. Even though this was to be their first meeting, he appeared to be genuinely concerned about Jane's condition.

"I'm about ready to order. You must join me for lunch."
He pulled out the chair for her and suggested the hotel's
specialty.

"That sounds delicious." Since Ardis had first found Jane
unconscious in the tomb, she had not taken time for a decent
meal. The rich aroma that surrounded them made her feel
sudden pangs of hunger.

Thomas gazed across the table at her. "I am studying in
London," he said, "working on my Ph.D. in Egyptology."

"My interests are similar," Ardis said, warming toward him.
"I've been teaching in Chicago."

"One of Jane Darvin's many protégés?"

"I have recently advanced from student to Jane's assistant.
I am here working with her on the newly discovered tomb of
Senmut."

His concern showed by the widening of his pale eyes. "Will
Dr. Darvin be able to return to work?"

"She's much better. I expect her to be released from the
hospital soon."

The waiter offered cups of "ahwa ziedda," very sweet
Arabic coffee. Thomas raised his cup in a toast. "Then we have
cause to celebrate."

"How do you know Jane?"

"We've never met, only spoken on the phone. When I saw
the article in the London papers about Jane Darvin's discovery,
I was so intrigued, I called her." With enthusiasm gathering
in his voice, he no longer sounded so primly British. "I didn't
think such a famous person would even bother to talk to me."

"Fame has not affected her. She is very much the teacher,
the Egyptologist."

"I guess I did most of the talking. I found myself pouring
out my life's dream to her. She was interested in my plans to
reconstruct the monuments of Thutmose III and to my surprise

she offered to help me obtain permission and support for my project from the museum director, Nihisi Khet. So here I am."

The waiter brought their food—beef kebabs with spicy dip, pita bread, and bowls of fresh fruit, oranges, melon, and grapes.

"I suppose you've read Jane's book, *The Vengeance of Thutmose III*."

Another grin revealed his prominent teeth. "Jane Darvin and I heartily disagree about Thutmose III. I'm convinced he was Egypt's greatest pharaoh. Greatly underrated. Thutmose III's name should stand beside the world's famed warriors like Napoleon, Alexander the Great, … "

"Ivan the Terrible," Ardis added with a smile. "Thutmose III hated Queen Hatshepsut so much he obliterated her name, destroyed her statues, built a wall to hide her obelisks, her dream." Ardis paused. "He even battered and destroyed her tomb and those of her loyal followers. Jane and I are both convinced that he had both Hatshepsut and her architect, Senmut, murdered."

"Well, love,"Thomas spoke with exaggerated British slowness, "they got just what they deserved, now didn't they? The Queen stole the throne from him and was in love with her architect. She didn't love his father, Thutmose II. Now who wouldn't resent that just a little?"

"A little too much,"Ardis laughed.

Their conversation continued in a pleasant, argumentative vein, the ancient mystery of Queen Hatshepsut's death a distraction from her worry about Jane. She found the dislike she had felt at the first sight of Thomas fading, being replaced with the beginnings of friendship.

After the pleasant meal, a long talk, and a promise to see Thomas Garrett again when he arrived in Luxor, Ardis felt very optimistic. She returned to the hospital to happily share with Jane her meeting with the young archaeologist. She was prepared to laugh with her about his defense of Thutmose III, the hated enemy of Queen Hatshepsut, who was always the center of Jane's thoughts and work.

Ardis sensed something was wrong the moment she entered the waiting room where Blake and Ramus stood talking in hushed voices.

"What's happened?"

"Jane's condition has grown much worse," Blake said, his dark eyes clouding.

Blake's announcement drained every vestige of light-heartedness from Ardis. Jane was dying! Disbelief, then overwhelming fear, rushed over her. "How could that be? She was fine when I left not over an hour ago. Can I see her?"

Blake and Ramus exchanged glances. "I don't think that's a very good idea," Blake said. "She won't know you." Lines tightened around his dark eyes. He turned his face abruptly from her as if trying to hide the agony of grief, loss, or some other emotion Ardis had no chance to interpret. Blake's eyes met hers just briefly, and the image of his grim features stayed with her long after he had strode from the room. His departure left in its wake a total emptiness.

"We had better contact Jane's family." Her words hung in the long silence with grim finality.

"What family?" Ramus answered at last. "We are her family."

She knew Ramus loved Jane, but had Ramus been more to Jane than a strong, loyal friend? Jane would have needed him—an old warrior, a faithful watch-guard to her daring dreams. But was he more?

"She has an ex-husband somewhere." Ramus spoke with caution as if he found the subject disagreeable. "Neil Darvin."

"Do you know where he can be contacted?"

"I understand he was originally from New York City. But Darvin is an archaeologist, like Jane. He could be in South America or any remote part of the world."

"Didn't you know him personally?"

"When they were first married, Jane and her husband came to Egypt and started working together. That was almost thirty years ago. At that time I had left Qurna and was employed by the Egyptian Museum. I saw Jane often when she traveled to Cairo, but I can't recall ever once meeting him."

For the first time she realized how little she knew about Jane Darvin's past. "Doesn't Jane have a child?"

His heavy lids drooped, shielding his large eyes. "Jane was pregnant when she left Egypt, but when she returned she had neither husband nor child." He paused, then went on hesitantly. "The baby must have died. It hurt Jane so much she never talked about it."

"You don't even know whether she had a boy or a girl?"

Ramus shook his head.

"Isn't it possible that the child stayed with Neil Darvin?"

"I don't think so," he said, then added with a solemn reluctance, "Rumor has it that the child didn't even belong to him."

So much time had passed, over thirty years. Jane's child, if one existed, would be about the age Blake Lydon was now.

Ardis noticed at once that restraints had been placed on Jane's wrists and across her waist, but she appeared so weak they seemed unnecessary. She stared up at the ceiling. Her wide-open eyes did not shift to Ardis even though she stood close to the bed.

Alarmed by the quick and drastic change in Jane's condition, Ardis called her name.

Jane raised a lean, brown hand as far as the cotton binding would allow. Her fingers locked tightly on Ardis' wrist, as if they were clutching at life.

Ardis brushed her free hand across the straight, thick black hair threaded with gray. Jane's forehead felt cold and clammy. Her eyes seemed even more dilated, her breathing thin and fearfully rapid … so close to death!

Ardis tried to disentangle the talon-like grip so she could summon the doctor, but the coiled fingers possessed strength, desperate and unnatural.

"Ardis!" The pitch of Jane's voice had an unfamiliar shrillness. "You know why I sent for you. You are the one I have chosen to take over for me!" The effort of speaking exhausted her, so that she finished in a raspy whisper. "All my papers, years and years of research, are stored in my files at the site. You, Ardis, are to finish my work!"

Ardis, afraid and choked with tears, replied, "You are going to complete it yourself."

"I won't be alive this time tomorrow. You have no time to waste." Jane's eyes began to burn with a feverish light. She managed to speak aloud once again. The forced volume gave her words a ring of hysteria. "Find the gold! That's what you've got to do!"

"Gold?" Ardis echoed. In Jane's mind Senmut's tomb was filled with gold, a hallucination, just like the snake Ramus had said she had seen and feared.

"Promise me, Ardis!"

Ardis knew she must go along with Jane's delusions to give her peace. Still, she hesitated to make so wild a vow.

Jane did not wait for her to speak. Her words poured out in a rapid stream. "I've searched for this tomb all my life. This is such an important discovery for Egypt!" The clutching fingers brought pain to Ardis' wrist. "The gold for the obelisks! Senmut hid the gold from Thutmose III before Thutmose killed him!

It's in the tomb! Wealth immeasurable … hidden in Senmut's tomb. I am dying and it is now up to you. Do you understand, Ardis?"

"Yes. I'll take care of everything." Tears, which she attempted to wipe away, slipped down Ardis' cheeks.

"The papyrus is the key! The papyrus within the obelisk!" Jane's eyes, wide and glowing like liquid metal, fastened on Ardis. "Ardis, I can't see you! Where are you?"

"I'm here."

The grip on Ardis' hand weakened. Jane's voice became fainter as she drifted farther and farther away, somewhere deep into the past, somewhere Ardis could no longer follow. Ardis was stunned to hear her final words, a plea that wrenched at her heart, "Please. I want to see my baby!"

Chapter 4

Ardis had taken a room at the Old Cairo Hotel when she had first arrived in the city. The solid stone building had the same aura of an earlier time as the Temple Hotel where she had met with Thomas. She imagined Howard Carter or Lord Carnarvon might have stayed here. They might have parted these same faded white draperies and opened wide, latched windows to the stifling evening heat and to the twilight view of the city.

Beneath her fifth floor window the street swarmed with vehicles, animals, pedestrians, a confusing mixture of Europe, Asia, and Africa. In darkened alleys, around the imposing, modern structure of the hospital where Jane had spent her last hours, souks remained open for evening business.

After Jane's death, Blake and Nihisi Khet had assured her they would see to the necessary arrangements. The reality of Jane's death had not had time to sink in; she felt only the numbness. How would she get along without Jane? Could she complete the work, so important to Jane and now entrusted to her?

So much had happened since Ardis had stepped on that plane in Chicago—so many changes. Jane, dead. Dead of natural causes. Even as she thought the words, she rebelled against Dr. Famey's impersonal explanation of Jane's death.

Jane's unexpected turn for the worse, after she had been so steadily improving, had caught Ardis totally off guard. Jane had seemed so much better. Ardis would never have left the hospital, not even for a minute if she had known Jane was only moments from death. Because of the brief respite, those few hours of hope and optimism, the reality of her sudden death became even harder to bear.

An image of Jane, sipping tea, talking so rationally about the day's business entered her mind. She had been so much better when Ardis had left her to meet with Thomas Garrett. What could have caused such a rapid change?

Again Ardis pictured Jane, the tea glass in her hand, and a sense of uneasiness stole over her. Jane had told her she had been drinking tea from her thermos in the tomb just before she had lost consciousness. Jane had also been drinking tea in the hospital just before suffering this fatal relapse.

Could there be some connection? From the first, Ardis had considered the possibility that someone might have wanted to purposefully harm Jane, but now it seemed a certainty. The way Jane had talked about the missing items in the tomb, the way she had spoken of her colleagues with such hesitation, as if on the verge of confiding some secret, strengthened Ardis' suspicions.

Ardis recalled Dr. Fahmy's words about how difficult it would be to detect some unknown toxin. Maybe Matthammed was not so far wrong in his wild speculations. What if Jane was the victim, not of some ancient poison within the tomb itself, but some insidious, difficult to detect substance intended to mimic the symptoms of "tomb dust"?

Someone, over a period of time, could have been slipping Jane poison, could have given her a heavier dose that day at the tomb. But surely this couldn't have happened at the hospital under the watchful eyes of doctors and nurses.

Even as she denied the possibility, Ardis found herself vividly recalling the half-filled glass of tea Jane had set on the nightstand just before Ardis had left for that meeting with Thomas. The doctor had ordered rest, and Ardis knew that Jane had been left alone for long intervals, uninterrupted except for the nurse's rounds and the short visits of her close friends, Ramus, Blake, and Nihisi Khet. Maybe not one of them, though. Anyone might have slipped into her room while Jane was sleeping and left the fatal dose of poison in her drink. And Jane, upon awakening, had quite naturally reached for the glass and finished the tea.

The glass would be proof. Traces of the poison would remain, and the killer, thinking no one would check, would simply leave it to be cleaned up by room service. Ardis leapt to her feet, her exhaustion suddenly forgotten.

As Ardis crossed the busy intersection, dodging an old car smelling of exhaust fumes that streaked past, she almost convinced herself that this was only a wild hunch. Still, knowing that she would never rest until she had done what she could to ease her troubled mind, Ardis entered the quiet, clinical atmosphere of the hospital and hurried down the long corridor to the room Jane had occupied.

In dismay, her gaze held to the vacant bed freshly spread with a smooth, white cover. The nearby nightstand was now cleaned and polished, the glass gone. Ardis opened drawers. All empty. Although it had been only a short time since Jane's death, all of her personal effects had been removed, all traces that she had ever been there erased.

Common sense told her that the glass she was seeking would be impossible to find or identify now. Still, she inquired of the young Egyptian girl who had cleaned Jane's room. Ardis followed her down to the huge kitchen where rows of identical glasses, hundreds of them, sat cooling on wire racks. The glass Ardis sought was somewhere among them, sparkling and sterile from the dishwasher, all traces of poisonous residue rinsed away forever.

Ardis, knowing there was little chance she would convince Dr. Fahmy to listen to her, nevertheless caught up with him just as he was leaving his office for the evening.

"May I help you?" he asked.

Tie loosened, suit jacket over his arm, he seemed much more approachable than the curt, professional figure in white she had spoken to earlier. Wearily he returned to his room and seated himself behind a desk near a photo of a woman and dark-eyed little girl. His gaze wandered to the clock on the wall as if he wanted to get home.

"I am not satisfied with the decision on Jane Darvin's death certificate. I can't accept the idea that she died of heart failure."

"Often we try to simplify the many causes of death into as few words as possible."

"Dr. Sirdi from Luxor did not know what had brought on Jane's illness. That's why she was sent here." Ardis drew in her breath and gazed at him with determination. "I want to know the exact cause of Jane's death."

"I have as much interest in finding out what happened to Jane Darvin as you do."

"In that case," Ardis replied quickly, "I believe an autopsy should be performed."

Ardis tensed, preparing herself for argument. After a long silence, Dr. Fahmy spoke. "No doctor likes unanswered questions concerning the death of a patient."

"Then you will request an autopsy?"

"The body has already been taken to the funeral home. There is much red tape involved … many difficulties. I can't make any promises. But I will call the mortuary before I leave here tonight."

Satisfied that she had done all that she could, Ardis went back to her hotel room to face a long, restless night.

"I had no idea we would run into this," Dr. Fahmy told Ardis the next morning. "There can be no autopsy. Jane Darvin's body has already been cremated."

The doctor's words struck Ardis like a blow. When she finally recovered, she demanded, "By whose authority?"

"It appears Nihisi Khet signed for the body to be cremated early this morning."

"But you phoned them. How could this have happened so quickly?"

"My call was left on the answering service, not received. I'm so sorry. I had no idea. These things never take place this rapidly."

"Then why did they?"

Dr. Fahmy's strong, capable hands spread across the desktop. "We're dealing with Nihisi Khet, who is a man of action. He immediately carried out Ms. Darvin's written requests, so it is all perfectly legal. Mr. Khet is the one authorized to take charge of her funeral arrangements."

"Why would he find speed so necessary?"

Dr. Fahmy looked suddenly uneasy. "Mr. Khet was evidently unaware that I had put in a request for an autopsy. A mistake. A regrettable, irretractible mistake."

"What if it wasn't a mistake?" Ardis returned bitterly. "What if he ignored the request intentionally?"

"In any event," Dr. Fahmy responded with an air of resignation, "there is little we can do about it now. Nihisi Khet is a very important man."

"What are you saying?"

He glanced up at her and the resignation in his eyes sent chills down her spine. "The powerful can pull many strings. Here," he said with a note of finality, "Nihisi Khet's word is not to be questioned."

As Ardis left the doctor's office, her fears intensified. It looked as if Jane Darvin had been murdered and that Nihisi Khet had conveniently arranged for the body to be quickly cremated to destroy the evidence.

"Ardis." As she entered the coolness of the hotel lobby, a familiar voice spoke her name. Green eyes blinking as they adjusted from blinding sunlight to the hotel's dim lighting, Ardis turned to face Blake Lydon. Hair as black as an Egyptians contrasted with the white linen jacket he wore.

"I've been looking for you," he said.

Ardis' resentment flared. "Why wasn't I consulted about Jane's cremation?"

"Let's find a place to talk." Blake silently guided her through the lobby, rose and tan, with elegance retained from the opulence of a by-gone era. Once the hotel had been a gathering place for wealthy adventurers with money for the leisurely pursuit of plundering Egyptian artifacts. Was it still?

In the dining area a few people, mostly tourists, lingered over breakfast. A young woman with curly brown hair glanced up from an adjacent table as they passed. After the waiter had brought coffee, Blake looked at Ardis steadily before saying, "Please don't be angry with Nihisi. For all their disagreements, Jane and he were very close. He was simply following the instructions Jane herself left. Why has this upset you so?"

Everything about the two seemed odd to her, even the way Blake referred to his father as Nihisi. Still, his words were spoken sincerely and caused Ardis to wonder if she had not misjudged them. "I had convinced Dr. Fahmy to request an autopsy."

Blake's eyes, so nearly black, widened. "Believe me, Nihisi and I didn't know anything about that."He drew a deep breath. "I'm afraid I don't quite understand."

"I believe there is much more to Jane's death … something the doctors have missed. Jane was drinking tea at the tomb when she became ill, and she drank tea again at the hospital before she died.This could be how she got the poison."

"Poison?"

In the stately dining room, beneath the swish of ceiling fans, it seemed unreal to Ardis that someone could have purposefully murdered Jane, still, she asked, "When you went back to the tomb, did you see the thermos Jane always kept with her?"

Blake frowned. "No." His look darkened. "In fact, most of Jane's things were gone. Her notes and … other items. I haven't been able to find out who removed them."

Ardis realized with a start that Blake was talking about the obelisk and the notes that she herself had taken. She glanced away from his close scrutiny.

"I must go now." Blake's hand closed around hers for a brief moment."There will be a small memorial for Jane tonight in the desert just outside of the city. Ramus and I will be leaving from the hotel lobby at sunset. I'll give you a call."

After Blake left, Ardis lingered, nursing the last of her coffee. Feeling as if she were being observed, she glanced up to find the young woman at the next table walking toward her. She looked vaguely familiar, but Ardis couldn't place her.

"Hi. I'm Faye Morris.You must be Ardis Cole. I don't want to impose on your sorrow, but I have just heard about Jane Darvin's death, and I wanted to offer you my condolences."Her uninvited companion signaled the waiter, saying,"It looks like you could use a sympathetic ear and another cup of coffee."

Ardis responded with a stiff smile, a forced attempt at politeness.

"I'm a freelance journalist," Faye said. "I've been closely following the story on the tomb."

"I've read one of your articles in the *International Reporter*."

The girl, as if flattered, slid boldly into the chair Blake had occupied. If she had heard a note of disapproval in Ardis' tone, she had chosen to ignore it.

She looked just as she had in the newspaper picture, the same scattering of freckles across the cute, upturned nose, the same pert, saucy smile. The printed page, however, had not captured the self-satisfied tilt to her head and chin or her air of being totally immersed in herself.

"I write for the *Reporter*, and several other publications as well. I've always been interested in archaeology, even took a few courses, before I decided journalism was more suited to my taste than digging up old bones."

"I'm sure it must be an interesting career."

A smile crossed the seemingly guileless face. The effect caused her to look much younger than she must be. Ardis guessed the young woman, clad in denims, a skimpy red tank top and a fashionably rumpled blazer, was probably somewhere in her late twenties or early thirties.

"Anyway, I saw you speaking to Blake Lydon." Faye leaned forward and said in a confidential tone," I thought you might be able to tell me something more about the missing artifact."

"I'm afraid I don't know what you're talking about."

Faye looked disappointed. "Of course, it's not common knowledge." Faye took a sip of coffee, than added importantly, "but we reporters always have our sources. I heard about it from one of the workers who's very close to Jane Darvin. He was there when the tomb was first opened. He told me he caught a glimpse of a small, white statue, a cat statue, he called it."

The tomb worker Faye referred to must be Matthammed. Blake or Ramus would not have spoken to this pushy, obviously very inexperienced reporter.

"I just checked with the Egyptian Museum," Faye added smugly. "It wasn't on the inventory, and it never showed up at the museum."

"Is there any proof such an item ever existed?"

A look of surprise crossed Faye Morris' face, as if she hadn't expected her words to be questioned. She shrugged. "Who needs proof? It's common knowledge Nihisi Khet makes a living skimming money from the museum projects."

Even though Ardis was wary of Nihisi Khet, she resented the girl's bold, careless statement. "What evidence do you have to back this up?"

Faye rolled her eyes. "As if I need evidence! No one could live like he does on the salary he makes. Blake's probably involved, too. No doubt it's turned into a father-and-son operation. There's money in stolen artifacts, you know. Blake Lydon's not talking, and none of the rest of them will either. But rumor has it a big investigation is on the horizon. Jane was no doubt involved in this, too." Confidentially, she added, "I wouldn't be surprised if you're right about someone slipping Jane poison. Thieves will fall out, you know."

Startled and angered, Ardis realized Faye had been eavesdropping on her private conversation with Blake. The thought, along with Faye's innuendoes, prompted Ardis to say sharply, "Jane would never have been a part of anything illegal."

Ignoring Ardis' statement, Faye asked eagerly, "Do you believe Jane Darvin was really a victim of the tomb's curse?"

"Certainly not."

Faye cocked her head to one side, considering. "Then the rumor that she was suffering a nervous breakdown must be true."

Ardis realized the girl was baiting her, but could not resist responding, "People do not die of a nervous breakdown."

Faye Morris' eyes widened, revealing the flecks of gold in the brown. "Then you <u>do</u> believe there was something more to Jane's death?"

"The truth behind her death has not yet been uncovered."

Faye smiled as if she had won a major battle. "I have just one more question."

"I wasn't aware that I was being interviewed," Ardis replied shortly.

Faye had come over to Ardis' table on the pretense of offering condolences, but now a deep, personal bitterness toward Jane was evident in her words. "Just how well did you actually know Jane Darvin? Do you know what kind of a person she really was?" As if seeking more ammunition for her attack on Jane's character, she added spitefully, "Everyone knows she had a child she just abandoned somewhere."

"That's only a rumor."

With an odd, questioning look, Faye insisted, "Is it?"

Ardis pushed the coffee cup, untouched, away from her and rose.

"Wait a minute." Overlooking Ardis' steadily growing anger, Faye asked bluntly, "Who is going to take charge of the project now that Jane is gone—you or Blake Lydon?"

Ardis didn't answer.

"Are you sure you're not afraid of this curse yourself?"

"I really must leave." Before Faye Morris could follow, Ardis abruptly walked out of the dining room. As she returned to her room, she tried not to allow the gossipy reporter's insinuations to influence her. Her instincts warned her that the girl was not to be trusted, no more than was Blake Lydon and Nihisi Khet.

A few miles from Cairo the desert once more claimed the land. Sunset shifted in moving colors across the barren earth tones of rock and sand. The scene before them was one of harmony, of oneness with nature, of peace. Ardis felt a sudden closeness to Jane and knew that remaining in Egypt was what Jane would have wanted.

Blake with an air of isolation stood alone gazing out across the desert. The wind blew his dark hair away from his somber face, a chiseled face with large, expressive eyes and high, slanted cheekbones. For a reason she couldn't understand, the thought came to her that Blake had understood the Jane she knew, had related to her in the same way Ardis had, as teacher, mentor, friend.

The rest of the small group clustered close together to pay their last respects to Jane Darvin. Ramus, his head bent as if in prayer, seemed to have aged ten years. Wearing a dark robe, Matthammed stood close by his side, offering words of consolation.

Matthammed turned to say something to Nihisi Khet. The dignified man, clad in a tailored black suit, appeared to brush off his words with a stony coldness. A sudden dislike for Nihisi Khet, such as she had experienced at the hospital, filled Ardis as she watched Matthammed, looking rejected, move away.

The ceremony began. The tears Ardis had been holding back now flowed. As she pressed a hand against her eyes, struggling to regain her composure, she sensed Blake's presence beside her. His strong arm slipped around her shoulder in a comforting way as Ramus, speaking in Arabic, solemnly scattered ashes over the land Jane had devoted her life to, making her one with the desert she had loved.

Chapter 5

A deep voice on the phone said, "This is Blake. I'd like to talk to you. Would you meet me as soon as you can in the dining room?"

Blake sounded very businesslike. No doubt he needed to discuss the work remaining on the Senmut Tomb. For some reason the desert twilight appeared to her, the feel of Blake's supporting arm around her. For a moment she wished she could trust him, that they would be able to work together to fulfill her promise to Jane.

Ardis selected from her suitcase a white cotton skirt and tailored jacket gave her an aura of professionalism, while a blouse of jade silk added a hint of softness that deepened her green eyes. She checked her appearance in the mirror, smoothing ash blonde hair that today she wore long and loose. Nothing she could do would successfully conceal the shadows resulting from many wakeful nights.

Blake was seated at a table near the window, his gaze fixed upon some distant point beyond the palm trees in the garden. No trace of a smile appeared as he faced her. She steeled herself for another siege of bad news.

"Would you like to order?" he asked, his eyes avoiding hers.

"No, just coffee."

An awkward silence, the tension of something that remained unsaid, hung in the air between them. Blake brushed a hand through slightly ruffled hair in an effort to delay whatever he intended to tell her. Then his shoulders squared, and his gaze met hers. "Since Jane is gone, I suppose you'll be leaving right away," he spoke gravely. "I wanted to take this opportunity to say goodbye and to wish you well."

"I have no plans to leave."

"Since Jane is gone," he repeated, "there's no need for you to stay."

His words struck her like a sound slap in the face. This time Ardis did not answer.

Blake regarded her solemnly, his expression, regretful, but firm. When he spoke, his words were hasty, as if he wanted only the quick accomplishment of some very unpleasant duty. "Let's make an attempt to put this all into perspective." He moved his hand forward as if he intended it to close over hers, but before he had touched her, he drew back. "Jane is the one who sent for you." He went on, in a cold, cutting way, "As for myself I have no need of an assistant."

"I won't leave here until Jane's work is finished."

"Unfortunately, there's simply no place for you now."

Not needed … no place for her … the import of his words stunned her. Last night she had almost accepted him as a friend. Something about his tone caused Ardis to think of her sister, how Lisa had failed to tell her she was going to marry Ardis' long-time suitor. Not that this was a betrayal on Blake's part; she had barely met him.

"Jane called me to her bedside before she died and told me that I was to take her place on this project. I have traveled many miles, giving up my own plans to be here."

"Nihisi will make certain your old job, or a better one, will be waiting for you," Blake replied respectfully. As if to soften the blow, he added, "Your expenses back to Chicago will all be paid, of course." Blake gave her a long, searching look. "I sincerely apologize for the … inconvenience."

"I have no intention of leaving."

A glimmer of something hopeful, a spark of understanding, even compassion, appeared in his eyes. She struggled to find the right words to explain her sense of duty, her dedication to Jane's work. She ended by saying, "Jane was a friend of my late father's. I'm not going to just walk away from her last request."

Last night she had begun to think they shared the same regard for Jane Darvin. She watched him closely, saw the lines around his eyes deepen. Then, as if to resist being swayed by emotion, he once more turned away from her.

"I'm afraid my decision must stand."

She studied his stony, set profile as he stared out of the window and knew whatever flicker of indecision had crossed his mind was gone. Still, she appealed to him one last time. "Would you go against Jane's own wishes?"

"Whatever passed between you and Jane is totally unsubstantiated." His voice, now flat and expressionless, reminded her of Nihisi Khet's. She wondered if his foster father had put him up to this abrupt dismissal of her. Or did Blake alone have some dark and sinister reason for banning her from the project?

Ardis rose slowly, saying with conviction, "Jane made it clear to me that she expected me to take her place on this project. And that's exactly what I intend to do."

"You may remain if you like," Blake answered, his voice equally unremitting. "But under no circumstances will I admit you to the tomb site."

Without another word Ardis pushed back her chair and left the table. She could sense Blake watching her departure but she did not look back.

Although Ardis had not expected him to welcome her as leader of the project; she had certainly never anticipated this action. Her only recourse was to go over his head and appeal directly to Nihisi Khet, but the chance that he would side with her over the decision of his own son was anything but hopeful.

Following up on what Jane was on the verge of discovering without admission to the site would be totally impossible. But she would, regardless of the Khets, stay in Luxor and find Jane's killer.

Matthammed Yusef entered the main lobby. She waved to him, continued to the elevator, and quickly pressed the button.

"Ardis! Wait! I've been looking for you!" His flowing robes billowed as he hurried down the rose-patterned carpet in her direction. "Have you read this?" he asked, waving a newspaper in front of her. "This morning's early edition."

Matthammed showed her an English edition of a local paper, whose sensational headlines likened it to *The International Reporter*. Matthammed pointed excitedly to an article written by Faye Morris. "You'd better hope Blake hasn't seen this. He warned all of us not to talk to her. I guess he didn't get around to telling you."

The elevator door suddenly swung open.

"Here, take it with you," Matthammed said, thrusting the newspaper into her hand. Once in her room Ardis sank into a nearby chair and with a sense of weariness scanned the title of the latest article Faye had written, "Jane Darvin—Victim of Ancient Tomb Curse—or Murder?"

The sudden death of famous archaeologist Jane Darvin remains shrouded in mystery. Her passing leaves in chaos the project of the newly-discovered tomb supposed to be Senmut's. Who will replace Jane Darvin? Why was Dr. Darvin, totally and solely in charge of the tomb, able to exclude all other Egyptologists and work with just a few very select people?

Rumors of a missing artifact have recently surfaced, posing many other, more serious questions. What was the real cause behind her death? Was Jane Darvin, a woman of often questionable ethics, involved in some illegal scheme and cover-up? Investigation of the alleged missing artifact is pending; however Blake Lydon, temporary head of the Senmut project, has refused to comment.

Scandals have followed Jane Darvin's long career, beginning when she first started working in Egypt thirty-two years ago. Another hush-hush incident involving missing artifacts, erupted around the time Jane Darvin found the alabaster Sphinx of Queen Hatshepsut in the desert beyond the Valley of the Kings. Items cataloged by the Egyptian Museum were "lost in transit" before reaching Cairo.

Does history repeat itself?

Jane Darvin's body was cremated early this morning under the authority of Nihisi Khet before a proper autopsy could be authorized. "People don't die of a nervous breakdown," stated Ardis Cole, an Egyptologist from Chicago who is attempting take over the project from Lydon. "The truth behind Jane Darvin's death has yet to be uncovered."

The truth, according to Ardis Cole, is that one of Jane Darvin's closest associates may have laced Jane Darvin's tea with a deadly poison.

How dare Faye Morris write such an article! Ardis' own words leaped out at her—words quoted out of context. They recklessly, boldly stated that Jane had been murdered, and that Ardis was pointing the finger of guilt directly at Blake and Nihisi Khet. Ardis slammed the paper aside and rose. The nerve of that brash reporter! If Blake had read this, then no wonder he had been so opposed to her joining the project.

When her anger began to wane, she began to have second thoughts. Surely Blake wouldn't allow himself to be influenced by an article penned by such a dubious source as Faye Morris. He must have another, more substantial reason behind his trying to bar her from the Senmut tomb. Ardis felt compelled to go back downstairs and try to find him. Just in case the article was behind his opposition to her joining the project, she would do what she could to set the matter right.

When Ardis returned to the dining room, the table where Blake had been sitting was empty. She searched the lobby where she encountered Faye Morris lounging on one of the pale pink chairs. She wore a skimpy outfit of denim shorts and matching jacket. A floppy hat bordered with flowers hid all but a few dark curls as she bent over her inevitable notebook.

Faye glanced up and noticed Ardis. "Have you read my article?" she asked cheerfully, almost as if expecting praise.

"Yes, I have. How could you write anything so shoddy, so unprofessional?"

"What are you so upset about?" Faye tilted her head to one side, looking incredulous. "I would think you'd be a little grateful to me for the publicity. Besides, everything I wrote is the truth."

"What you wrote is an ugly distortion of the truth! Don't you care what damage you do?"

Faye shrugged. Her defiant look warned Ardis of the uselessness of trying to get her to accept any responsibility.

"I didn't use anything but your own words."

"You quoted me on things I did not say to you."

Faye pointed the tip of her pen at Ardis. "But you did say them."

"I say a number of things I don't want to have published!"

"Bad policy," Faye answered, returning to her notes.

Outraged, Ardis drew closer. "You had no right making those libelous statements about Jane. She stood head and shoulders above the rest. She was a person of real character." Ardis couldn't resist the sarcasm that followed. "Perhaps you have trouble understanding the word."

Several people in the lobby had begun casting curious glances in their direction. Ardis lowered her voice. "You attack people who can no longer defend themselves."

Faye's temper flared. "You think Jane Darvin was some kind of a goddess. You don't have any idea what kind of a person she really was." Faye quickly turned the table on Ardis, hurling accusations as if she were the injured one. "She was a devious snake, capable of anything! She ruined my whole life. That's what Jane Darvin did to me!"

As Ardis watched Faye leap from her chair, clutch her notebook and storm away, she wondered what Jane had ever done to her to cause hatred so bitter it outlasted even Jane's death.

Ardis sank into one of the lobby chairs. After a while the inquiring eyes of those who had overhead the confrontation turned to other interests. Ardis remained, hoping Blake would appear.

Time passed and there still no sight of him. She finally began ambling around, ending up at the entrance to the small adjoining room that contained displays of Egyptian artifacts. The gold-embossed sign above the door, "The Griffith Collection, 1920" told her the contents had been purchased from some private party before laws came into effect regulating the removal of such objects into the hands of collectors.

Her attention moved from an alabaster jar to a small figure she recognized as an ushabti. Sometimes hundreds of these diminutive figures, likenesses of the deceased, were buried with the dead. Their purpose was to keep the dead company on their journey and to work for them in the underworld.

Ardis skimmed displays of glass and faience pottery, her gaze settling with revulsion upon a withered mummy's hand. Perhaps some early adventurer had snatched it from some unknown tomb to sell as a curiosity. Since Napoleon's time, a fascination for Egyptian artifacts had increased their desirability as collectors' items. The gruesome relic so carefully preserved under glass served as a reminder of the recklessness with which the tombs had once been plundered, the mummies desecrated, and many of the treasures winding up in foreign museums and private collectors' homes.

Despite the strict rules and regulations that now guarded against it, the smuggling of artifacts out of Egypt was still a lucrative business. And entirely possible if one had the right connections. The disturbing thought entered Ardis' mind that Faye might have come closer to the truth in her article than Ardis was willing to admit. The real reason Blake didn't want her near the tomb was because he couldn't risk her finding out that Nihisi Khet and he were involved in smuggling artifacts out of the country.

Jane, of course, would have been no part of it herself. More likely she had been on the verge of uncovering some illegal scheme between Blake and Nihisi Khet and that was the reason behind her murder.

Ardis realized how easily the word *murder* now slipped into her thoughts. She must be careful about drawing hasty conclusions. She still had no proof that Jane had died of anything other than natural causes.

Still hoping to speak to Blake, Ardis wandered over to the desk and asked the clerk to ring his room. After several attempts, he shook his head. When Ardis finally returned to her own room, her eyes fell to a single glass of iced tea that had been placed in her absence upon the stand near her bed.

It rested on a silver tray such as room service provided. But somehow she knew that its presence was not the compliments of the Old Cairo Hotel.

Woodenly she moved forward and inspected the drink. The ice clinked as Ardis swirled the amber liquid. She raised the glass closer, then recoiled from the sickening smell, metallic and minty.

Poison!

Ardis stared into the dark contents and, fully comprehending its message, became immersed in fear. Because of Faye Morris' article, Jane's killer had become wary of Ardis' presence here. He intended to frighten Ardis away, to avert any investigation into Jane's death. The iced tea had been left for her as a clear and sinister warning.

Ardis knew without doubt that Jane Darvin had been murdered the moment her gaze had locked on the iced tea left in her room. She fully understood the threat, as real and terrifying as if it had been a message scrawled in Jane's blood across the wall.

Ardis had failed to convince Dr. Fahmy of it. She had taken the glass of tea to him at once and had insisted that it be analyzed. After some time he had agreed but only to calm her.

"This process takes some time," he had said. "I'll be in touch concerning the results. Will you be staying in Luxor?"

"Yes, I'll be returning there today."

She would be in no better position in Luxor, however, than she was here. She needed access to Jane's journals and records, the lifetime of Egyptian research Jane had told her was stored at the site. Unless she could gain admittance into the tomb, she would have little chance of finding out who had killed Jane.

Before she left Cairo, Ardis decided to contact Nihisi Khet. Nihisi had the final say concerning all activity around the tomb sites, though Ardis thought it unlikely that he would overrule the word of his own son and allow her to finish Jane Darvin's work. Moreover, if Nihisi Khet had read Faye Morris' article, he would probably slam the door in her face.

In any event, the very idea of appealing to him filled her with distaste. She did not like him and even believed he might be the one behind her sudden dismissal. Ardis had dealt before with people who possessed such a rigid state of mind—nothing but an act of God would be likely to change his opinions once they were formed.

Ardis wasn't used to using this aggressive sort of approach, but her desperation called for such a measure. Ordinarily, she would have called for an appointment, yet she had this odd feeling that he would not see her unless she was on hand to insist.

So much depended on this meeting. Perhaps, if nothing else, she could get his sanction for her to remain on the site as any ordinary worker—if Blake had not talked to him first, if the two of them were not co-partners in some deadly, covert activity which involved Jane Darvin's murder.

The thought increased her apprehension. To lessen it, she turned to look out the taxi window. She was bombarded with colors, smells, sounds, and with the jostling of strange and varied types of people and customs. What a mixture—men in business suits, women hidden beneath shapeless black robes and veils, dignified holy men, peasants in rags—all of them moving, lugging burdens, calling.

The cab driver, catching her eye in the rear-view mirror, said, "Life here is lived in the streets."

"I'm sure that's the very spirit of Egypt," she answered.

They passed cafes and tables spread out into the walkways. Egyptians lingered in entrances and alleyways. Ardis leaned forward to look through beaded doorways into quaint little shops protected from the sun by faded and torn awnings.

The cab careened into the middle of the city. She would have been tempted to fear the fast approaching meeting with Nihisi Khet were it not for more present worries, the dangerous nearness of trucks, and the yelling of a man as the taxi brushed against his cart.

"I'm not in any big hurry," she said to the driver.

He slowed a little, but soon picked up speed again until they were going as fast as before. She clung to the back of the seat, bracing herself against the sudden bumps that caused a rattling under her feet.

Shaken by the wild ride, nauseated by the strong fumes, she paid the driver and stood for a moment in front of the famous Egyptian Museum. Even at this early hour tourists streamed into the huge, stone building. Ardis, still feeling queasy and uncertain, joined them.

From the doorway she could see two huge, granite statues toward the rear of the great hall. Their looming height momentarily overshadowed her qualms. She took time to pause and study them, to look up at the serene faces that had found some small way to survive a mortal time frame. Feeling steadied by familiar stirrings of interest and awe, she turned to the guard who stood nearby and asked almost casually, "Where can I find Nisihi Khet's office?"

At least he understood the name, for he directed her toward a stairway. On the second level Ardis wandered through another vast room filled with displays. Through an open door beneath an arched stone entrance, Ardis caught sight of Nihisi Khet seated behind a desk. Opposite him sat an Egyptian man, who swung around at her approach. His eyes, underlined by deep pouches, narrowed with agitation.

Nihisi brusquely closed the folder in front of him and rose. Because he waited without even a word of greeting, Ardis said, "Would it be possible for me to talk to you this morning?"

Instead of answering her he addressed the other man in rapid Arabic. Irritated over what was probably a quick dismissal, the Egyptian man began stuffing papers into his briefcase. After he left, Nihisi still waited.

His frigid manner caused Faye's article to flash across her mind. "I'm sorry to have interrupted you," Ardis said.

"That's quite all right."

Only the words had politeness; the coldness remained plain on his face, a face that would have been handsome if not for the permanent etch of a frown between his dark eyes, the judgmental set of his thin lips.

She was dealing with a much different man than Blake. She had sensed in Blake the presence of deep emotion that was likely to guide him. Not so with his foster father—whatever Nihisi Khet felt was private and hidden, kept totally separated from his actions.

This knowledge caused her to hesitate, to reconsider her approach. She studied him a moment longer, then deciding he would appreciate directness, said, "I'm here because Jane Darvin asked me to take charge of her project."

Nihisi Khet's dark eyes remained expressionless. The only change in him was the tightening of his lips. As the stillness hung around them, Ardis thought of the glass of tea with its strong, minty smell left in her room, of rare poisons, of Jane's hasty cremation that this man had ordered. Even in the busy museum with the door wide open she felt strangely isolated and frightened.

"I've run across a problem," she went on. "Blake tells me he is now in charge and that he will not allow me to work with him even as an assistant. I'm not going to ... "

Nihisi broke in, "It doesn't matter what Blake tells you. I am appointed by the Minister of Antiquities and that makes neither of you in charge. Not without my authorization."

The harshness of his voice caused anger to rush over her. She had known trying to talk to him would be a waste of time, but this sharp manner, this rudeness, had been unanticipated. He was much worse than Blake, who had at least been willing to listen to her.

Nihisi turned his back to her and looked from the window. Taking this for a gesture of dismissal, Ardis' anger mounted. "Don't think I'm giving up. I will never abandon Jane's work."

Even as she spoke, she felt defeated. What else could she do? They both knew his decision would be final.

When Nihisi did not respond, she added with determination, "I gave my word to Jane. I'll never break it, no matter what measures I must take."

"Drastic measures would not be advisable," he replied.

Ardis took a step back toward the entrance.

"The project would benefit most," Nihisi spoke slowly, "if Blake and you could find some way to come to terms, to work together as partners."

"That's out of the question."

"When it comes to hieroglyphic translation, there is no expert more knowledgeable than Blake. He has had the advantage of two worlds, which gives him an insight *outsiders* will never have."

"I'm not denying Blake's qualifications. He is the one refusing to work with me."

Nihisi began almost grudgingly to explain, "Jane meant a great deal to him—to us all—and quite naturally he wants to be the one to finish her project for her."

"I'm not big on titles," Ardis said. "Give Blake whatever position you wish. My only concern is staying here."

These words apparently sparked some approval in him. After a moment of consideration, he asked, "Has some conflict arisen between Blake and you that you're not telling me about?"

"I didn't know there was any problem between us at all until he told me that I would not be admitted to the site." She paused. "It might help if you talked to him."

"No," he answered in a resentful way, "Blake should have come to me."

Once again he looked from the window. This time she waited for him to speak, and the wait was long and anxious.

"Jane and I," he said at last, his voice strangely distant, "go back many, many years. Regardless of our little differences, there was great trust between us." He slowly turned back to her. "She knew whatever plans she had, I would set in motion."

"I assure you, Jane's plans included me. Jane wanted ... "

"I know," he interrupted. "When I saw her that last time at the hospital, she told me that she had sent for you to complete her work, in the event that she could not. That makes me ... honor bound ... to appoint you. Although," he added, "I do not think it is the wisest course."

It took Ardis some time to fully comprehend this unexpected turn-around. Despite his careful wording that indicated that he had been intending all along to keep his word to Jane, Ardis felt as if he had just decided on the spur of the moment to do so. Trying to keep her surprise and her sudden suspicions from him, she managed to recover and say, "I would like Blake to stay. Would you tell him that?"

"Blake will expect me to side with him."

"Even against Jane's wishes?"

"This decision will be sure to anger him." Nihisi said shortly. "But so be it."

"Maybe he will listen to reason ... "

"Blake will ask to be transferred."

The certainty present in Nihisi's cold statement left Ardis feeling a sense of loss instead of triumph.

"I am going to draw up papers that will put you in charge of all of Jane's projects here. I'll send them to you at once. You're staying at the Oasis in Luxor, aren't you?"

"Yes."

Nihisi's dark eyes met hers in a solemn appraisal. "Being held in such esteem by a person like Jane Darvin speaks very well for you. No one would need a higher recommendation."

Chapter 6

Good fortune—or was Nihisi Khet's decision allowing her to head Jane's project good fortune? Ardis felt too weary, too alone, too saddened by the loss of her friend and mentor, to even consider the immense task that stretched before her, or the danger that she was so certain that it involved.

The crowded Ramses Station gleamed, a splash of noise and color against the Cairo sky. Egyptian men in blue and white jellabas with their heads wrapped in turbans and peasant women wearing black dresses and gauzy black scarves began to fill the ancient green train during the last-minute rush. Ardis found consideration and helpfulness, rather than the push and shove of ordinary crowds.

As Ardis wandered past rows of seats, she noticed carefully styled gray hair among white turbans and black-haired Egyptians. For a moment Ardis wondered if the attractive, older man with the trim mustache, whom she had selected to sit near, was the same British man she had asked for directions just outside the Cairo Hospital. Something about the sharp, distinctive profile seemed vaguely familiar. Still, she couldn't be certain. The faces of doctors, of people in the waiting room and on the street, seemed to blend together into one big haze.

As if sensing her curious eyes, he glanced up from the newspaper propped across his knees and nodded. Whether the nod was a sign of recognition or only a gesture of casual politeness, Ardis could not be sure. Maybe it was only that he was so obviously British, that he looked as out of place on the local train as she felt, that caused her to think she had seen him before.

The train started off with a jolt. The gray-haired gentleman frowned as he attempted to concentrate on his newspaper. Ardis settled back and watched Cairo blur past the filmy train window—lighted Coca Cola signs in Arabic script, high-rise apartment buildings, slum areas of crowded streets and markets. Tall buildings grew smaller and finally disappeared, replaced by fields interspersed with mud huts. Ardis had the strange feeling that the rattling train was moving them back in time. Soon all that surrounded them was endless, shadowy stretches of desert.

This man across the aisle put aside his paper and spoke to her, "You've found your way, I see. Not lost any longer."

He was the same man who had directed her to the hotel where she met Thomas Garrett. She smiled at him, "Surprisingly, I now know exactly where I'm going. I'm on my way to the Valley of the Kings. To Luxor."

"That sounds so exciting, doesn't it? I'm bound for Luxor, too. I've always planned to tour Egypt, but I have a hard time believing I'm actually here."

Ardis leaned back in the seat again scanning the crowd in front of her. She noticed a man dressed in a tan safari jacket—another tourist, an American, perhaps. Her eyes left him, then returned suddenly, recognizing the broad set of shoulders, the thick, black hair. She felt a sudden, apprehensive catch in her breath.

Having become aware of her gaze, Blake looked back and their eyes met, his steady and opaque. He must know about her talk with his foster father and was attempting to conceal his anger. Or had he intentionally taken the train because she had?

Blake arose, his hand gripping the backs of seats as he came down the aisle toward her. His scrutinizing gaze had vanished into a thin smile. "May I join you?"

Ardis' voice sounded as formal as his. "If you wish." After a period of uneasy silence, Ardis spoke again, "I suppose you've read the article in this morning's paper by Faye Morris. I want you to know that I ... "

"I'm quite familiar with the way she operates," he interrupted. "There is no need to explain." He eased his arm across the back of the seat as he turned toward her. "I looked for you at the hotel to say goodbye. I hadn't thought that you must return to Luxor to retrieve the rest of your luggage."

Ardis, with a quick, sideways glance, determined that Blake had not talked to Nihisi before he had left Cairo. She faced him, prepared to tell him about the outcome of the meeting, but his smile had become genuine and radiated a warmth that stopped her. That, or the emptiness left from the funeral, the draining pace of the days before it, prevented her words. She needed a period of calm. It would not matter if she temporarily put off the unpleasant confrontation she knew must soon take place between them.

Besides, as of yet she did not possess the papers that gave her the authority to take over Jane's work. Although Nihisi had spoken of Jane's implicit trust in him, it was not trust Ardis herself felt. Nihisi Khet may or may not follow through with her appointment. He may be using this tactic as a delay until he could devise some scheme that would get her out of the way, a scheme that Blake was right now helping him carry out.

Blake spoke sincerely. "Ardis, there's something I want you to understand. What I said to you this morning had to be said."

Feeling a return of animosity toward him, she looked away.

"I want you to know, Ardis, if we had met under different circumstances …" His voice trailed off. "If you're ever back in Egypt, I want you to give me a call. I can show you the real Egypt, what tourists never see."

Ardis did not answer. Blake was looking beyond her into the murky void of desert. She could see the reflection of his dark eyes in the window.

"We'll be traveling for a long time," Blake said. "It's 400 miles to Luxor by rail." His voice had lightened. "People are in such a hurry these days that most of them fly. But ever since I was a child, the train to Luxor has always fascinated me."

Ardis could see nothing here to fascinate. The seats felt hard and uncomfortable, the air as stiflingly hot and motionless as the tomb of Senmut. As time passed in casual conversation, Ardis found herself beginning to be comforted by the sound of Blake's deep voice, by the soothing motion of the train.

"I wish it were daylight," Blake was saying. "Traveling through the countryside, you can best see the real Egypt, my Egypt, Jane's Egypt."

Ardis' heaviness of heart returned at the mention of Jane's name.

"Wherever I go, I'm drawn back," Blake went on. "I've always felt it my destiny to do my life's work here. Do you believe in destiny, Ardis? All my life I've felt it calling me. I am destined to do something important here in Egypt."

Ardis had heard Jane make almost the same remarks. Poor Jane, dead now, before she had accomplished all of her wonderful plans. Ardis felt a sudden unworthiness. How could she ever expect to take over for Jane? She could never replace her, even though for a moment watching from the window she had felt that strong call of Egypt, too.

A land of change, of mystery, of blackness spreading endlessly across the long horizon—she turned back to Blake, noting the same contrasts in the chiseled lines of his face. At any other time she would have been attracted to his tall, straight frame, his high cheekbones, the hint of Egypt in his eyes. But she must not allow for such feelings. She had far too many questions about Blake Lydon.

"Jane sent for me that day at the tomb," she spoke. "Had she also sent for you?"

"We all take a break in the hottest part of the day. Actually I had come out to see if I could convince Jane to take a rest." His voice dropped to a tone of regret. "I had been worrying about her a great deal. I keep thinking now that I might have prevented this."

Whatever Jane had discovered in the Senmut tomb, she had intended to share with Ardis but not with Blake. That fact alone confirmed Ardis' suspicions. Jane had not trusted him, and Ardis warned herself that she must not, either.

The lapse in their talk was filled with the noise of the train, the sound of steel wheels against track. Ardis' thoughts flitted to the obelisk that Jane had been working with the day of her collapse. She could hardly wait for the chance to examine the papyrus hidden inside it. The key, Jane had called it. Thank goodness Ardis had been able to secure it in the safety deposit box at the hotel. The minute she arrived in Luxor, she would take a look at this ancient scroll.

"Whenever I take the train," Blake was saying, "I pack a lunch." He rose and from an overhead compartment took a thermos and a small paper sack from his carry-on. Settling in the seat beside her again, he said, "Won't you join me?"

He poured her a paper cup of coffee and handed her a roast beef sandwich. Even the smell of the strong coffee braced her. She had forgotten how many meals she had missed. They finished their lunch with a rich pastry Blake called konafu, flaky strips of dough soaked in honey.

"How did you and Jane become such solid friends?" he asked.

"My father was a professor, an Egyptologist. He had met Jane on one of his trips to Luxor. When I signed up for her course, she recognized my name. After she found out Father had passed on, she took me under her wing." Ardis remained silent for a moment before she added, "My mother died when I was very young." Again, she paused. "Jane became almost a mother to me."

"How fortunate you are. Jane Darvin is certainly a legend around here. I always felt honored to work with her."

"Your father is another legend," Ardis stated.

"My foster father." A shielded look fell across Blake's face. "Yes, Nihisi Khet is a man who commands great respect from everyone."

Ardis had already noted the unnatural lack of rapport that existed between Blake and Nihisi. She guessed that Nihisi Khet would be more successful in commanding respect than love, even from his own son.

"Who are your real parents?" she asked.

"I've tried to find my natural parents, but I always reach a dead end." With that same shuttered look, Blake added, "I'm convinced Nihisi knows more about them than he's telling me."

The lack of closeness and affection between Nihisi Khet and Blake was no doubt the driving force behind Blake's search. Nihisi's strength, his hardness, were not the qualities of a good father. Maybe he was a man void of feeling or perhaps he, like her own father, merely refused to let his emotions show.

"All Nihisi will tell me is that my parents are Americans. I think my mother," Blake added speculatively, "was one of Jane's associates, a young student, probably. I always had a feeling Jane knew her very well. Anyway, I know that Jane was the one who visited the orphanage in Luxor and talked Nihisi and Lami into taking me when I was still a baby."

Another silence fell."Lami was a great woman,"Blake said. "Nihisi married her when she was a girl of fifteen. She died when I was twelve."

"Then Nihisi saw to your education."

"With Jane's advice," Blake said, smiling. "Between teaching assignments, Jane always managed to return to Egypt. Every time she did, she always visited us first."

Ardis thought about Jane's going to the orphanage and finding a home for an abandoned baby. At the time Jane might have been thinking of her own child, who, as Ramus had said, might have died at birth. Wondering about Blake's background, she gazed questioningly at him. The conversation lapsed into silence.

Across the aisle the gray-haired gentleman had folded his paper and was staring out of the window. The small man in front of him, who wore a turban, leaned back and closed his eyes. Ardis' own vision blurred with sleepiness and fatigue. Hours of forced wakefulness were taking their toll—and the food had increased her drowsiness until she had difficulty keeping her eyes open.

Through half-closed lids she was barely aware that her head rested upon Blake's shoulder. She attempted to move away, but a gentle, yet firm hand urged her to relax. She thought she saw Blake smile down at her through the fog of sleep before she drifted off into a world of blessed oblivion.

The darkness, the gentle rocking of the train, must have lulled Ardis to sleep. She awoke with a start and found that Blake was gone. Ardis felt a slight jolting of the back of her seat. She sat up, fully awake, to see the older, gray-haired gentleman bracing his hands against her seat to prevent the swaying of the train from pitching him forward.

"Pardon," he said in a clipped, very British accent. "I didn't mean to disturb you."

Her hand rose to steady him while he attempted to regain his balance.

"Thank you." He swung awkwardly around to his seat and sat down hard. Leaning across the aisle, he confided to Ardis, "Wretched train. If I had known how blasted primitive this ride would be, I would have waited for tomorrow's flight."

"We'll soon be in Luxor," Ardis replied. She guessed that he must be a professor, one accustomed to a soft life, unused to the rigors of travel in a foreign land.

"That is, if we get there in one piece after all of this rousting about." He flashed her a faltering smile, as if the jostling of the train had actually made him ill. She had thought him an attractive man. On closer look, she observed traces of a faded handsomeness, but a definite worldliness that in some way detracted from his good looks.

Blake returned and slipped into the seat beside her. "I came to wake you," he said with a flash of white teeth. "But I see now that I won't have to." He pointed to bright lights beyond the window. "We'll be pulling into the Luxor station in a few minutes."

Once they arrived, Blake asked, "Would you like to stop for coffee or something to eat?" Blake suggested. "I know a quaint place that is still open at this hour."

Although Ardis had slept a good portion of the train journey and was now wide-awake, she let Blake believe that she was still tired. "No, thank you."

The taxi pulled up to the Oasis Hotel, which shone white in the moonlight. Blake stepped out to escort her to the door. "Then I'll say good night to you here," he said. Still, he lingered a moment by the entrance as if reluctant to let her go.

Ardis watched Blake's taxi disappear from sight, momentarily wishing that she had accepted his offer for coffee and something to eat, although she was neither thirsty nor hungry. She had been so anxious to arrive here, yet upon his leaving she felt a great sense of dread and a return of despondency.

Even though it was not yet midnight, the vast chandelier that dominated the center of the lobby was no longer lit. Only a dim light glowed above the hotel desk, making the room, usually brisk with activity, seem singularly empty.

The clerk, Essa BenSobel, who had previously been so friendly, stood immobile behind the counter … His face, smooth and dark as ebony, remained void of any greeting. Everything looked so foreign, so frightening. Her plan to take a look at the papyrus could wait until morning. She moved slowly toward the elevator and pressed the button.

"Good to see you again, Miss Cole," Essa BenSobel's voice sounded more soft-spoken in the deserted room. "We were so sorry to hear about Mrs. Darvin. That probably means you won't be staying."

"I will be staying," she said, changing her mind and walking back to the desk. "I need to get into my safety deposit box."

With a cat-like response the desk clerk moved to the wall and a flick of his hand filled the small room behind him with brilliant light. With a sweeping gesture, he said, "Go on back."

Ardis entered alone and placed the key into the metal box marked 45. Quickly she removed Jane's battered, canvas bag, heavy with the weight of the obelisk. Nervously, she took it out, holding the long, slender statue tightly in her hands. This closer look at it convinced her the obelisk was an authentic and priceless treasure possibly dating back to the time of Queen Hatshepsut. She could not take the time tonight to study the rows of script so deeply embedded in the granite that would give her some clue to its authenticity.

The obelisk seemed perfectly solid. She studied the stone base, but could find no catch that would free the base and admit her to the hollow space inside where the papyrus was safely stored.

"Do you need any help?" Essa BenSobel's voice, even lower than before, drifted to her from the doorway. Before she could conceal the obelisk, his gaze fell upon it.

"No, I'll be just a while longer."

Ardis again tried to turn the stone base, but it remained firm. She studied the row of symbols along the bottom edge. It took her some time to identify the same exact design on two of the sides—the pointed ears and faded image of some animal, possibly a cat. Ardis pressed these two images simultaneously and felt something give. This time, pressure triggering a release from inside the stone walls, the base swung free.

Relieved, Ardis lifted the obelisk so she could see into the hollowed column. With disbelief she ran her fingers inside to assure herself that her eyes were giving her a correct message. She found no hidden script, only a vacant place where the papyrus had once been hidden. The papyrus, the key to Jane's life's work and perhaps even to her death, had been stolen.

Chapter 7

The British man Ardis had met in Cairo and again on the train stopped in front of the lobby desk, setting down his luggage and saying breathlessly, "Laurence Tolliver. I have a reservation."

Essa BenSobel, looking distracted, cut short his talk with Ardis and checked the hotel records. "Yes. Room 209."

"I'll be staying for at least seven days." Then to Ardis, "So we meet again."

If his hurried entrance had not interrupted her questioning of the hotel clerk, Ardis might have been glad to see him, still she managed to smile and answer, "I'm Ardis Cole. Welcome to Luxor."

With a lift of thin, white eyebrows, he leaned closer to her and said speculatively, "Not a tourist, are you?"

"No, I'm an archaeologist."

"Where are you working?"

The sudden dropping of his brows over keen, gray eyes caused Ardis to believe that he already knew the answer. "I was called to assist Dr. Darvin at the Senmut Tomb."

"I don't suppose that it's open to public viewing."

"No."

Appearing to have lost interest, Laurence Tolliver turned to the clerk and exclaimed, "I'm going to be doing some sight seeing starting early tomorrow. Where is the best place to begin?"

Essa BenSobel, grateful for the delay, launched into a detailed account of available tours.

"To tell you the truth," Tolliver said, "I'm not one for guides. I like to go out on my own, find and explore everything for myself."

"If you change your mind, just drop by the desk." BenSobel smiled broadly. "Leave your luggage here, Mr. Tolliver. It will be brought up to you."

The moment Laurence Tolliver disappeared into the elevator, BenSobel's smile abruptly vanished. "You say what you lost was priceless. What was it?"

"A document."

"I am the only one who has the keys to the safety deposit boxes," BenSobel said adamantly, "and they never, ever leave my possession."

Ardis watched Laurence Tolliver walk along the open balcony upstairs. He drew to a halt in the center, leaning against the railing to purposely listen. She asked in a lower voice, "How does anyone get admittance to the boxes when you are off duty?"

He drew himself up. "I live in this hotel. When that happens, I am paged."

"Could anyone have jimmied the lock?"

"Absolutely not."

Ardis looked deeply into the black depth of his eyes which had grown sullen. He could be bought off, she decided. While she was in Cairo, he could have taken the papyrus at the bidding of any one of them—Blake, Ramus, Matthammed, Nihisi Khet.

"Whatever it is that you're missing," he said, his defensive voice ringing loudly, "was not stolen from the Oasis."

From the hallway above Laurence Tolliver straightened up, his face merging with shadows.

BenSobel reached for the phone. "I'm going to call the police."

Ardis had no way of knowing whether or not the papyrus had even reached the hotel. Just as likely, it had been stolen at the site, taken by whoever had poisoned Jane. At any rate, she did not want to discuss the papyrus or its possible contents with anyone. "No, don't involve the police. It would do no good."

When Ardis reached the second floor, Laurence Tolliver ambled back toward her.

"Couldn't help overhearing," he said. "I hope you didn't lose anything of great value."

"It was of the greatest value."

"A pity." He seemed genuinely sorry. "I never trust hotel securities myself. I've traveled far too much for that. But I don't think that clerk had anything to do with it. He seems a good bloke if I know anything about people."

They began walking down the hall together. "Might be a good idea to talk to the police," he said before she went into her room.

Her surroundings here, ultra modern and luxurious, contrasted greatly with the antique decor of The Old Cairo Hotel. She crossed to the window, looking out at the Nile, much nearer than she had remembered. The darkness of the water merged imperceptibly into the night sky.

Finding the papyrus would be impossible, but it had been in Jane's possession so many years, Jane must have shared its existence with someone, a person she trusted, likely Ramus. She would contact him tomorrow and ask him what he knew about it.

Ardis did not drift off to sleep until nearly dawn. She awoke with a start hours later to find that the morning was almost gone. At the sound of the ringing phone beside her bed, her thoughts flitted to Blake.

"Surprise."

Ardis could not identify the pleasant, masculine voice. "Who is this?"

"Thomas. Thomas Garrett. Don't tell me you don't remember me?" The British accent gave him away before he added, "We met in Cairo."

"Of course. Did you get to see Nihisi Khet?"

"Don't mention that name to me," he moaned. "I would have had a better interview with the Great Sphinx. Begrudgingly Khet did make a couple of small concessions which allows for some kindergarten work at Karnak."

Ardis laughed.

"But good luck does follow me a little. I've just found out that we're staying at the same hotel." Thomas went on in his jovial way, "Would you consider having lunch with me, love?"

For an instant Ardis was tempted to accept. It would be good to talk to Thomas again. She had liked him; he was so open and uncomplicated. "I'm sorry," she said, "but I have some business I must see to. Perhaps another time."

"I'm going to hold you to that, Ardis Cole. Expect another call very soon."

Jane's killer now had possession of the papyrus, but Jane might have among her records some reference to that ancient writing. At any rate Ardis must waste no time gathering the papers in Jane's makeshift office before they, too, disappeared.

Ardis drove much too quickly, Jeep bumping over rough patches of road. She passed the little village of Qurna and began following the rim-line of buff-colored cliffs. Already her throat felt parched, and her lips were covered with a fine layer of dust.

Ardis drew to a stop at the fenced line between the canyon walls. At once two guards appeared from the shelter and stood, one in front of her Jeep the other at her window. She recognized the man who had admitted her on her last visit.

"I won't be long," she told him. "I need to pick up some of Jane Darvin's papers."

"You can not go any farther," he said in choppy English.

"You must remember me? I was here just the other day. I showed you the pass Jane Darvin had given me." She began shuffling through the contents of her bag.

"You can not be admitted," the man repeated.

"Why not?" Ardis demanded, anger rising and settling around her like the thick layers of heat. "I was called here to assist Jane. You can not keep me out."

"We have instructions that you are not to pass through this gate." He stepped back a little. "I am sorry."

"Whose instructions? I have a right to come and go as I please."

The man spoke slowly as if trying to explain in words that were not familiar to him. "Blake Lydon. He is in charge now, not your friend, Jane Darvin."

Ardis thought for a moment of backing up and swinging the Jeep around the blockade across the road. They certainly wouldn't use those guns on her, but they probably could and would physically prevent her from reaching the tomb.

Fury rose again, then eased into logic. She simply had to wait until she received the papers from Nihisi Khet. When or if they arrived, she would be quickly admitted. No one could possibly refuse to acknowledge his written orders.

She tried again to convince the guard, but he remained adamant. Having no other choice, Ardis turned back. Ramus lived in Qurna. She would stop and talk to him, perhaps convince him to do what she had just failed to accomplish, to secure Jane's life-long work.

Ardis' anger had subsided long before she reached Qurna. She had slowed the vehicle to a pace suitable for the barren, lifeless surroundings. Although Ardis had passed through Qurna before, today she really saw it for the first time, the way it perched on the edge of the Theban Hills. One good road led through it. Mud-brick houses were scattered here and there, some precariously clinging to the jutting slopes.

Because of its proximity to the tombs, Qurna was internationally known as a haven for medieval tomb robbers. These people had lived in tight little groups since before the thirteenth century. Once they had sworn to keep the secrets of the tombs and had kept their fortunes stowed away to sell a little at a time. Were the descendants still operating in the same way?

Ardis could somehow picture Ramus as head man among them. He knew more about the tombs than any of his professional associates and would be able to extract the best prices and keep the profit for those who stubbornly remained in Qurna despite years of government opposition.

Jane had spoken of the villagers, how they refused to be transplanted to the new Qurna imposed on them by the government. From Ramus' attitude, Ardis supposed he had led the opposition and, if so, Dr. Jane had helped him. They would both know men of power in the government, men like Nihisi Khet.

Around her she saw only deprivation and squalor. Men on donkeys, Arabs in jellabas and turbans, raggedy children— the whole town stopped and watched her approach with a boldness that was anything but secretive. She stopped in front of an ancient-looking building with an amateurish sign signifying authentic antique treasures. Two men stood under the sun-battered awning. She inquired about Ramus.

The taller of the two pointed up a steep, rutted road. Although she was tempted to try to drive the Jeep, Ardis decided to walk. She could feel their eyes on her as she stopped at the machine to purchase two sodas. Because of the blistering sun, she walked slowly up the great incline. Dust hung about her, intermingling with the insufferable heat.

Ramus' home, not a wealthy man's estate by any means, seemed so compared to the others. Enclosed behind a low, stone fence, masses of palm fronds created a cool oasis in the blinding sunlight. Apparently Ramus lived here alone, even though the house seemed vast, suited to an extended family, a prosperous family.

Ardis drew to a stop at the gate. She knew nothing at all about Ramus Montu. It was absurd to trust him, to ask him to protect Jane's research for her.

The fence shut out the dry barrenness of the hillside. She crossed the large yard. A tiled fountain filled with steamy water set in the center. Beside it stood a hand pump, a proclamation of status. The house was so open it seemed unnecessary for her to knock. Instead she called, "Ramus."

Ardis could see the fine furniture inside, the silver teapot, the tiny porcelain cups with green twisted-vine designs. An ornamental buffet was covered with granite statues, with pots of clay and crudely fashioned metal. She gazed through a beaded doorway into another room, cool and dark, filled, no doubt, with even more exquisite treasures.

Ramus suddenly appeared. She had expected him to be in the same mournful state he had been in at the funeral, but today he was composed, a frightening composure, worse than any exhibition of grief. His house appeared to be so abundantly supplied, she felt foolish offering him one of the sodas she had just purchased.

Ramus accepted the drink graciously and said with a chilling control, "I don't know how we're going to get along without Jane."

"We have no choice. And that's why I'm here." Ardis stopped, searching the broad, strong face for some sign of friendship. "We must work together, Ramus. That's what Jane would have wanted."

Ramus' eyes, hard and fixed, gave no hint to his thoughts. He took a drink from the can and invited her to be seated on the wicker couch.

Ardis had not intended to accept the offer, but because of the room's protection from dust and glare, because of the air stirring around her from the overhead fan, she allowed herself to be seated. The drink began to quench her awful thirst. Almost against her will, her gaze wondered to the statues spread across the rosewood buffet.

"Knick-knacks," he said. "I paid almost nothing for that statue of Queen Hatshepsut. They give me a good buy because I am one of them. We have some excellent craftsman here in Qurna."

Ardis studied the placid face of Queen Hatshepsut. Even with close inspection it would be impossible to attach any date to it, but the limestone looked very smooth as if worn by centuries of desert wind. Close beside it loomed an enormous, alabaster scarab—the beetle so sacred to the Egyptians and beyond that set a picture of Ramus, Blake, and Matthammed, displayed in a bright, filigree frame. Her eyes lingered on the photograph of Blake, his handsome, smiling face, his arm thrown in comradeship around Matthammed's thin shoulder. Such a tight little group.

"Do you recall the miniature obelisk that belonged to Jane?" she asked, indicating the twelve or fourteen-inch height of the stone work.

"I've seen it." He frowned as he set aside his drink. "It was part of Jane's father's collection." He hesitated before adding, "He was able to purchase authentic items before all the laws forbidding it."

"Then you don't think it's a reproduction?"

Ramus hesitated again. "I would have no way of knowing. But I do know Jane treasured it, just as she did that award Nihisi presented to her from the Egyptian Museum." He stared at her a long time before adding, "Since I've returned from Cairo, I have been looking for the obelisk, but so far I haven't located it."

Ardis finished the soda which had grown almost warm in the short interval since she had purchased it. She placed the can on the coffee table. "The obelisk isn't what's important," she said. "Jane told me that hidden inside it was an ancient scroll. Do you know anything about it?"

"The Senmut papyrus," Ramus exclaimed, turning and walking around the room. "This papyrus was what prompted Jane to keep up that endless search for Senmut's tomb. I knew of its existence, but I have never laid eyes on it."

"What exactly did Jane tell you about the scroll? What was in it?"

He shrugged heavy shoulders. "Jane believed she would find in the tomb the gold Senmut had gathered for the obelisks in Karnak. She could never be swayed from that idea, preposterous though it is. Before she died, she was busy looking for secret chambers."

"Secret chambers could exist." Ardis went on excitedly. "Jane might have discovered one and that is why she left that note for me to meet her at the tomb."

Ramus shook his head. "I talked to Jane early that morning. She was using the obelisk the very day she died, comparing its inscriptions to those on the tomb wall."

Pain filled his large eyes whenever he spoke of Jane. Ramus had loved her so much, Ardis thought suddenly, he would never have harmed her. For that reason, he was likely the only one she had met here whom she could trust. "I have the obelisk."

Ramus' dark eyes could change rapidly, the same way Blake's did.

Ardis had not intended to confide in him, but now that she had, she might just as well tell him all. "When Jane was in the hospital at Luxor, she wanted me to pick up the obelisk from the tomb. I secured it for her. I didn't know about the hidden papyrus until she told me about it in Cairo. I looked inside the obelisk the minute I returned last night, but the papyrus has been removed."

Ramus' features remained impassive.

"If it does give some clue to a hidden chamber and there actually is gold, as Jane thought, then we are in great danger of losing it." She paused. "The guarding system leaves a lot to be desired. Is there some way to make the tomb more secure?"

"There is little need for that. Those sheer, circular cliffs give natural protection. The men at the main gate guard the only accessible entrance."

"Couldn't a person find a way down the cliffs?"

Ramus shook his head. "Only if he had a death wish. The cliffs are solid rock and drop straight down. Even if anyone was able to perform such a feat, it would be impossible to haul artifacts from the tomb. Such a maneuver would be spotted immediately by the guards at the gate."

"Since the scroll is missing, we need to make sure Jane's papers are secure."

"Her records, over thirty years of them, beginning with her first work here in Egypt, are stored in the shack near the tomb entrance. Jane was there day and night. Since she's gone, I've had one of my men take her place. But I think I'll start staying there myself until this project is finished."

Ardis arose to depart, and Ramus followed her from the house. "You could have driven up here easily," he said.

"I felt like walking."

Ramus stood beside the colorfully tiled fountain and watched her leave. The sun's rays beat down on her, stronger after the pleasant coolness of the house. Trickles of sweat trailed across her face as she descended the slope.

Midway, pausing for breath, Ardis looked back. To her surprise Blake now stood beside Ramus at the fountain. In astonishment she wondered where he had come from, if he had been there all the time or if he had arrived unnoticed while they had been talking.

Even though Blake was taller than Ramus and more American in appearance, the two men, standing side by side, looked very much like father and son. Their features possessed the same angular lines, their dark eyes, the identical slanting slope. Their strong resemblance, magnified in the wavering sunlight, went far beyond the physical. Both of them were men of mystifying contrasts—open, yet hidden, strong, yet vulnerable.

Ardis hesitated. She wanted to return and talk to Blake, yet she was infuriated by the instructions Blake had given to the guards at the site. Blake's head moved in a barely perceptible gesture of greeting. She thought for an instant that he intended to stride down the slope toward her, but he did not.

She managed a quick wave before hurrying on to her Jeep. The image of the two men remained firmly stamped in her mind.

Blake had told her on the train that he had been trying to locate his natural parents. What if he had found them? If Blake were Jane's son, he would feel it was his right to take over her work. If he had recently found out that Jane Darvin was his mother, Blake's feelings would quite naturally be confused—

love and admiration tainted with the bitter edge of hatred because of her abandonment of him.

True, Ardis had not known Jane when she was young, and people do change drastically over the years. Perhaps, back then, Jane had met some force she had been unable to cope with, a force strong enough to cause her to give up her child. Jane Darvin's child—but who was the father? Ardis suddenly had the clear notion that the baby had not belonged to Jane's husband, Neil Darvin.

Chapter 8

Shielding her eyes from the glare, Ardis looked up into the unblinking stare of a ragged Arab driving a cart. His narrow face, brown and marred by harsh sun and endless drudgery, jolted her from her own thoughts and filled her with pity for him. She detested the squalor scattered everywhere amid the thriving tourism of Luxor. She waited while the scruffy donkey pulled the heavily-laden wagon by her. The stench of half-spoiled fruit lingered in the air, hanging over her like dust, as she crossed the road toward the Temple of Karnak.

Under the watchful eye of BenSobel, Ardis had taken the obelisk from the deposit box, carrying it with her in Jane's canvas bag as she headed toward the tallest monument in Egypt. Once the great temple complex had been surrounded by the thriving city of Thebes, which no longer existed. As Ardis walked between a double row of ram sphinxes representing the god Amon, an uneasy feeling overtook her, as if eyes other than the huge stone ones of the sphinx were watching her.

Ardis hastily bought a ticket and paused in the shade of the ancient wall to look back. She saw nothing out of the ordinary, only large groups of tourists and robed salesman peddling trinkets. She took a deep breath of the still, hot air and assured herself that no one could possibly harm her amid such swarms of people.

Ardis began walking again, thinking of the last phone conversation she had had with Jane Darvin. "When I was lowered into the chamber, I knew at once I had found Senmut's tomb, what I've been looking for all my life! When I discovered his signature inside, it was the greatest moment of my life!"

"Greater," Ardis had ventured, "than finding the perfect sphinx of Queen Hatshepsut buried so long in the desert?"

"Different," Jane had replied. "The difference between a lifetime of search and a moment's chance."

Why hadn't Ardis asked her the many questions that had then arisen in her mind? What had she expected to find in the tomb? Had she found it? But Jane's enthusiasm had flared and vanished in an instant, leaving her voice filled with a great weariness that had worried Ardis—a weariness that she had never recognized in Jane before.

The last time Ardis had seen the Karnak Temple, Jane had been with her. They had stood in the recesses of the Hypostyle Hall where great columns towered. "One-hundred-thirty-four of them," Jane had told her as she had paused to sip iced tea from her colorful thermos. "Each column is so wide it would take about twelve people to reach around it."

They had moved on to the wall Thutmose III had built after he had overthrown his stepmother. Once it had loomed high enough to prevent travelers through the temple from viewing the obelisks, now the crudely cut stones had fallen, eroded by age.

"Such an evil little man," Ardis had exclaimed, abhorred by the thought of betrayal. "This wall stands as a protest against her greatness."

The evidence of Thutmose III's spitefulness had spanned centuries. Ardis found the wall appalling, more appalling now that she knew exactly the same situation had existed for Jane

Darvin. Thutmose-like hatred had reared its head in precisely the same way, in the form of Faye Morris and others, who were doing all they could to obliterate Jane Darvin's work and her dream.

Ardis, again feeling apprehensive, glanced over her shoulder. She scanned the jagged temples, the great, black entrances, and the shadowed depths between columns and statues. She felt none of the awe she had experienced when Jane had been beside her. The immensity of the temple left her feeling dwarfed, oppressed by the heaviness of her fears.

Once more convincing herself that no one was spying on her, Ardis walked around the wall and gazed straight up, almost one hundred feet, to the tip of Queen Hatshepsut's obelisk.

"Red granite," Jane had stated with wonderment. "Three-hundred tons of it. Can you imagine these heavy stones floating on rafts from Aswan?"

In the stillness surrounding her, Ardis could visualize slaves dragging the obelisk to the temple on ropes, pulling the shaft upright while others dug away the sand from the base. What a super-human feat Queen Hatshepsut's architect, Senmut, had accomplished! What a demonstration of limitless power!

Ardis tried to picture what the temple had looked like when Queen Hatshepsut had first dreamed of obelisks entirely sheathed with gold, an extravagance beyond any pharaoh's wildest dreams. Queen Hatshepsut had written that she couldn't sleep, so dear to her heart was the Temple of Karnak.

Probably because of the threat of Thutmose III, the queen had been forced to compromise her dream of golden obelisks by gilding only the tips with an electrum mixture of silver and gold, for which she inscribed at the base of one of the obelisks, an apology to "my father Amon." She had written, "It was my wish to have them cast in electrum." But had Queen Hatshepsut ever lost sight of her greatest dream, obelisks actually covered with gold?

Ardis stepped closer. The hieroglyphic writings remained clear and sharply cut … The inscriptions were etched in thirty-two horizontal lines, eight to a side. They paid tribute to four kings, Thutmose I, Thutmose II, Thutmose III, and "King" Hatshepsut. She knew that they were telling of the earthly and divine events surrounding the erection of the obelisks, and the loyalty of the queen to her beloved god, Amon Re.

"How like her it is!" These words, so deeply inscribed in rock, united the queen and the obelisk. In another place Ardis interpreted the reference to Queen Hatshepsut as "more beautiful than anything."But nowhere did she see the signature of Senmut.

Ardis took the small obelisk from the bag and began making comparisons. She studied markings, first on the large obelisk, then on the one she held in her hand. Every line matched exactly. Ardis felt a moment of exhilaration. The small obelisk was too detailed, too perfect, to be a fake.

On the small obelisk Ardis found inscriptions that were not on the large stone that towered before her. Etched deeply near the base was the symbol of a writhing crocodile with a snake piercing its heart. The same curse that had been discovered on the tomb wall. The presence of the curse led Ardis to believe that Senmut himself had fashioned this small obelisk after he had finished the tomb. Inside he had stored the papyrus, which would contain clues which could be used to unravel the mystery of the tomb—its contents, its purpose, so carefully planned by the queen's master craftsman, the great Senmut.

Ardis checked the small obelisk for other differences. The only dissimilarity she noted between the large and small obelisks was the worn animal figures near the bottom of the one she held, the ones she had pressed to release the base from the space where the papyrus had been stored.

Once again feeling eyes on her, Ardis whirled around. As she did, she caught sight of a man with carefully styled gray hair disappearing behind a wall. This man she had seen near the hospital in Cairo, on the Luxor train, rooming beside her at the hotel, and now, here. Obviously, he had trailed her from the Oasis. Just as obviously, Laurence Tolliver did not want her to know of his presence.

She hurriedly replaced the small obelisk in the bag and attempted to follow him, but he had already become lost in the crowds of people. For a long time she wandered around trying to locate him, until finally the search lost its edge. The intense heat made her uncertain of all of her conclusions and slightly ill.

"Ardis." Thomas, looking very casual, was seated on the base of a stone pillar reading from a small notebook … Behind him the ocherous rocks, like fireplace stones, emitted waves of heat. He rose, tall and lanky in jeans and a tight T- shirt. He stuffed his pad into his back pocket. "Follow me … I want to show you the Thutmose III temple."

Ardis smiled. "I'd rather see the refreshment stand."

Thomas caught her arm as they walked around a group of tourists whose Egyptian guide was telling them about the sculptured lotus. "… a water lily, sacred to the Nile and symbol of Upper Egypt." The guide's voice grew distant behind them. "The papyrus symbolizes Lower Egypt, and is used in the union of the two lands. In this very place, over one hundred different pharaohs planned and built."

"I spent almost an hour looking at one wall," Thomas said. "I counted over one hundred victories that Thutmose III claimed."

"Queen Hatshepsut's monuments claim none. I think that is what I like about her, over twenty years of peace."

Thomas gave a small, British chuckle. "You don't do my man Thutmose justice, do you? He was the important one here. He built an empire. Do you know that he stretched Egypt's borders from the Euphrates to the desert beyond Napata? He controlled not only the Nile Valley, but also the entire Mediterranean. A real military genius." He stopped to grin at her. "Admit it, Ardis, he out-did the old girl!"

"Only if conquest is better than peace," Ardis answered. She liked the pleasant argumentative pace of their talk. It caused the anxiety she had felt over seeing Laurence Tolliver to slowly recede.

Thomas led the way through rocks and ruins into an imposing, columned hallway at the east end of the temple. "This is one of the great architectural beauties of Thebes," he said with satisfaction. "The Festival Hall of Thutmose III. See how it runs transversely across the axis of the temple."

Ardis saw nothing except the imagined image of Thutmose III lurking in the shadows, full of hatred, on fire with selfish ambition—sulking, jealous, dangerous. "He even took credit for all that Queen Hatshepsut accomplished."

"They all did that, dear. But she was the treacherous one!" The shadows from the columns fell across him. "How would you have liked to have been Thutmose III? It was his right to seize the throne. His heritage had been ripped from him. Stolen!"

"But he used the throne to destroy, to murder. The queen referred to him as a 'raging crocodile whose jaws snap, and there is no escape for him whom they seize.'"

Thomas' voice rose in strong opposition. "For twenty years his stepmother subordinated him! She stole his inheritance, what was his by birth, by right! Of course he hated her! She flaunted Senmut, a commoner, a traitor to the true king, in front of both him and his father. If he had tolerated it, he wouldn't have been a man!"

Ardis, a little startled by his harshness, did not encourage him to continue.

"Thutmose III was only Hamlet, seeking a just revenge."

"However," Ardis added, "I will never be able to think of him without shuddering."

All of a sudden Thomas laughed. "Say, this blasted sun is getting to us. I think we'd better head for shade and drink."

They began walking toward the sacred lake. Ardis had begun thinking of Blake, wondering again about his parentage. If Jane were his real mother, Blake could very well feel exactly the same way that Thutmose III had felt; he could be seething with the same resentment and hatred which Thomas had just a short time ago so unyieldingly described. She thought about how Blake might be seeking revenge for Jane's not wanting him, for stealing <u>his</u> heritage. Hot air and wind-driven sand stirred around her making it difficult for her to catch her breath.

Thomas had resumed his pleasant chatter. "The chapel of Thutmose III interests me the most. It needs the most reconstruction. That's where I plan to start working."

Near the gigantic statue of a scarab at the turn of the trail, Ardis caught sight of Laurence Tolliver again. She put a restraining hand on Thomas' arm. "See that man over there. He has been following me."

Once again Laurence Tolliver had ducked out of sight behind crumbling stone walls. Thomas, however, had seen him and now stood staring at the empty space where he had stood. "He's staying at our hotel. I ran across him at breakfast this morning. He's probably just looking around, too."

"He's been watching me."

Thomas frowned. "That man does look familiar to me. You know," he said suddenly, "I think I saw his picture in the *London Times*. He's some sort of a big-shot investigator."

He must be working with the Egyptian authorities concerning the flow of illegal artifacts from Egypt. Hadn't the girl, Faye Morris, spoken of such an investigation?

"I'm sure he's not on any vacation," Ardis said. "He seems overly interested in my work and what I'm doing."

Thomas raised his eyebrows. "I wouldn't be surprised if he's tracked some thief right here to Luxor. The illegal flow of antiquities into Great Britain goes on all the time. The old boy seems to ask a lot of questions, but not about projects, if he's as interested as he claims. He asks about people."

"Who does he ask about?"

"Mostly about Blake Lydon," Thomas said, "but he's also mentioned you."

After lingering over cool mineral water under the shade of an open-air refreshment stand, they started back to the hotel.

"You know Nihisi Khet is going to be spending a day or so at the Oasis. That's a piece of luck. They say his lectures are a college education in a nut-shell. Not anything you would want to miss, I imagine."

"I didn't know anything about them." Ardis said.

"Dr. Assari was scheduled to speak this weekend at the convention hall at our hotel … He had to cancel, so Nihisi Khet volunteered to fill in for him. He should draw in a big crowd. All the details will be posted on the hotel bulletin board."

Ardis fell silent at the thought of seeing Nihisi Khet again.

"What are you planning for this afternoon?"

Ardis headed off the offer she knew he was about to make by saying, "Work. I have to work."

"All work and no play," Thomas chided. "You American's already know how tedious that makes one."

They had reached the street. A group of shabby children began scampering after them, ever so often approaching Ardis with hands outstretched. Ardis, smiling, reached in her bag for change.

"Don't do that, love," Thomas said. "They'll follow you from here on out."

"Hey, you, don't walk by here!" Matthammed, wearing a woven black and tan jellaba, stood in the archway of a quaint-looking store with a false, mud-brick front. "Come on in. It's cool inside." He ushered them into a room overflowing with Egyptian goods, saying exuberantly, "Welcome. I run this shop at odd hours as a little sideline."

Ardis turned back to the entrance to divide her change among laughing, grasping children. Matthammed spoke to them sharply in Arabic and shut the heavy door.

The closed door created depths and shadows in the room. Ardis first noticed the clusters of rugs that hung from the ceiling. The dim light added a dimension of value to the deep reds and blues. Shelves rising to the ceiling were crammed with clay pots, urns and statues. On one a sign read "antiques." The *antiques* were doubtless fakes, Ardis decided, very high-priced ones.

A scrawny black cat leaped from its seat on a padded cushion and followed Ardis as she wandered over to where Matthammed was explaining a papyrus. "Here," he pointed out, "is a dead man joining his gods, becoming a part of the company of Amon and Osiris."

"Will they be meeting Ardis and I, too, when we make our final journey?" Thomas inquired. "Or do they only meet Egyptians?"

A slightly resentful glint appeared in Matthammed's black eyes, quickly driven away by a smile. "You will probably be met by your own gods, a representative from Chase Manhattan," he said. "Or Lloyd's of London."

Matthammed cast an approving glance toward Ardis as she laughed, then his glittering, black eyes followed her gaze to a row of shelved statues. "You like Queen Hatshepsut?" He didn't have to be told which one she liked, he had already reached for it.

"No, she doesn't," Thomas spoke slowly. "She likes this." He lifted one of the famous statues of Thutmose III, carved of gray granite. The thin body leaned forward, one long leg far ahead of the other, poised to action, a stance somehow immensely intimidating. Thomas took glasses from his breast pocket and studied the base. "See this," he indicated four bows lying at the right foot of the statue, five by his left. "That represents the nine nations subject to Egypt during Thutmose's reign. How much is this?"

"That is very expensive," Matthammed said. "But I have another …"

"I want this one."

"Then," Matthammed said, smiling, teeth white against his dark skin, "you must pay the price. Eighty-five dollars."

"It's worth ten," Thomas said. "But, because I like you, I'll give you twenty."

Matthammed lifted a very poorly carved Thutmose III head. "This one I can sell for twenty. That one is eighty-five."

Thomas handed the statue to Ardis. "I'll give you thirty dollars. For Ardis. She admires him so much."

"Why didn't you say it was for Ardis?" Matthammed's beaming gaze settled on her. "For Ardis, I'll cut the price to forty."

While Thomas paid him, Ardis regarded the statue. How could she keep from Thomas how much she despised it? The head set forward on a short, stout neck. A large, arched nose caused great hollows in the thin, elongated face—a face so evil in its arrogance and power.

"You'll grow to like him, love," Thomas drawled, starting to the door.

"Wait. I'm going to show you what I never show anyone else, my private room. I don't keep anything of real value out here. Luxor is not what it used to be."

Beaded ropes clinked together as Matthammed parted them and gestured for Thomas and Ardis to follow into the back section of the shop. On a back wall, he pressed one of a long series of lotus decorations, and a heavy wooden door slid open.

The secluded room, darker than the first one, was lit by bare bulbs above a huge table. Ardis was dazzled for a moment by the contents of the room ... She stepped close to a larger-than-life statue in front of a glass case. The eyes were of turquoise, the pupils of black obsidian.

"That is not for sale," Matthammed said, clicking on a ceiling fan against the stifling heat. "This is actually my workshop."

"I would like to see what's in those boxes stacked against the wall," Thomas said, starting toward them.

"Those are not mine," Matthammed said.

"I'll bet they're filled with treasures from ancient tombs." Thomas wound around display cases toward the cartons.

"Please don't touch those!"

Thomas, surprised at Matthammed's sharp tone, halted abruptly.

"Look at that picture," Matthammed said in a consolatory tone.

The painted face with the large dark eyes, the handsome, regular features, looked very familiar to Ardis.

"That's Abrahim Khet, Nihisi's father, Blake's grandfather. A truly great man." He added sadly, "He would still be alive if he had listened to me."

The quietness was filled with the whining of the overhead fan. "What happened to him?" she asked at last.

"He died from the curse."

Thomas laughed.

"It's nothing to laugh about." Matthammed's playful voice had become toneless.

In the darkened room, crammed with priceless treasures, Ardis felt just as she had in Senmut's tomb the day she had fallen and heard that muffled, warning voice that had seemed to be coming from another world.

"Their spirits linger in the tombs. They *stay*." He shot a warning glance at Ardis. "There's a power locked in those tombs! I tried to tell that to Abrahim. I tried to tell that to Jane. And now I'm telling it to you. You have just come to Egypt, Ardis. I have to make sure you understand."

Both Thomas and Ardis remained silent.

"No one is strong enough to defy the curse of a pharaoh!" Matthammed said. "Or the curse of Senmut!"

"I wouldn't even try," Thomas joked. "I certainly wouldn't want the old boy's wrath to fall upon me."

"Neither would I." Matthammed's answer was short, clipped, but spoken with a dead-certain resolution.

Chapter 9

As Ardis reached the tomb site, she noticed a commotion at the gate. Faye Morris, camera strapped around her neck, argued heatedly with one of the guards. Thomas, looking ill-at-ease, hung back near his vehicle.

"I am a member of the press." Faye's words became more distinct as Ardis switched off the Jeep motor. "And I demand you let me through this gate!"

The guard, who had so firmly turned Ardis away yesterday, appeared menacing and formidable as he stalwartly blocked the entrance. "You have no papers."

Faye, not intimidated by his burly form or by the heavy gun strapped across his chest, stepped closer to him. "I have a press card."

"That is no good."

Faye drew herself up indignantly. She wore shorts and a bright yellow T-shirt. A straw hat with a big, white brim perched on her head at a devil-may-care slant, tied under her chin with a huge, yellow ribbon. The effect resulted in her looking somewhat ridiculous, like a little girl playacting.

"Being associated with the *International Reporter* should be all the authorization I need."

"Real credentials," Thomas spoke in a low, skeptical tone. He had some time ago approached Ardis' Jeep and now leaned his elbow against the door, saying, "Don't blame me for this. I hardly know her. We just met at the hotel this morning, and she talked me into driving her out here. Against my better judgment."

The guard and Faye had squared off again. Just behind them the make-shift shade of yesterday had been replaced by a sprawling white tent, whose immense flaps were probably open on the side facing the tomb. A second guard, alert to the rising voices, appeared momentarily; then, as if satisfied that he was not needed, he ducked back inside.

"I told her she'd never get past security." Thomas shook his head, his expression a mixture of amusement and embarrassment. "I should have known she'd make a scene."

"You must leave now!" Losing patience, the guard spoke in rapid and slightly broken English. "If you don't, I will … I will … put you on report."

"Oh, you do that!" Faye flounced around, yelling, "Hey, Thomas, he's going to jail me!"

"I wish he would," Ardis said under her breath.

Thomas flashed Ardis one of those appealing smiles, then called back to Faye. "He can do it. I suggest we go now, love. Peacefully."

Noticing Ardis, Faye hurried forward. "You're a big shot around here. Can't you do anything about this? All I want is to get inside and snap a few pictures."

"The site is closed to the public," Ardis said.

"You sound like you're right in with them."

"Time to go," Thomas intervened. "Give up, Faye. Let's journey on to Karnak. You can take all the pictures you want there." He added as if to pacify her, "My little project could use some publicity."

Faye stomped back to the guard. "You think this place is so secure. I don't even need to ask your permission. I can sneak in and out of here like Senmut's ghost."

As an added gesture of defiance, Faye raised the camera. "OK, Mr. Smart-guy! Smile!" The guard glowered as she defiantly snapped a picture of him. "Be prepared, Buddy, to read all about yourself in the news." With a flash of bare legs Faye whirled away from the gate and grudgingly climbed back into the car to wait for Thomas.

"Will you be at the hotel tonight for dinner?" Thomas asked Ardis.

"I'm not sure."

"I'll call you just in case."

After Thomas and Faye left, Ardis opened Jane's canvas bag. She had left the obelisk in the safety deposit box at the Oasis, but had taken Jane's recent writings to use in her work today. She shuffled through them now to find the papers she had received this morning, special delivery from Nihisi Khet, authorizing her to head Jane Darvin's project.

The guard, a glare remaining on his broad face, watched her as she climbed from the Jeep and headed to where he still blocked the road. "You can not enter," he said.

In reply she handed him the papers that gave her authorization to enter. As his eyes fell across the signature, Nihisi Khet, his attitude changed. "Please come this way."

He led her around to the side of the tent, wide-open to the cliffs. There, Ardis stopped, face to face with Blake Lydon.

Blake sat at a folding table amid stacks of papers. He was dressed for work in a faded shirt rolled up at the sleeves, a tan vest, and desert boots. He gazed at Ardis with surprise.

The guard handed him the papers, legal and formal and properly signed by Nihisi Khet. As Blake skimmed them, his jaw set with tension. His black eyes met hers accusingly, and in their depths she identified a look of hurt, of betrayal. It surfaced only for a moment, then was lost in anger. He arose and tossed the papers down on the table. "Why is it that neither you nor Nihisi saw fit to inform me of this?"

Ardis recalled the way she had felt when Blake had told her there was no place for her on the project. He must now be feeling these same emotions. But surely he could understand that he had forced her to go over his head.

Nihisi should have told him. On the other hand, she should have, too. Not telling him the outcome of her meeting with Nihisi Khet during the long train ride from Cairo now seemed coldly planned and extremely unfair. She could not possibly explain to him now why she had remained silent—that she had been enjoying his company and hadn't wanted to spoil the evening with news that would bring an inevitable conflict.

"This matter is far from over," Blake said, swinging away from her.

Remembering that Nihisi had told her that Blake would ask for an immediate transfer, she said, "Having access to the site and Jane's research is really all that concerns me. I have no desire to interfere with your plans."

Blake faced her again with hostility, his eyes not moving from hers. "You know quite well my feelings on the matter, feelings you have chosen to ignore."

Obviously, he wasn't going to listen to reason. "Other people have feelings, too," she said, crossing to the table and taking back the papers Nihisi had sent her. She had reached the edge of the tent, remaining just inside the shade. "If we are to successfully complete this project, we should be working together."

"You do all right on your own," he answered flatly.

"Then I'll find out what I need to know from Jane's papers."

Ardis was used to holding her own in verbal battles. Clashes with co-workers in the field could never totally be avoided.

This one was no worse than some of the others she had experienced. She wondered why she continually over-reacted to Blake Lydon's displeasure, why this man was so capable of hurting her.

She drove the Jeep through the gate without glancing to where Blake now stood in the full sunlight. She was never-the-less aware of his straight posture, the intentness of his features.

Ardis began driving much too fast on the deeply rutted road, her thoughts whirling ahead of her. Her first stop would be the cabin where the bulk of Jane's research was stored. Reading Jane's notes concerning the tomb would surely bring her up to date. Then she would go into the tomb, taking with her the papers Jane had been working on the day she had found her unconscious. Ardis would continue with whatever line Jane had been pursuing. She also wanted to compare the curse written just below the entrance of the tomb with the one inscribed on the small obelisk.

Ardis swung the Jeep to a stop near Jane's shack. Generators were running, suggesting that activity had been going on recently. She would probably find Ramus seated inside in front of one of the buzzing fans. Feeling upset from her conflict with Blake, not wanting to talk to Ramus or to anyone, Ardis decided to start with the work inside the tomb.

The step that had caused her earlier fall had been repaired. Still, she tested it before allowing it to support her full weight. A flood light glared against a back wall where Ramus must have been transcribing the writings on the ancient wall.

The harsh light threw shadows back into the far corners of the chamber, across the sarcophagus and the looming stone statues guarding it. Ardis visualized Jane slumped over the desk where Ardis had found her unconscious. Ardis mustn't think of Jane; she mustn't give in to the tears that unexpectedly stung her eyes. She must think instead of Jane's mission.

She placed the canvas bag bearing Jane's papers on the desk and taking pen and pad, returned up the steps until she was eye-level with the Curse of Senmut. She carefully copied each marking, complete with the writhing crocodile, then returned to the desk. The passages were identical to the one on the base of the small obelisk except for several markings representing some specific word or phrase.

She believed the curse of Senmut on the obelisk was as old as the tomb itself, both of Senmut's own design. But what explained the difference in that one section? She had much less knowledge of hieroglyphics than Blake, she wished she could have asked him to interpret this for her. As it was, she was faced with hours of study to find out what might prove insignificant.

Once more absorbed in Jane's papers, she slowly became aware of the dimming lights. She waited, prepared for the dreaded possibility that they would go out. Prepared for the blackness of the tomb, for that chilling chant to surround her, she held her breath. Finally, to Ardis' relief the lights brightened again.

Most of what Jane had written made little sense to her. Besides using her own kind of shorthand, Jane's penmanship was little better than the typical doctor's. Deciphering the fragments of broken sentences that filled cramped pages was about as easy as reading an Egyptian scroll. But gradually, after much concentration, Ardis began to make progress.

Scattered sketches and hieroglyphics that Jane had copied from the walls covered many pages. In one place Jane had hastily scrawled, "obelisk is key" and in another, "obelisk and papyrus—authentic." These random notes were interrupted by a short passage of text that appeared to have been transcribed directly from one of Jane's history books "From Senmut's journey to Punt, a land in Africa, he brought back for the Queen treasures such as the Egyptians had never seen. Among these treasures were ebony and fragrant woods, ivory, and rare animals. Senmut brought back, to the delight of his Queen, a live white cheetah, one of the first ever to be seen in Egypt. But most importantly, he returned with gold, enough gold to fulfill Queen Hatshepsut's dream of gilding the twin obelisks at Karnak in honor of her god, Amon."

The notes on Punt abruptly ended. The next entry was just a continuation of the hieroglyphics. Ardis leaned back in her chair and took a drink from the bottled water she had stuffed into Jane's canvas bag. She must have spent more time than she had thought for the water had grown warm.

In this interval of repose, Ardis became more conscious of the surrounding tomb and the fact that she was seated at Jane's desk. She listened intently, as if she would again hear that muffled voice rising from some unknown black depth. That voice—where had it come from? Had it been a human sound or just the muffled hum of the generator above, magnified by the tightness of the tomb and altered by her fears? She listened, but no unearthly voices sounded, only silence. With an undercurrent of disquiet, she took another drink and turned again to Jane's notes.

A crouching, cat-like figure had been sketched in great detail. Ardis studied the long, thin face, the elongated ears and the stylized form. Beneath it Jane had scribbled "cheetah—ivory." Then the notation, "Now I know for sure."

Ardis suddenly realized the sketch was not of a wall painting, but of the missing statue. The regal creature was not a cat, but a cheetah, an ivory cheetah, a carved likeness of the one Senmut had brought back from the land of Punt.

Stillness enveloped her, deep and frightening. What did Jane know for sure? That the item had been stolen, that one of her select and long-time associates was a thief?

A faint noise echoed around the tomb. Ardis jumped to her feet. Was the same person who had been in the tomb when she had come after the obelisk in here now?

She tried to tell herself that was impossible. She had witnessed the tight security. The guards at the gate would allow only those properly authorized to enter the area, but that thought did not make her feel any safer.

The tomb became totally quiet. After a while she sank back down at the desk again, her gaze once more on the cheetah. This time she made the connection. What Jane had written had nothing at all to do with the statue's theft, but with its origin. Senmut had brought back a live cheetah from Punt for the Queen. Since neither ivory nor cheetahs were common in Egypt, the statue, must have been brought back from that same expedition. The missing ivory cheetah was the first definite link between this tomb and Senmut's journey to Punt.

Someone else had figured this out, too, and that was why the small statue had been stolen. The tomb had contained one item that came directly from Punt. Were there more? How many other objects had also vanished from the tomb? The missing ivory cheetah suggested proof that other treasures from the same expedition—possibly even the gold—had once been hidden by Senmut within this very tomb.

Excitement filled Ardis as she realized that the animal shapes on the obelisk exactly matched the image of the crouching cheetah statue. The appearance of the cheetah on the obelisk definitely proved its connection to this tomb.

Jane had told Ardis that her find might be more important than anyone realized. Ardis was certain now of the path Jane had been pursuing. If only Ardis had the papyrus! The vanished papyrus must hold the key to some clue that would lead to a hidden chamber, a chamber that might hold rare treasures—a wealth of gold from Senmut's journey to Punt.

When Ardis finally rose again, her back ached and she felt exhausted from long hours spent bending over the notes. She realized that, like Jane, she had lost all track of time. But enthusiasm over her progress overrode any pangs of physical discomfort. Ardis had a sudden urge to share with someone what she had discovered, but she realized, just as Jane must have, that there was no one here she could trust. Ardis would continue on her own and examine the research stored in the filing cabinets in the cabin. She had intended to go through those papers today, but it was growing late and she was getting tired. Ardis decided instead to gather some of the most recent files to take back to the hotel room with her to study.

When Ardis emerged from the tomb, she was surprised to see that the hot, yellow-orange sun was blazing its last fiery path across the sky before sinking behind the jagged cliff side. Long shadows fell across her path as Ardis headed toward the empty cabin. She wondered if Ramus might still be inside, but there was not a soul in sight and no vehicle except for her own Jeep.

Lights from the shack glowed through the many cracks in the old wooden frame of the building. "Ramus," she called as she pushed the door open.

Aghast, Ardis stared at the havoc spread before her. Tables, fans, and the cot were overturned. The filing cabinets, once overflowing with Jane's precious years of labor, gaped in emptiness. Much of the contents, soaked in water or some liquid, set in a soggy heap in the center of the room. Other files had been hurled in all directions, many a lying in shredded disarray at her feet.

Whoever had murdered Jane already had possession of the Senmut scroll, so he must be searching for something else—or was this an act of pure vengeance? Ardis remained motionless, appalled by the viciousness apparent in the damage—the ravages of rage that stemmed from the deepest vein of hatred.

Her gaze shifted with alarm from the ruins around her to the empty shelf where the rose-granite sphinx that Nihisi Khet had awarded Jane from the Egyptian Museum had once set in proud display. She located it in a far corner, shattered and broken. Ardis stepped around the disorder and lifted it. Throwing it might have cracked the stone, but the statue had suffered a far worse fate. It had been furiously pounded, the pulverized face of Queen Hatshepsut, totally obliterated. Ardis continued to hold the statue, and as she pressed it against her, tears filled her eyes.

Where was Ramus? Or Blake? If she couldn't find them, she would report this to the guards at the gate. She set down the sphinx. As she started to the door, her eyes fastened on a piece of white cloth, half buried under torn papers.

The fabric, yellowed with age, had been slashed through time and again with a sharp blade. She had no trouble recognizing what it had been—part of a baby outfit. Beside it, in the rubble, she found an old snapshot of a baby, ripped in a jagged line through the center. She could not tell whether the faded image was a boy or a girl, just a small figure with tiny, curled fists. Tightness gripped her chest. She knew she found a picture of the baby Jane had lost. Jane had kept the picture and the shirt all these years, tucked away in some private place.

Jane's baby wore a white cap and shirt—maybe even the shirt that she now held in her hands, an item that caused the baby to be real to her for the first time. In the stillness Jane's voice seemed to ring out, just as it did before she died, "I want my baby!"

Ramus had indicated that the infant might have died, but Ardis had always thought otherwise. She was now convinced that the person in this picture was very much alive. Ardis had an eerie feeling that Jane had not needed to seek for the child. The child had found her.

Outside the cabin heavy wheels crunched against rock and a noisy engine faded into silence. Hurriedly Ardis stuffed the baby shirt and photo in Jane's canvas bag and swung toward the opening door.

Ramus abruptly halted, surveying the disaster, then his countenance changed. His short-necked, stocky form resembled one of the huge, sacred Egyptian bulls—a dangerous bull ready to charge. He spoke with measured slowness. "Who did this?"

"I don't know. When I came in, I found everything in total ruin."

"I spent the night here. I left early this morning. I should have known better!" He stooped to scoop up a handful of paper, wadded and wet. "Jane's research, her irreplaceable years of work." He stared down at the indecipherable pages, then with fury hurled them across the room. They thudded against the back wall. "History is repeating itself. History runs in cycles, until it runs its course. No one is safe from its curse."

What was he talking about? Had this same sort of trouble happened in the past? Or was Ramus not thinking of Jane at all; but reacting to some plot that was going counter to his own plans?

"Someone is going to pay for this," Ramus said relentlessly. He did not appear to be addressing Ardis; he did not even look at her. He spoke no other words, just whirled around and left the cabin.

Ardis waited, hearing the skid of tires as his vehicle pulled away. Then she began lifting some of the papers. Torn rubble was scattered everywhere. She could not begin to put any pages in order.

Ardis had not heard the door open so Blake's words startled her. "I've just talked to Ramus. You shouldn't touch anything until the police arrive." He wondered around the room, looking strangely calm in contrast to Ramus.

"Why would anyone do this?" Ardis asked tearfully.

"Vengeance," Blake replied.

Vengeance—that word always brought forth images of Thutmose III, his brooding face that spoke of cruelty and the corruption of power. Ardis watched Blake uncertainly, wondering what emotion he was shielding.

"Jane was successful enough to have her share of enemies, but I would have expected revenge to subside with her death."

"Nothing was gained by destroying her work," Ardis said. "It was a vicious act of hatred. Why would anyone hate Jane this much? Whoever did this must have felt betrayed or cheated."

"Or rejected," Blake added. "Jane was a person who inspired great love. Unfortunately a person with those qualities also inspires great hatred." As he spoke he lifted the broken statue of the sphinx, placing the smashed award back in its place of honor on the shelf above him.

The pathetic sight of the queen's face, battered to pieces, caused Ardis to shudder.

"That journalist, Faye Morris, tried everything to get admitted to the site today. Maybe she did manage to get through."

"She wouldn't have any reason to do this."

"Who has passes to the site?" she asked him.

"Ramus, Matthammed, Nihisi, myself. Others are admitted to help with special work, but are never allowed in alone."

"What about the guards?" Ardis asked. "Could they be persuaded to look the other way if the price were right?"

"I know all of them personally. I would vouch for them."

"Then there must be another way into the tomb area."

Blake shook his head. "Ramus and I have gone over every inch of those cliffs looking for a possible way down. There is none."

"That doesn't leave very many suspects, then, does it?"

"Not many," he replied.

Ardis paced around the room. "Jane's work meant so much to her," she said, her voice revealing the vast emptiness she felt.

Blake drew closer to her. His hand, warm and comforting, reached to cover hers. "We can save some of her writings, Ardis. After the police have gone over the room, we'll try to put some of her files back in order."

They waited for the police, but Ardis' meeting with them proved futile. After numerous questions, they told her she could leave.

"I rode out with Ramus," Blake said. "May I catch a ride back with you?"

The setting sun had extinguished the intense heat. The night was lit by a wash of moonlight that streaked across the star-spattered sky.

"Aren't you staying with Ramus?"

"At times, I do. Usually I reside in Luxor at one of Nihisi's estates." Blake slowed at the gate and said something to the guard in Arabic. Then they continued, jogging along the rough road lit by the Jeep's headlights.

Her eyes strayed to Blake's profile, and she thought of the baby's shirt and the picture in Jane's bag lying at her feet. Then, trying not to think at all, she gazed from the window.

Night rendered the area totally unfamiliar, an endless dark plain where cliffs rose in black silhouette. At any other time Ardis might have thought the scene enchantingly beautiful and would have been gripped by the majesty of the desert. But not tonight. Ardis, exhausted and deeply saddened, said more to herself than to Blake, "I wonder where Ramus went."

"He's a very solitary man. Ramus often goes off by himself. He makes his decisions alone without discussing them with anyone."

"Do you think he knows who wrecked Jane's cabin?"

"I hope not," Blake answered shortly, his gaze not leaving the road.

"You've known Ramus a long time, haven't you?"

"Since I was a child. Matthammed is his nephew." He glanced at her. "Matthammed is no one to worry about. He's very trustworthy."

"I think he might have been the one to leak the news to Faye Morris about that missing artifact, the cat statue."

Blake paused, as if trying to think of a way to justify this. "He was infatuated with the girl and wanted to impress her. But I think he knows better now."

"What do you think became of the statue and the other missing artifacts?"

Her question was met with silence. Finally he said, "I don't know."

The village of Qurna seemed totally asleep, except for the milling of goats and donkeys. Blake pulled the Jeep off the road at the shop where Ardis had stopped to buy sodas the day she had visited Ramus. Blake studied the outline of Ramus' house where it perched on the steep hillside. "There's no lights," he said in a worried tone.

As they turned back on the road, Blake spoke again, "Ramus is a force to reckon with. He's always been very protective of Jane. Anyone who injured her in any way became his personal enemy."

"Ramus seems very emotional."

"Let's say Ramus is from the old school. Except he adds a few of his own rules. Instead of an eye for an eye, he wants two eyes for one."

At the thought, a chill crept down Ardis' spine. If Ramus knew who had ransacked the cabin, he would definitely take matters into his own hands.

Blake checked the Jeep back into the compound, and they began their long wait for the ferry. In the semi-darkness, his hand found hers. "We have gotten off to several wrong starts," he said, "which was never what I wanted."

"We could begin again," Ardis said, smiling.

"I guess I am going to stay with the project, to protect you," he said. "But that does not mean I have changed my mind. I still do not think that you should be here."

The ferry arrived at last and they boarded. Blake looked different in the lighted boat. The rugged desert clothing accentuated his tallness and the width of his shoulders. They seated themselves near a window.

The huge deck was empty except for a small Egyptian man. He sat perfectly motionless without even a glance toward them. Ardis watched the vastness of the river and the ever-changing shoreline. Palm trees grew near the water's edge and gave the landscape an unreal appearance, like some exotic travel poster. Her stormy whirl of thoughts slowly began to recede and to be replaced by the haunting beauty of the night.

The spell of Egypt, Ardis thought—the spell of the great, dry wasteland cut by the life-giving river. She could feel the power of the Nile stirring around them, its deep undercurrents passing beneath the boat.

"You have never been on the Nile at night," Blake said, pleased by her rapt attention.

"No. It is very lovely."

Feeling the warm breeze and the gentle splashing of waves against the side of the ferry, Ardis began to relax a little. For the moment Ardis attempted to distance herself, as much as she could, from the dark tomb of Senmut and its secrets, from the wreckage of Jane's cabin. Together they watched their slow progress toward the landing at Luxor.

"Egypt," he said with awe.

The star-filled night seemed a precious luxury. The glow of the moon and the lights from the ferry cast golden hues across the water, causing the whole world to take on an air of mysticism.

"This is the Egypt I want you to remember," Blake spoke softly, "no matter where your journey in life takes you."

Ardis could picture Queen Hatshepsut, beautiful and delicate, but possessing great strength and dignity, amid the pomp of unbelievable wealth. She could see her gliding down the Nile, just as she was doing—Hatshepsut, with Senmut close beside her.

Ardis glanced toward Blake. He had never looked more attractive to her than he did at this moment. As his dark eyes held to hers, Ardis had a strange vision of herself as Queen Hatshepsut and of Blake as Senmut, her strong and faithful protector.

If only she could trust him! Ardis longed to tell him the secrets she was keeping to herself, her knowledge that the ivory cheetah could be a valuable link between the tomb and the voyage Senmut had taken to Punt. She wanted to search with Blake for hidden chambers, for unimaginable wealth brought back from Senmut's wondrous expedition. But Blake's obvious attraction to her combined with his resistance to having her here could have only one meaning—Blake was involved in whatever was happening at the Senmut tomb, deeply entangled in some type of fraudulent conspiracy.

As if he could read her thoughts, Blake said, "For your own safety, I should be wishing Jane had never sent for you." His voice was lower this time, strong and certain. "But that would mean we would never have met. And I could never wish that."

Chapter 10

A rdis and Blake spent the next morning cleaning up Jane's cabin. The work had availed nothing. Even back in her hotel room, her thoughts kept returning to the slashed baby shirt and the ripped photograph. Those seemed the only clue linking the destruction of Jane's cabin to any particular person.

Ardis placed a long distance call to her father's old friend, Dan Hall, a chief investigator for the Chicago Police. After they had discussed Jane's untimely death, Ardis said, "I want you to do me a favor, Dan. I need to know what became of Jane Darvin's child. He ... or she ... would be just about my age now."

"I didn't know Jane ever had a kid."

Ardis could almost see Dan seated at his desk, pursing his lips as he weighed all the information carefully. His gray hair and sturdy build as well as his affable manner made her think of Laurence Tolliver

"Your father was in Egypt around that time," he said. "Jane and he kept in close contact, you know. Craig spoke often about Jane and her search for the Senmut tomb, which was little more than a pipe dream back then." After a long hesitation

Dan said, "As much as your father always talked about Jane, he never mentioned any offspring."

"I'm certain Jane had a child."

After another long pause, Dan stated, "I'm going to start by trying to locate Jane's husband. I met Neil Darvin once in Chicago years ago, just after he and Jane married. If I remember right, he was associated with the university then. When they left Chicago, he took a job at a museum in New York City. That was before he and Jane went to Egypt. It's possible the museum will know of his whereabouts now."

"The baby may not belong to Neil Darvin," Ardis said cautiously. "Jane and he were in the midst of a divorce around the time the baby was born."

"He'll still know what became of Jane's child," Dan said, "if I can locate him."

"This is very important, Dan. Please call me the minute you find out anything."

"Will do."

Ardis left her room anticipating a quiet, leisurely lunch. As she entered the dining room, Thomas Garrett noticed her and waved. His smile, because of the slight protrusion of large white teeth, looked boyishly appealing.

Faye Morris sat close beside him. She wore a bright yellow sundress set off by an assortment of heavy, primitive jewelry. The exaggerated dress accentuated her girlish looks and the slightly upturned nose, and mass of short, brown curls.

"Come join us," Thomas called.

Faye eyed Ardis boldly and said with a false smile, "We've already eaten, but hate to leave the air-conditioning."

Ardis sat down across from Thomas. "Did you both stay at Karnak yesterday?"

"I did," Thomas said, "I'm sold on the work ethic, you know."

"I never stay anywhere long," Faye said breezily.

The waiter promptly arrived, and Ardis ordered a beef sandwich, fresh fruit, and coffee. Shortly after the waiter disappeared into the kitchen, Matthammed came in through the same double doors.

"Here he comes again," Faye sighed. She leaned closer to Thomas, the wooden elephants on her earrings jingling.

"Bad pennies, you know," Thomas responded with a sparkle in his eye.

As Matthammed joined them, he lifted his cup. "I have to go after my own brew." He slipped into the chair beside Ardis. He was dressed in a long robe minus his customary turban. Because of its absence, his black hair made him look much younger than the forty-odd years he must be. "They know me in the kitchen," he went on importantly. "It is my second home."

He shot a glance toward Faye, but she ignored him, instead she lifted a white leaflet which had been left upon each of the linen-topped tables. "Look at this, Thomas, The Great Khet from Cairo will be arriving in Luxor today. He's giving a lecture tonight right here at this hotel."

Matthammed's tall, thin form leaned forward, adding a sort of eagerness to the alertness that characterized him. "I'm going to lock up my shop so I can attend," he said. Nihshi knows more about our history than anyone in Egypt."

"Have you met Mr. Khet?" Ardis asked Faye.

"Not yet." With that annoying air of self-importance, Faye added, "But I think I'll take this opportunity to interview him. I have questions concerning that missing artifact."

Her words caused Matthammed to lean back in his chair, enthusiasm vanishing. Telling her about the statue had gotten him into trouble once. He didn't want Faye to bring the matter up again, especially not to Nihisi Khet.

Ardis' lunch arrived. Faye began to read aloud the schedule of events. "This evening, a banquet, seven o'clock, followed by a lecture at the Oasis Convention Center; Friday, lecture at Deir el-Bahari. Monday through Wednesday, students-only seminar. Thursday, the grand finale, poolside barbecue, eight o'clock, Oasis."

"Are you going to attend the banquet and the lecture tonight, Faye?" Matthammed asked hopefully.

With a shrug, she continued to study the brochure.

"How about you, Thomas? Or will you be too busy working?"

"I set my own hours," Thomas answered with a clipped shortness.

"He's doing reconstruction on one of the Thutmose temples," Ardis inserted pleasantly.

Matthammed's shrewd, black eyes acknowledged her words with interest. Once again he addressed Thomas, "How's it going?"

Thomas' brief reply, "Fine," appeared to snuff out the possibility of further conversation. Thomas seemed different when he was around Faye. This certain arrogance, a side to him Ardis had never seen before, greatly diminished his appeal. She wondered what it was about the snippy little journalist that succeeded in bringing out the worst in everyone.

Faye tossed aside the brochure and burst out pretentiously, "So how does Ardis feel about your great love for Thutmose III?"

"Why, Thutmose is one of her heroes," Thomas said with a grin. "She keeps a statue of him, I understand, up in her room."

"A very beautiful work," Matthammed broke in, undaunted. "I hope you are enjoying it."

"I would very much like a refund," Ardis commented lightly, slanting a smile at him. Although she would always detest the statue, she was by now used to its presence on the bed stand, and had come to think of it as hers.

Matthammed had drawn a small black briefcase from the floor beneath the table and now placed it in front of Ardis. "Did you notice the cartouche Faye is wearing?"

Ardis glanced at the cartouche, an item prominent in Egypt's history, a royal signature used by pharaohs and other important dignitaries. Faye extended the golden necklace with pictures from the hieroglyphic alphabet that spelled out "Faye."

"She didn't buy it from me," Matthammed said. "Which was a mistake." He paused. "What did you say you paid for it?"

"One hundred and eighty dollars."

"Two times more than what I charge," Matthammed's smile shot back to Ardis.

"I pay more for quality," Faye retorted.

Matthammed tore a slip of paper from a notebook. "Ardis," he said, and wrote the letters of her name in a downward row, returning to sketch in the pictured symbol beside each. He held it at arm's length, beaming appraisal. "I like your cartouche!" he said.

Faye laughed loudly. "I bet he does!"

"I mean, look at these symbols—A, a falcon. This means you are a very strong woman." He cast her a playful glance. "Like Queen Hatshepsut. Like Jane Darvin." His long finger traced the next letter. "D, a snake. This means royalty."

He started to go on, but Thomas said, "Please spare us the rest, old boy. We're not into the supernatural."

"Do you make these yourself?" Ardis asked, trying to compensate for Thomas and Faye's sniping remarks. She had grown accustomed to Thomas' rather droll sense of humor but sensed Matthammed felt a little hurt.

"I am not a salesman, my dear, I am an artist. I hand make each cartouche and personally do the inscribing."

"All for three-ninety-eight,"Thomas persisted in a jesting, yet vaguely condescending way.

Faye laughed again, encouraging him.

"For you, eighty-five,"Matthammed said,"no, seventy-five dollars. I give you a ten dollar cut."

"What a deal," Faye Morris burst out rudely."Guaranteed brass. Special for you."

Ardis did not like the way Thomas and Faye continually made Matthammed the brunt of their jokes. She directed a disapproving glance at Thomas, who had the good sense to look sheepish."I'd like to order one,"she said."Would you like a deposit?"

"No." Matthammed put a hand on hers to stop her from reaching for her purse. He rose quickly, his bold glance sliding from Thomas to Faye. Even though he remained extremely affable, his black eyes snapped, giving clue to his deep feelings of resentment.

"I'll bring the cartouche to you the night of the barbecue. I won't be present when it starts. I'll wander in about eight-thirty or so."With that, Matthammed left.

"Who invited him to the barbecue?" Faye asked, looking after him.

Instead of responding to Faye, Thomas said to Ardis, "I hope you're going to be there. It will be a great chance to mingle. Faye tells me many important people are flying in for these events." With a grin that included Faye, he added, "Or better yet, what do you say we skip all those boring lectures and spend our time in the pool? Wear your bikinis, girls. We'll have a great time."

At the sight of Essa BenSobel approaching the table, looking very grim and formal, the smile vanished from Thomas' face.

"Miss Cole, you have a long-distance call. You may use the phone on my desk if you like."

Ardis quickly excused herself and followed him. The caller must be Dan. She had not expected him to call right back, but she was anxious to know what he had found out.

In the lobby, Laurence Tolliver lounged on one of the comfortable chairs near the desk. He shuffled his morning paper to one side and watched Ardis approach. "They always call at mealtime," he remarked with a chuckle before going back to his news.

Instead of returning to his post behind the desk, Essa BenSobel headed to the doorway where Blake stood. They started talking in hushed voices like two conspirators.

"Hello. This is Ardis Cole."

"Dr. Fahmy, from the hospital in Cairo."

"Dr. Fahmy," Ardis responded, surprised. "Thank you for contacting me."

As Blake spoke with BenSobel, his dark eyes strayed to Ardis. Laurence Tolliver lifted his head slightly from the paper as if suddenly taken by curiosity. Because of the total lack of privacy, Ardis wished she had accepted the call in her room. Lowering her voice slightly, she asked, "What did you find out?"

"I've just received the results from the tea you brought to my office to be analyzed." He paused, as if studying a report. "It's just as I thought. No foreign substances were found, merely tea strongly flavored with mint."

Across the room she met Blake's gaze. Even though it was impossible, she had the uncomfortable feeling that he, BenSobel, and Laurence Tolliver had all heard what the doctor had told her. "I see," she said.

"I hope," Dr. Fahmy returned tersely, "that this puts your mind at ease. About a lot of things," he added before he hung up.

Dr. Fahmy had probably read Faye's article and concluded that Ardis was either a trouble-maker, a fool, or both. Feeling irritated over the doctor's shortness, which seemed almost a reprimand, she stepped away from the phone.

"Ardis." Blake drew forward. "I need to take a look in your security locker."

Ardis' gaze wandered toward Essa BenSobel, remembering his veiled glance at the obelisk that night she had returned from Cairo. Apparently he'd lost no time telling Blake what he'd seen. Ardis felt a sense of warning, a keen distrust of both of them, still she gestured to BenSobel, who as if awaiting her summons, stepped forward and supplied her with a key. Blake and she entered the small room where Ardis unlocked the box and handed him the obelisk.

Blake studied it for a while, saying finally, "I've found out what I need to know."

"And what is that?"

"I'm certain this was designed by Senmut himself."

He ran his fingers over the engravings, pausing as he located the two worn animal figures. Then he applied pressure upon the carved figures and the obelisk opened.

"The papyrus is gone," Ardis said.

Blake, not reacting to this, returned the stone carving to Ardis. After she had once more secured it, he said, "Now I will share something important with you."

They reentered the lobby. Laurence Tolliver's chair empty. BenSobel remained at his desk, watching them depart, his manner revealing alertness as it disclaimed interest.

"Where are we going?" Ardis asked.

"Not far," Blake said. "I can't be gone long as I have to help Nihisi make last minute preparations for his talk tonight."

Bright sunlight beat down upon the sun-dried buildings. The smell of freshly-baked bread wafted from a nearby bakery, mingling with the scent of exotic spices. They cut through a market where vendor's tables were stacked with fruits and vegetables and where whole animal carcasses hung upon hooks.

Blake stopped in front of the arched entrance to Matthammed's shop and drew out a key from his pocket. The door opened to a cool semi-darkness. Once they were inside, Matthammed's scrawny black cat pattered forward to meet them, mewing plaintively.

Blake parted the swinging ropes of beads that led to the back of the shop. He pressed the release button and the wooden door opened to the secret room where Matthammed had taken Thomas and her. Blake switched on the light that cast a glare over the display cases. Ardis' gaze moved uneasily toward the shadowy mound of boxes stacked along the wall.

She recalled Matthammed's anger when Thomas had wanted to look inside one of them—cartons filled with … what? She thought of conspirators, of tomb robbers. What better front than a shop with a hidden room?

Blake worked the combination to a small safe and drew out a roll of yellowed paper.

"I found this scroll among Jane's papers the day she collapsed."

Jane had told Ardis it would be inside the obelisk, but she had been unclear then about so many things. Jane must have removed it right before she fell ill … if Blake were telling the truth.

Blake carefully unrolled the scroll and pressed it flat on a table. "I believe it's authentic, Ardis. I think we're looking at the Senmut papyrus."

Was the scroll authentic, or a skillful reproduction intended to fool her? Beneath the glow of the overhead light the papyrus looked stiff and fragile with age. Ardis could barely decipher the royal stamp and the cartouche of Queen Hatshepsut. Beside it was the royal signature of Senmut.

"The body of the papyrus is written in hieratic script."

Ardis was basically familiar with this abbreviated form of hieroglyphics, a cursive form, which was used in the eighteenth dynasty, around Queen Hatshepsut's time.

"This first section I have been able to fully translate. This passage is simply a litany of royal titles belonging to Senmut." Blake read for her the rows of writing in faded characters of black and red. "I was a noble beloved of his Queen who entered upon the wonderful plans of the Mistress of the Two Lands. I was the superior of superiors, the chief of the chief of all works. I was in life beloved of the Mistress of Two Lands, she who was Queen and King of Upper and Lower Egypt, Hatshepsut."

Ardis felt a rush of hope. If the papyrus were authentic, then, Queen Hatshepsut's architect, Senmut, was speaking to them from over three thousand years ago. He wrote of himself with the lavish self-praise that characterized this favored of royalty, the architect who had dared to love a queen.

"It's very difficult to interpret," Blake was saying. "There's so much damage to the scroll. So far, I've only been able to make out a phrase or two. 'From the land of Punt I, Senmut, have returned with enough gold to guild the obelisks for Amon.' He indicated another passage 'to make my Queen's dreams come true …' And this one refers to Thutmose III, but the writing is so worn, it's impossible to translate."

Blake pointed out three distinct passages that formed a decorative, triangular border written in hieroglyphic form around the body of the script. These passages, too, were so faded it was virtually unreadable.

"This one you'll recognize," Blake said, pointing out a writhing crocodile. He translated slowly, "Death will devour he who disturbs the eternal duty of Senmut."

"The curse on the tomb wall reads 'the eternal *rest* of Senmut." It had taken Ardis hours of work to decipher the variation in the markings. "Here, as well as on the obelisk, it translates as 'duty'. Do you believe there is any significance in this slight difference?"

"I'm sure there is." Blake's dark brows drew together. "But I'm not sure just what it all means, not yet."

Blake showed Ardis a faded image of two felines facing one another. "As I was studying the small obelisk, I realized that this scroll has these same, identical figures. I think the same symbols may appear somewhere in the tomb. If so, they may open the way to a hidden chamber, much like the opening of the obelisk that concealed the papyrus. If these symbols do exist, it may take weeks, even months, to find them. We will have to go over every inch of the tomb again."

We—all of a sudden *they* had become partners. His gesture of sharing this scroll with her served to invite her total trust. If the papyrus were real, why was Blake showing it to her now? Why was he confiding in her this valuable information after his initial resistance to her even joining the project? Regardless of his reasons, Ardis could not help being caught up by the excitement of such a possibility.

"Then Jane was right," Ardis said. "This hidden chamber will contain the gold."

Blake's words seemed carefully chosen, as if to prepare her for disappointment. "I believe we may find the chamber Senmut designed to hide the gold from Thutmose III. But I doubt if the gold was ever actually hidden there." He turned his attention to the papyrus again, saying, "From what I can interpret, this writing indicates that Senmut *failed* in his mission to secure the gold. In fact, this scroll was most likely penned at a time when he knew he was helpless to hide the treasure from Thutmose's invasion."

"But we don't know that for sure."

Blake indicated the third border at the very bottom of the papyrus, obelisks, spaced in a neat row of five, each confined within a square. Beneath was a faded inscription. "Take a careful look at this, Ardis," he said. "I'm sure this is where Senmut declares his own failure."

Blake's voice grew more serious, as if the message he found recorded there dashed his hopes just as they had Senmut's. "I'm not entirely clear on the true meaning, but as close as I can come to a translation it reads like this: Queen Hatshepsut's dreams have turned to stone."

Chapter 11

Hours later, arriving early for the lecture, Ardis entered the hotel lobby. Nihisi Khet, immaculate in an expensive brown suit, stood just outside the dining room surrounded by professors and students who clung to his every word. As Ardis passed by him, she noticed the deep frown that cut between his eyes, the rigid straightness of his thin form. He looked even more unapproachable than he had when she had first met him at the Cairo hospital.

A worried man wearing a jellaba was telling him, "Your son has sent word that he won't be able to introduce the lecture. We still have time to get a substitute."

Nihisi, as if his entire life had been spent in constant combat with problems—delays, bribery, ignorance, or inaction—met the news head-on and returned a snap decision. "We won't need one. I'll speak without an introduction." Preoccupied, he abandoned his entourage and stepped toward Ardis, "I should have arrived earlier," he said curtly. "I'm finding everything totally disorganized."

Ardis wondered if his arrival in Luxor served some purpose other than a generous willingness to fill in for Professor Assari.

"How are you getting along with …?" Nihisi Khet left the sentence dangling as if he had intended to add "with Blake?" but had stopped himself.

"We're recording and translating hieroglyphics," Ardis replied. She avoided mentioning the papyrus Blake had shown her.

"A tremendous task for so few people. I can send all the skilled help you need."

"At this point, we would prefer working alone."

Nihisi gazed churlishly toward the table where he was to sit. "If you run into any trouble, don't try to handle it yourself. I will be here for at least a week."

Ardis watched Nihisi walk toward his table, his regal bearing suggesting that he took for granted the work the hotel had gone to for his behalf, the two statues of Queen Hatshepsut they had acquired in his honor.

The room was already packed, a colorful mixture of race and dress, however most of the guests were male and Egyptian. Surrounded by noise and by the guttural sound of the Arabic language, she circled back toward the main doorway. As she did, she thought of Jane and she wondered if Jane had ever felt as Ardis did now—an intruder, a stranger in an unfamiliar land.

Above the murmur of the crowd, a voice called her name. Ardis looked around, spotting Thomas and Faye seated at a table positioned the nearest to Nihisi Khet's. Thomas rose and pulled out the chair beside him. The seat required her to look right across the table at Faye Morris, which made her feel even more out of place.

"There's that Tolliver fellow," Thomas remarked as Laurence Tolliver entered the dining room and paused to look around for an empty seat.

"I keep running across him," Faye said. "He's really interesting. Let's ask him to join us." Not waiting for consent,

Faye called, "Mr. Tolliver. Over here. We've saved a place for you."

"Right nice of you," Laurence Tolliver said. His gray hair was slicked back and glistened with oil that did little to control the tiny curls around his temples. "What a bit of luck, to hear Nihisi Khet speak on my favorite subject." He sank heavily into the seat beside Faye, smiling at each in turn. "Have any of you gotten the chance to talk to Mr. Khet yet?"

"I gave it a try." Thomas smiled humorously. "I think the old boy must have studied personality from one of the mummies at the museum."

Faye burst out laughing. Her sleeveless black cocktail dress left her arms bare except for silver bracelets that clinked together whenever she moved. Her hair, short and springy, accentuated her pert nose and the sprinkling of freckles.

"Silent people," Ardis sprang to Nihisi's defense, "often have the most to say."

Tolliver nodded in agreement. "Mr. Khet's living proof of that. Brilliant man. I've read everything he's written."

"What about what I've written?" Faye asked boldly. She quickly reached in her bag and supplied Laurence Tolliver with a clipping. "Just off the press."

After Laurence Tolliver read it, he rubbed a hand across his trim mustache and pursed his lips before he spoke. "I'd think you'd be a little afraid to take on a legend like Jane Darvin."

Thomas, reaching for his glasses, accepted the clipping. Ardis avoided Faye's impudent glance and the guarded one of Laurence Tolliver. Her heart sank. What had Faye written this time?

Thomas, a little shocked, removed his glasses and passed the clipping on to her. Ardis glanced down at the bold black print which read, "Who Mourns Jane Darvin's Passing Most?'

What an absurd headline! She skimmed the lengthy details of the article, which was crammed with insinuations concerning Jane's private life. Surrounding the print were photos of Jane and Ramus, of Jane and Nihisi Khet. In the first one Jane wore khaki shorts, her black hair drawn back. Ramus stood beside her amid ruined stone walls with one arm on her shoulder. In the second, sleek in a dark dress, Jane dined with Nihisi Khet at some expensive restaurant. He was gazing at her with one of his rare smiles.

Ardis could feel a flush rising to her face. Was there no end to Faye's pointless prying? How was she going to sit at the same table with Faye Morris and pretend that she could tolerate her? She quickly passed the newspaper clipping back to Faye.

"You didn't even give it a good read."

Ardis tried hard to control herself. "I don't like gossip columns."

Faye thrust her chin forward. "Everyone else does. You know, people are more interested in Jane Darvin, the person, than they are in that old musty tomb!"

"I'm interested in Jane's personal life, too. But not in the same way you are. I'm in the process of tracing her background." Ardis gazed levelly at Faye, gauging her reaction. "I'm going to find out exactly what happened to her child. I want to know where he … or she … is right now."

Faye responded with an uneasy laugh. "If you do find out, let me know. That would make a very interesting story. Jane Darvin's love life, that's what people want to hear about. And I'm going to supply them with just what they want to read." Her voice grew louder. "Who were Jane Darvin's lovers?" She rolled her eyes in that sassy manner of hers. "I can get story after story out of that, can't I? I'm going to start with Ramus Montu; he's a sure bet." Faye stopped short, gaping toward the doorway.

Ramus—no doubt he'd read the article—had taken several steps into the room and halted. The taut set to his lips, the anger in his large dark eyes, alarmed Ardis.

He began striding relentlessly forward. If Ardis didn't intervene, an ugly clash was certain to take place. Ardis intercepted him before he reached the table. "Ramus, I must talk to you. Alone."

Ramus continued walking.

How was she ever going to stop him? His vengeance seemed very physical. No telling what trouble would come of it.

"Ramus," Ardis stated in a low, calm tone. "Please, listen to reason. Faye is not worth answering back. Don't give her the satisfaction of a response. Jane wouldn't, and she wouldn't want you to."

The mention of Jane caused him to stop. After a while, he turned back to the lobby. Ardis followed him.

"I think she found some way to get into the site," Ramus said. "I think it was that blasted girl who ransacked Jane's cabin."

"We don't know that, Ramus. It would be quite a feat getting past those guards."

"Don't think I'm going to let her sully Jane's memory!" He stopped short, his deep anger taking on an even more frightening form, silence and resolve.

Ramus had faithfully defended Jane while she lived, and he would continue to do so. Unlike Nihisi Khet, Ramus possessed a humanness that touched her. Ardis groped for some appropriate words. "It isn't possible for a person like Faye Morris to tear down all Jane has accomplished."

"But why?" Ramus demanded. "Why would anyone want to do this to Jane?"

He did not wait for Ardis' answer, but turned on his heel and strode outside. Ardis stood in the doorway until his form had blended into the darkness. She had done the impossible, turned a whirlwind from its course. At least for now.

Ardis caught the end of Laurence Tolliver's sentence as she slipped into the chair beside Thomas." ... a fair amount of time in London."

"My people come from Harwich. It's beautiful by the sea," Thomas said.

"I've been there many times," Laurence agreed. "Splendid place."

Faye leaned aggressively forward. "You didn't have to run interference for me," she said to Ardis. "That old man doesn't scare me any." She waited a while for Ardis to reply. When she didn't, Faye said impulsively. "Watch this. Nihisi Khet refuses to discuss the tomb project with me. He says he will not be interviewed. I'm just going to go over to his table right now and force him to answer some of my questions."

Her announcement left them dumbfounded. They all watched as Faye snatched a notebook from her velvet bag and started toward the head table.

Laurence Tolliver's chair creaked as he turned around, his gray eyes intent and curious. Out of the corner of her eye Ardis caught a glimpse of Thomas. His slightly protruding teeth caught against his lower lip, as he gave a disbelieving shake of his head. Around them, groups of people, caught up in their own private conversations, seemed unaware of the havoc about to take place.

Nihisi Khet's eyes followed the girl's bouncing step and remained sternly fastened upon her as she drew to a stop in front of him. Even if there had been truth in Faye's statement and she hadn't been afraid of Ramus, then she should, Ardis decided, be afraid of this man.

"I thought everyone might enjoy a question and answer sort of thing before dinner," Faye stated in a loud, aggressive voice.

"Who are you?" Nihisi asked coldly.

"Faye Morris."

"From where? Whom do you represent?"

Faye had not expected Nihisi's total control of the situation. She disliked having the tables turned. She wanted to be the one asking the questions. "I work for several local papers."

"Which ones? Do they all have the same status as *The International Reporter?*" Nihisi's clipped words cut though the stillness that had fallen around them. "No, I don't think any questions from you are by any means in order."

Undaunted, Faye tried an outright attack. "Why don't you tell us why you're keeping the work on the Senmut tomb so very private? Why can't these people … " Her hand swept around the elect group of Egyptologists that surrounded him. "Why don't you allow them to help interpret this find?"

"I have nothing to say to you. If you think I want my name associated with your kind of journalism, you're dead wrong. Now, will you please leave."

"What I'd like to know is why you gave Jane Darvin's project over to Ardis Cole instead of to your own son?"

Nihisi's eyes, cold as frost, stared at her. He did not speak.

"There's something funny going on here. Why are you refusing to talk to me?"

"I do not," he said disdainfully, "cast pearls before swine."

Faye bristled, then whirled around, and swished back to their table. "Who does he think he is?" she demanded. "He'll be coming to me and begging to talk to me, before I'm through with him."

"Nothing is as relaxing as a peaceful dinner," Thomas observed.

Laurence gave a weak smile.

"Mr. Big-Man Khet had better watch out for me! I'm used to being on my own. My mother dumped me with my grandmother when I was just a baby. No one ever cared what

I did. So I grew up on the streets of New York, fighting my own battles and defending myself."

"You're not defending yourself," Ardis challenged. "You're tearing someone else down. You're intentionally trying to ruin Jane's name both as a person and as an archaeologist."

"She was a failure at both," Faye said. "As an archaeologist, she was obsessed. She just wanted glory for herself! She tried to shut everyone else out. And <u>he</u>," she pointed to Nihisi, "let her do it!"

"Here comes our first course," Laurence said with relief. Everyone except Ardis eagerly watched the waiter's approach.

"I could have been a famous archaeologist, just like <u>her</u>," Faye said bitterly once the dish was placed before her. "Jane Darvin took a dislike to me and washed me out of the program. I had my heart set on that field; and I'll never, ever forgive her for what she did to me. She had no reason at all, except for her petty dislike of me."

"That doesn't sound like Jane."

"You just didn't know her. She was a cold-hearted woman, capable of anything."

Ramus could have been right. Faye could have been the one who had smashed and torn up the contents of Jane's cabin. Her deep, personal hatred of Jane could be because Jane's child had not been a son, but a daughter.

All evening Ardis had expected Blake to return, but she didn't see him until the lecture was over. He stood by the doorway, dark, well-cut suit flattering him, blending with his hair and eyes.

"Let's walk," he said, ushering her from the lobby out into the dark, still night.

"Faye's written another article about Jane. Even worse than the others. We barely avoided a confrontation between her and Ramus." Fearing the course Ramus' vengeance might take, Ardis added, "Ramus left, but this isn't over."

"We have much bigger problems," he told her. "The papyrus that I showed you has been stolen."

"Stolen?" Ardis stepped away from him, shocked. Most of Jane's papers had been destroyed and now they had lost the papyrus, too. The entire project seemed to fall around her in ashes.

As the first impact of the news subsided, suspicion took its place. Ardis had only Blake's word that the papyrus he had shown her had been the original one hidden inside the obelisk. And now it had quickly disappeared before Ardis had had time to decipher those vastly important words for herself. How could she trust him? With Nihisi's help he could have come up with a replacement for the genuine papyrus, a ruse fashioned to supply her with false leads that would give them time to remove the gold and other treasures. "How would anyone know where you kept the papyrus? How did the robber gain access into Matthammed's back room?"

"He crashed through a side door. Somehow he found the door to that private room and broke into the safe. Matthammed is there now with the police."

"What else is missing?"

"Gold, but that's not what the thief was after. He wanted the papyrus."

"There won't be any fingerprints," Ardis said. "There weren't any in the cabin."

He met her gaze with that shuttered look she had often noticed in his eyes. "No, whoever is doing this is very careful, very professional."

He did not speak for a long time. The quietness between them contrasted with the buzz of talk from the hotel lobby.

"We didn't report the missing papyrus to the authorities," Blake said. "We have enough trouble without this leaking to the press. It's of utmost importance that we remain silent about the scroll, about how valuable it is."

If the papyrus she had seen had value, Ardis thought. It seemed an uncanny coincidence that it had been stolen at the same time Nihisi Khet had arrived in Luxor. She studied Blake hoping she was wrong. Could it be possible Nihisi was working alone, that he used Blake as a pawn—the way he must have used many other people in his lifetime? Ardis' words cautiously bridged the silence between them. "Did your father know about this scroll?"

Blake's lips compressed. "Jane would have told him. But what does that have to do with what happened to it?"

"Even if someone followed us, they couldn't have seen into that back room. Who else knew the papyrus existed or where you had hidden it?"

"Besides you," he answered gloomily, "just Ramus, Matthammed, and me."

Chapter 12

Ardis gazed down from the balcony into the hotel lobby which was alive with commotion, noisy with the buzzing blend of voices from the large crowd gathered for this morning's scheduled trip to Queen Hatshepsut's temple, Deir el-Bahari. The startling news of the stolen papyrus, the narrowly avoided clash between Ramus and Faye at the banquet last night, created in Ardis a sense of impending disaster that made her dread rather than anticipate today's excursion. With steely determination she gripped her bag, packed with mineral water and notebooks, and started down the stairs.

Thomas, with a lopsided smile that brightened his irregular features, jostled through the crowd toward her. "Saw you standing on the balcony," he said. "Thought for a minute you weren't going to join us."

"I heard the call of duty," she answered lightly.

"What about just having fun?"

As they fell into step with the group streaming from the hotels toward the main street to the ferry landing, Ardis looked for Blake, disappointed by his absence. On the way, they met up with Faye, who had stopped to pick out a hat from a vendor. "Which one do you like?" she asked Thomas.

He pointed to a floppy white hat with Egypt spelled out across the background of pyramids. "We'll take two of these," Thomas said, reaching for his billfold. He arched a brow at Ardis. "That's what it will take for you to look like perfect twins."

For a moment Ardis didn't know what Thomas was referring to, then she noticed that Faye wore tan shorts and a white cotton blouse almost identical to her own.

Busy adjusting her new hat, Faye called out a thank you and scampered off. Thomas and Ardis slowly strolled down the plank walkway to the ferry, where they found empty seats near the window.

Blake, at the last minute, boarded. His dark eyes swept across the crowd, settled on Ardis and then moved to Thomas. Then he turned and left the cabin. She could see him on the deck gripping the railing and moodily staring across the water.

The huge motor ground into the seabed as the craft eased away from the dock. She watched Blake, his dark hair slightly ruffled by the wind, and felt a painful sense of estrangement. She wondered if the great gulf between them had been caused by the stolen papyrus or by Thomas' presence beside her.

Ardis forced her eyes away from Blake, toward the deep, churning water, sparkling with brilliant early morning light. On the opposite bank a row of battered mini-busses waited that would take the tour group toward the Valley of the Kings.

Once the boat had stopped, Ardis lost sight of Blake in the crowd. Thomas and she were swept toward the center bus where they hastily boarded. Faye in the seat opposite them, adjusted the camera that hung on a strap around her neck.

"I'm glad I got on this bus. Ramus Montu keeps giving me those murderous looks." Faye leaned across the aisle to Thomas. Her face was already shiny from the heat, and her dark curls were sticking to her damp forehead. "That's how I know when I'm really successful," she added smugly. "When people single me out for persecution."

Thomas adjusted his long legs under the seat in front of him. "That may be OK for you," he commented, with a droll glance toward Ardis, "but I, myself, enjoy keeping a low profile, like a deer in hunting season."

Faye laughed. "You British miss out on all the emotional ups and downs. Too bad. They're what gives life a flare."

Ardis, not in the mood for Faye, watched from the window as the buses filled.

Their driver had started the engine when Matthammed, wearing a white robe, entered. He paused on the step. "Ardis," he called, "the *head honcho* wants to see you. He's on the first bus, first seat. I'll trade places with you."

Thomas rose to accompany her.

"Sorry, no room for you," Matthammed said, gesturing for Thomas to slide over and make a place for him. "Only Ardis."

Ardis hurried toward the leading bus. She stopped at the front where Nihisi sat with Ramus. "What do you want?" she asked him.

Nihisi looked up at her blankly.

"I'm the one who sent for you," a deep voice said from the opposite side. Blake stood up, gripping the overhead railing.

The bus moved forward with a lurch. Blake reached out to steady her into the only remaining seat, the one beside him.

"Does Matthammed always refer to you as the *head honcho*?" Ardis demanded.

"I only asked him if he would invite you to sit with me." A sparkle appeared in his eyes. "The message sometimes changes according to the messenger."

Laurence Tolliver in the seat behind them leaned forward to say, "What bloody good luck, my getting to tour Deir el-Bahari with Nihisi Khet."

Tolliver wore a khaki hat, a light cotton shirt, and carried a canvas bag beneath his arm instead of a suit jacket. "This may be my grand finale," he proclaimed with a little regret. "In a short time I must return to London."

"So soon?"

"I had to pull strings to get this brief holiday. I'm afraid my next one will be three years from now when I retire." As he spoke, his gray eyes shifted away from Ardis suggesting a certain insincerity. Even though he spoke the words to her, he seemed to be directing them at Blake, as if he were trying to convince Blake that he was just an ordinary tourist.

Tolliver's intent gaze now locked on Blake. "You ever been to London?" he inquired.

"Many times," Blake answered.

Tolliver went on talking about the British Isles, but Ardis barely heard him. She could always sense approaching trouble, but wasn't sure whether it would come from Tolliver or from Ramus and Faye.

The trail of buses pulled to a stop in the wide parking lot. People poured out and assembled in front of Nihisi at the base of the great monument. He led the way down the long, wide stone path to Deir el-Bahari. Blake and Ardis lagged behind the group that moved silently, like in a procession, toward the temple.

Theirs was the first of the day's onslaught of tours. They had arrived before peddlers and vendors had yet invaded the stillness to set up their shades and wares. Soon, the yellow rays of sun would be scorching, unbearable. But now, for a brief time, the heat was gentle and quietness dominated the golden sand and sky.

The pleasant stillness was broken by Faye calling out shrilly, "Ramus Montu! I want to interview you today!"

Ramus was walking alone just ahead of Blake and Ardis. At the sound of Faye's voice, he turned back. Disdain tightened the creases around his mouth and eyes. This, along with his stony silence, gave him a threatening aura that made Ardis' breath catch.

"What do you say?" Faye asked. When Ramus continued to glare at her without answering, Faye raised the camera mockingly as if to snap a picture of him. A muscle in Ramus' jaw clenched. Ardis' earlier dread changed to fear. Before the day was over the mounting tension between the two of them was sure to erupt into a violent, angry scene.

Blake, as if he had not noticed the near clash, caught Ardis' hand and drew her on ahead of the others.

Bright morning sunshine played upon the faded apricot walls of Hatshepsut's temple, blending the colors and making it seem almost an extension of the steep, jagged cliff beyond. Sunshine crept into dark corners spreading brightness over hidden niches, arched chapels, and slim, white columns. Hatshepsut's graceful temple seemed a part of its surroundings. Ardis delighted in its openness, the doors and windows that freely admitted light. Ardis remembered the words used so many times by the Egyptians to describe Hatshepsut's graceful buildings and monuments, "How like her it is!"

"This portico," Nihisi said, "once held a huge statue of the queen." His voice rose to accommodate the scattered crowd. "As you know, Thutmose III attempted to obliterate Queen Hatshepsut's name and image wherever it appeared. His vengeance was so great that the sphinxes were heated and then cooled until they burst; the fragments were tossed over the edge of the cliff. The statue which once stood here probably met a similar fate."

Ardis stared at the empty place where the statue had once been. She could imagine the slender grace, the placid features of Queen Hatshepsut. Statues of the queen portrayed a determination, a quiet strength that reminded Ardis of Jane

Darvin. She was another great woman who had devoted her life to the study of the enigmatic queen.

Ardis' tragic sense of loss at the statue's malevolent destruction deepened and mingled with sadness as she thought of Jane. The tour to this grand place seemed empty without her. Jane had known every inch of the temple, every faded mural, every stone, by heart. She had loved Deir el-Bahari in the same way that Queen Hatshepsut had loved it.

Nihisi paused on the steps outside the monument to tell the story of Hatshepsut's "divine" birth. "Queen Hatshepsut believed that she was no ordinary mortal, but the actual daughter of the god, Amon." Quoting by heart what was inscribed upon the temple walls, he said, "The god came who is lord over all, even over the throne of the two lands, and he approached the queen in the shape of her husband. Amid the splendors of the palace, he found her sleeping …"

"What a convenient story," Thomas scoffed.

"It worked, didn't it?" Faye spoke up. "It caused her to become the first woman pharaoh to rule Egypt. She tricked the entire male population with her story of being the daughter of a god. The first women's libber. Let's applaud, girls."

"She invented this story to steal the throne from its rightful heir, Thutmose III," Thomas protested, with a teasing, challenging glance toward Ardis. "She used the Egyptian's religious superstition to her own advantage. Who could deny the throne to the daughter of the great Amon? A self-seeking conniver, if you ask me."

"Which we didn't," Nihisi said sharply.

"Of course she was a fraud," Faye burst out. "An even worse one than …"

Faye's words died in her throat. Ardis looked toward Ramus, whose narrowed gaze watch her, as if only waiting for Faye to speak the word *Jane*.

Faye quickly turned away.

"Queen Hatshepsut believed in her own divine birth,"
Nihisi went on. "She was deeply devoted to her god, Amon.
I'm certain Queen Hatshepsut was convinced that she and
only she was the chosen one to rule Egypt."

"Who are we to question her?" Matthammed asked with a
rush of emotion.

"I'll bet you believe in mummies rising from their tombs,
too," Thomas retorted mockingly.

"I'm not asking you to second-guess the queen's motives,"
Nihisi spoke again. "Queen Hatshepsut represented herself
to be the daughter of Amon. That's all that matters from a
historical perspective."

Subject closed, Nihisi moved on, pointing out one of the
series of many murals that decorated the temple. "One of Queen
Hatshepsut's greatest accomplishments was the journey to
Punt," he said. "Please follow me to the other side. The murals
covering the southern walls of the colonnade have been the
least damaged by erosion and Queen Hatshepsut's enemies.
There, we can better see the ships and painted figures."

As they moved along, the pressure of Blake's hand stopped
her. "Look at this," he said showing Ardis a place where Queen
Hatshepsut's name had been hacked out with a vengeance,
erased from her own monument by her angry successor.
"Only one of the hundreds of desecrations found here in this
temple."

"How he must have hated her," Ardis said with a little
shudder.

The look on Blake's face was indecipherable—was it
outrage or some other emotion that darkened his eyes as he
said, "Doesn't it remind you of what was done to Jane's cabin?
The same sort of hatred."

The sight of the ugly gashes in the stone, along with Blake's
words, sent a shiver through Ardis despite the smothering heat.
She could see Faye though the blistering haze of light smirking

at some remark she had made to Thomas. The smug image of the journalist prompted Ardis to think of Jane's enemies—one who had set out to ruin her and had done so with as much ruthlessness as Hatshepsut's mortal foe had done so many centuries ago.

With agitation, Ardis wandered away from Blake back toward the group gathered about the series of faded wall paintings. Nihisi's words once more became distinct. "These murals were designed by someone who was capable of describing in detail the journey to Punt to the artist—probably Senmut himself."

"Here you see five ships sailing past the cliffs of the Red Sea. The next mural depicts the Somali coast and the settlement of the Puntite kings. Notice the huts shaped like beehives? The arrival of their ships in a place so remote was so unexpected the king of Punt asked, 'How have you come here to a land no one knows of? Have you fallen from the sky?'"

Ardis wondered how Nihisi could look so immaculate with the terrible heat clamping down upon them. Ardis fell back a little, adjusting the white hat Thomas had bought her against the burning sun.

"Something to drink?" Matthammed asked from his seat in the shade. He offered her a can of pop he had just drawn from a small thermos pack.

"Thanks," she said. "I brought water, but it will probably be boiling by now."

Nihisi was pointing to the painted image of an enormous figure of a woman astride an obviously overburdened donkey. "Queen Ati was monstrously obese, so much so that archaeologists believed her to be the victim of some disease. However, the Puntites regarded their queen as a great beauty." Without even the trace of a smile, he added, "Beneath the small, inadequate-appearing donkey she rides, you see the words,'The ass that carries the queen,' a rare touch of Egyptian humor."

"And they say our British humor is lacking," Laurence Tolliver remarked, his words elicited a dry laugh from Thomas.

Nihisi moved over to the next mural. "These five ships are loaded with the exquisite treasures of Punt—ivory, ebony, myrrh, resin, incense, kohl, and cinnamon wood. Exotic trees, the skins of the southern panther, and great quantities of gold were also brought back to delight the queen. Live animals, too, including a rare white cheetah."

Senmut had tried to bring Punt to Egypt for his queen—the fragrance of myrrh trees, gold and ivory, and the white cheetah in a cage. Hatshepsut and Senmut had walked, here in their garden paradise, under the watchful, jealous eye of Thutmose III. He was eagerly waiting to snatch their happiness and their power. What became of their paradise ... and of the gold Senmut had gathered for the obelisks at Karnak?

"What's wrong with Ramus?" Matthammed asked Ardis, as he gazed sharply at his uncle, who stood grim and solitary in the shade of a huge column. "He's usually so absorbed in these lectures. Today he's hardly even listening." Matthammed's black eyes became crafty in his hawk-like face. "When he looks like that," he said wisely, "you can be sure there is going to be trouble."

Nihisi and the others had moved inside the temple, with the exception of Faye. She was scampering like a goat along the edge of the monument, scaling high stones with long, nimble legs. Ardis saw her slight figure, with the floppy white hat identical to her own, disappear behind a column of stone.

Ramus, as if aware of Matthammed's and Ardis' close scrutiny, followed the others into the hallway. Ardis drank the last of the soda and joined the group. Beyond the portico lay a pillared hall, sanctuaries, and the funeral chapel of Queen Hatshepsut. Caught up in Nihisi's words, Ardis forgot about

Ramus for a while. When she thought of him again, he was gone.

Ardis left the monument, spotting Ramus at once. He stood squarely in the center walkway. Behind him were the tents and canvas shadings of the peddlers and an ever-increasing line of buses. From a distance, his heavy frame appeared slightly distorted, like a mirage. He was staring up toward the cliff area, his eyes, squinted from the brilliant light, following Faye's every movement, almost as if he were stalking her.

Ardis started toward him, but as she drew closer, his total appearance seemed to change. With sagging shoulders he half turned away from her. The sadness of his solitary figure caused her to stop.

Ardis could not bring herself to intrude upon his grief. She had misinterpreted his actions today. Ramus' thoughts had not been centering on Faye at all. Ramus, like Ardis, was missing Jane. Deciding not to disturb him, she returned to the group.

"The innermost sanctuary of the temple is carved deep into the rock of the cliff." Nihisi began to tell of the excavation work around the temple in which tombs for Queen Hatshepsut and Senmut were discovered—both disturbingly empty.

"It is known that the Queen had two tombs; the lesser one was abandoned at the time she became Pharaoh. A grander tomb in the Valley of the Kings led to Deir el-Bahari by a secret passage. In both instances the sarcophagi were found empty.

A deep shaft was also discovered in 1927, which began a long distance in front of the temple and descended to a great depth. The shaft was traced to the end and was found to lead to a vault, which lay directly beneath the spot where Queen Hatshepsut intended to be buried. This was a secret tomb of Senmut's."

Nihisi continued. "The sarcophagus within this tomb was found smashed into a million pieces. Neither the mummy of Queen Hatshepsut nor Senmut's have ever been found. It remains a mystery to this day where either one was actually buried, or if they were both murdered and their corpses destroyed by Thutmose III."

Ardis' thoughts turned to the recently-discovered tomb bearing Senmut's signature. She was anxious to go back to work, to search for the cheetah symbols apparent on both the papyrus and the obelisk. Would some undiscovered chamber lead to missing mummies? Did it hold within its depths some clue about what had happened to the handsome, daring architect?

"I find all this talk about secret tombs and hidden passageways fascinating." Laurence Tolliver remarked.

"Are there really secret chambers in the tombs?" a thin, young girl, obviously a student, asked.

"The ancient Egyptians were masters of illusion," Nihisi said. "A touch of the hand upon some obscure symbol has often unexpectedly resulted in the discovery of a hidden chamber. The Egyptians were often very creative in their concealment of such passageways. In one tomb I helped to excavate, a huge black scarab upon the wall concealed a catch, which, when pressed ever so lightly, caused a spring-loaded door to open. Sometimes the Egyptians used a series of numbers or symbols to provide admittance into a certain chamber, similar to the combination on a modern-day safe. Other times an object, such as a piece of metal or stone, had been fashioned to be fitted and turned within a depression upon the wall like a key in a lock."

Ardis' thoughts strayed from Nihisi's talk to the matching cheetah symbols that had appeared both on the obelisk and the papyrus. She must find them before the person who had stolen the scroll did, symbols Jane had been searching for and might have discovered the day she had sent for her.

"I've heard these chambers are often booby-trapped," the student said.

Nihisi nodded somberly. "An unexplored chamber is more dangerous than an empty mine shaft. Heavy rocks balanced from above, deep pits, or jagged stakes used to discourage tomb robbers often await the unsuspecting explorer."

"I wouldn't risk going in one," the young girl exclaimed.

"Now if you'll follow me to the right, we will take a look at the hieroglyphics along the far wall. There, you will see the image of the goddess Hathor, the god Anubis, and the sun god, Amon Re."

As Nihisi motioned the group over to the side, Blake impulsively reached for Ardis' hand and drew her away with him. "Since we're here," he whispered, "I want to share something special with you. Something not included in Nihisi's lecture tour."

Blake guided her further back into the temple. They had soon wandered so far away from the others that she began to grow uneasy. Deep in the heart of the temple, an ever-increasing darkness began to close around them as the walls began to narrow. She could feel the rough, uneven stones beneath her feet. Curiosity kept her following him through the shadowy dimness. He led her, at last, into a small, windowless room.

Blake shone the flashlight he carried along the walls. "Ah, there it is."

Ardis looked at him quizzically. The light fell upon on a little wall carving set close to the rock floor.

"See that small likeness of a man." In a space so obscure as to go virtually undiscovered, Blake pointed out a tiny, crude relief, a portrait carved in stone.

"Senmut." She looked with awe at the diminutive carving, the rough profile hewn in stone. A space beneath the primitive picture bore the proud signature, Senmut, Steward of Amon.

"If he had been caught, he would have been put to death for daring to place his likeness here, in a temple reserved for the gods," Blake said. "Senmut must have worked here alone, under cover of night. He was willing to risk divine anger in his desire for a chance at everlasting life with his beloved Queen."

Ardis glanced up from the carving of Senmut to Blake suddenly imagining an uncanny likeness between the two of them. An unexplained feeling of fear swept over her, almost like a premonition. The fear was not for herself, but for Blake. She sensed that his showing her this small statue held some deeper meaning. Was he another brave Senmut, forced into a situation beyond his control? Would he, like Senmut, meet some ill fate? She suddenly felt very much afraid for him.

"Other statues of Senmut have survived, like the large one in the tomb Jane found. This was a little extra insurance." Blake paused. "The Egyptians believed that as long as a likeness was preserved, the person had a chance at everlasting life. That's why Thutmose tried to destroy everything that even in a vague way related to Queen Hatshepsut and her consort, Senmut—her royal name, her sarcophagus, her statues, possibly even her mummy. Thutmose thought he was denying her and Senmut eternal life."

"He almost succeeded."

Blake smiled. "Thutmose couldn't destroy everything. Senmut's everlasting state would have been assured by this tiny, surreptitious portrait, carved in haste in the dead of night. And Queen Hatshepsut's image lives in the undamaged sphinx Jane found in the desert, among other places."

"So according to their beliefs, both could still be blessed with eternal life?"

"By the Egyptian way of thinking, yes." She could see Blake's strong features, shadowed and handsome in the semi-darkness. "But there was one thing even more important that Thutmose could never destroy."

"What was that?" Ardis felt hypnotized by his deep gaze.

"Their love."

Chapter 13

The group gathered around Nihisi on the stone terrace. It took Ardis a moment to grow accustomed to the shock of heat and of the dazzling sun so bright she could not look directly up at the fierce blue sky.

"For those of you who are interested," Nihisi was saying, "there is a path that leads up into the cliffs where you can get a magnificent overview of the area. From this vantage point, you can see the Theban valley, the Nile, Luxor, and Karnak. However, since it is a very steep and rugged climb, some of you may choose to remain behind." He checked his watch. "We will all plan to meet back here in around forty-five minutes."

From below, the surrounding wall of cliffs looked almost vertical, impenetrable. Nihisi Khet and Ramus took the lead. Most of the group dropped back. Only a few scattered participants started up the uneven heights behind the temple.

Blake called back to Matthammed, "Aren't you going to join us?"

"Not me," Matthammed responded, wiping his turbaned brow. "I've seen that view hundreds of times. I'm going to hang around down here and wait for the bus."

"Matthammed and I used to wander these cliffs as children," Blake told Ardis. "The desert was our playground."

The direct rays of the sun emitted an appalling heat. Sweat dampened Ardis' forehead as she and Blake began the arduous climb up the spiny ridge of rock.

As they scrambled over the stone-scattered path, Ardis noticed that Faye and Thomas had paired off and were walking together a few steps ahead of them. Thomas turned back to wink at Ardis, "Only the hardy are attempting this climb," he said jovially, but as he regarded Blake his eyes lost some of their friendly warmth.

Laurence Tolliver lagged behind them. He paused, puffing. "This climb isn't for sissies," he said. "If I'd known what I was in for, I would have stayed with Matthammed."

When they reached the first level, Laurence, looking strained and out of breath, sat down upon a huge, flat stone to rest.

"I'll bet that's as far as you go," Thomas yelled back teasingly. Faye had sprinted on ahead to snap some pictures from the top of a smooth, brown boulder.

"Sitting at a desk all day doesn't qualify one for all this strenuous activity."

"It isn't much farther," Thomas encouraged. "I can see the top from here."

"Don't worry about me," Laurence replied. "I'll be along after a bit."

Ardis glanced up, started to see Ramus standing high and alone upon another ridge keeping a grim surveillance on Faye as she scampered from rock to rock. The tense set of his heavy form put her in mind of a tawny, solid-stone statue. The way he glared at Faye warned Ardis that in Ramus' mind the journalist had been pronounced guilty of some crime and only the execution of the sentence remained.

Blake came up beside Ardis, slipping an arm casually around her shoulder as if he sensed nothing wrong. "Ready to go on?" She wondered how Blake could gaze up at Ramus and fail to interpret Ramus' chilling thoughts.

After a breathless climb over huge boulders they reached a level plateau. Nihisi drew them all together, saying, "Where is Mr. Tolliver?"

"Couldn't take it," Thomas answered. "Probably turned back."

Nihisi, frowned, then began to orient the small group. "What you are seeing now is the ancient city of Thebes." He indicated the very top of the distant ruins of Luxor and Karnak. "Thebes was in reality a twin city. Located in the Nile valley was the *city of the living*, and in the desert was *the city of the dead*. The two were once connected by wide avenues of sphinxes." Nihisi pointed out the winding strip of the great river. "Men crossed the Nile in holy barges to pay homage to the 'City of the Hundred Gates.'"

With that abruptness common to him, Nihisi checked his watch. "Fifteen minutes to wander, and then we'll all start back down together," he said.

Ardis looked for Blake, but he had left her to join his foster father.

"Go ahead and look around," Blake called to her. "I'll catch up with you later."

Ardis paused to pull damp hair back from the nape of her neck, twining it into a loose knot, which she held in place by readjusting her hat. Seeing that Nihisi and Blake were still immersed in deep conversation, she wandered off by herself to admire the view.

Ardis reached the very edge of the cliff and gazed down at the Deir el-Bahari gorge. Stone walls, sheer and steep, dropped straight down, broken only by spiny outcrops and narrow ledges of sand-colored rock.

Ardis would have enjoyed the scene were it not for the intense heat, which made her feel slightly ill. She stepped back and looked away from the dizzying height. As she did, she saw a stocky form emerge from behind a jutting boulder, a bare outline that appeared briefly, undulating in the heavy air.

She guessed the man was Ramus. He had always been friendly to her, but sometimes he seemed like the desert, hard, empty, and immensely frightening.

Ardis turned her full attention back to the view, endless miles, a panorama of fields and desert. She raised her hand to shield her eyes from the glare and attempted to identify the shape of a towering obelisk within the ruins of the temple of Karnak.

Focusing on the distant temple, she stepped forward slightly. Her foot was braced against the rock that lined the cliff's edge. At that moment, an Arab cry broke through the quietness, terrifyingly muffled. Startled, Ardis attempted to whirl around, but was struck a slamming blow to her back. A shattering pain exploded between her shoulders. Ardis had no time to turn, no time to look around at her attacker. Frantically she struggled to regain her balance. Her hands flailed into the vacant air in front of her.

She could feel herself falling, falling though a great, empty space.

Not far below the cliffs Ardis hit a solid promenade of rock. She clawed desperately at smooth stone and roots that broke away in her hands. She could find no hand or foothold, no way to break her rapid descent. She hit the jutting stone platform and began to slide toward the edge. She slid faster and faster down the slick rocks.

Ardis gasped as she smacked into another rock surface. When the intense pain subsided, she became aware of her precarious position. A narrow ribbon of rock had stopped her fall. Only this fragile ledge had prevented her from plummeting straight down to certain death.

Trying to remain calm and still, Ardis wiped the streaming blood from her forehead. Her ankle, previously injured in the tomb, seared and burned.

Ardis slowly changed positions to ease the stabbing pain. As she moved, the ledge beneath her, traumatized by the impact of her fall, began to crumble. Aware of the shifting surface beneath her feet and the shower of falling stones, she grabbed for the shelf of rock just above her.

She totally lacked the strength to pull herself to the top. Ardis tried again to raise herself up. The sudden shift of position caused the ledge beneath her to give way entirely.

With a cry, Ardis struggled to maintain her grip on the stone's sharp edge.

Echoing her terror, a shrill voice from far above her screamed out, "It's Ardis!" Through a blur, Ardis saw Faye staring down at her. Her white hat slipped from her head and fell far into the gorge.

Faye shouted, "Blake! Over here! Help us!"

"Don't move!" Blake cried. "I'm coming down after you!" Using the jutting stones for support, Blake began the perilous descent to the first outcropping of rocks. From there he eased himself downward until he reached the second ledge. Then, on hands and knees, he stretched his arm as far as he could toward her. "Ardis, I can't reach you. Not without your help."

She felt too weak to move.

"Ardis! You're not going to be able to hang on much longer. You must try to grab my hand!"

She had to take the only chance she had, even though it might mean falling to her death. The stiff, aching fingers of her left hand kept frantic hold to the rock, while her right hand reached up. Blake caught her wrist. For a brief time she felt suspended, a short reprieve before disaster.

"Slowly, now. Slowly!" he said.

Blake now clutched both of her hands. Still she had to use her feet as leverage in order to make it to the top. He pulled her to solid ground and into his arms, saying with agony, "Darling, I almost lost you forever!"

Blake held her close against him as they made their slow ascent to the top. Ardis was only barely aware of being passed upward and received by unidentifiable arms. After being hoisted again in the same manner, she found herself lying on a hard, level surface. A sea of faces floated above her. Faye, Thomas, dear Blake, who had saved her life! Blake's face faded and darkened until it disappeared entirely.

Ardis gradually became aware of hushed voices, but had no idea of what they were saying. Someone had placed a backpack beneath her head like a pillow. Blake wiped her forehead with water from his canteen, a look of fear in his eyes.

Faye Morris dropped to her knees beside her. "What happened, Ardis?"

"She fell," Thomas said.

A sick feeling settled in Ardis' stomach. Was she going into shock? Or was it simply the heat bearing down, burning like a torch all around her.

Thomas' strained voice cut through the insufferable rays of sun. "We should have all stayed together. Places like this are wide-open for accidents."

"It wasn't an accident," Ardis managed to tell him. "Someone pushed me."

Faye stared toward the fast approaching figures of Nihisi Khet and Ramus. As she did, her face paled, and for the first time since Ardis had met her, the cocky boldness drained away and left genuine fear. "He did it!" Faye said in a panicky voice, gaze holding to Ramus."He was trying to kill me, and he mistakenly pushed you instead!"

Ardis shifted uncomfortably on her chair in front of her hotel room window. The medicine Dr. Sirdi had given her had made her doze for a few hours, but now she was awake again and in pain. Ardis guessed by the amount of light outside that it was still early in the evening.

She remembered how Blake had held her tightly during the long bus ride to the hospital and had waited as Dr. Sirdi had examined her and X-rayed her ankle.

"You are lucky," he had said. "Your head injury is not serious, and you have only a sprain, no broken bones." With the instructions that she keep her ankle tightly bound, Dr. Sirdi had released her.

The events of the day replayed in her troubled mind. She remembered leaving Blake with Nihisi and wandering over to the cliff's edge. Hazily, as if in a dream, she recalled seeing a stocky figure that looked like Ramus momentarily appear and then duck back to a place of concealment. But the image she had glimpsed so briefly had been only a wavering outline she could not positively identify as any specific person.

The fact remained that Ramus hated Faye, and Ardis had sensed that he had been stalking her all morning. Faye and Ardis were of the same build and had been dressed similarly. With Ardis' hair covered by an identical white hat, it was possible Ramus had found her in a vulnerable position, had mistaken her for Faye, and had given her what he would consider a well-deserved shove.

No, she thought suddenly. The push had been intended for her, not Faye Morris.

An unexpected knock caused her to start. She rose, her entire body feeling battered. She limped forward and opened the door. Laurence Tolliver, looking worried and concerned, stood outside. "Thought I'd stop by and see how you are," he said.

Instead of replying Ardis looked down the corridor to where a burly form quickly disappeared into the elevator.

Laurence followed her gaze, saying, "Ramus Montu, wasn't it? He was probably going to check on you, too." Laurence added with a chuckle, "I must have scared the old boy away." His gray eyes turned back to hers. "You are doing all right, then? Didn't want to sit and worry about you when I walk right past your door."

"Why don't you come in," Ardis said. "I'm feeling a little jittery after all that happened today. I wouldn't mind having some company."

Laurence stepped inside and eased himself into one of the overstuffed chairs near the window. He had changed his hiking clothes and had donned a light, summer suit. "Nasty accident," he said. "When I think of those sheer cliffs and what could have taken place … All I can say is thank heavens it wasn't worse."

Ardis' thoughts had returned to Ramus, and what had brought him up to this floor of the hotel. Could he have felt guilty and been intending to inquire about her?

Laurence Tolliver's gray eyes studied her. "It _was_ an accident, wasn't it?"

Ardis could not bring herself to reply.

"Were you with anyone at the time?" He added impatiently, in an almost interrogative manner, "Who or what did you see before you fell?"

"Nothing," she managed.

Laurence seemed dissatisfied with her reply, but he did not pursue the subject. Instead, he said, "That Montu fellow, he lives in Qurna, doesn't he?"

"Yes. He has a little oasis on a high hill just above the town."

"Must be great living in that famous valley. That town's got quite a reputation, so I hear." He paused, then went on affably, "For years and years it's been a hive of tomb robbers. Story is they are all related and pass their torch from father to son."

Her pain growing worse, Ardis wished she had not invited him in.

"Father to son," he repeated, then again, "father to son. Some set-up. I wonder, does this Ramus Montu have a son?"

"I'm sure he's not associated in any way with the town's background," Ardis said. "He's well-educated and respected. A very professional man."

With a wave of his hand, Laurence said, "I'm sure they all are … these days." He gave another of his short chuckles. "Most all the big-time thieves and rascals have a degree or so to wave under our noses."

What was he trying to communicate to her—a warning about what was behind her accident today? He seemed to like her, to trust her. She wished he would just confide in her, tell her exactly who he was and what he was doing here. It would be better if he could talk to her straight-out, and they could help one another.

That, of course, would spell out grave danger for him. He would be in great risk if she or anyone else happened to blow his cover. She wondered about his exact title, about the department he represented, about his real name.

As if tuning into her private thoughts, Laurence leaned closer and said sincerely, "From what I've been hearing, you took over quite a bombshell heading this Senmut tomb." He gave a significant pause. "It's the seat of a good deal of illegal activity, so I'm told. I wouldn't blame you if you handed the whole project right back to Mr. Khet and left the country."

Chapter 14

When Ardis arrived at the site the following morning, she found Blake already within the tomb. He rose in startled haste from where he knelt near the huge, stone statue of Senmut. Brushing off his hands, he stepped toward her saying in a distant way, "I didn't expect you to return to work so soon."

Face to face with him, Ardis couldn't help recalling the crushing pressure of his arms around her yesterday, the emotion in his voice as he had murmured, "darling!" Confronted with Blake's unapproachable formality, their closeness, his concern about her near-brush with death on the cliff at Deir el-Bahari seemed but a distant memory.

Suspicion seeped in to replace the sense of trust that had been gradually building between them. The reason he was working at the tomb so early must correspond to her own; he had come to search for the cheetah symbols that had been inscribed on the papyrus and the obelisk. No doubt Blake was hoping to discover some secret chamber, while she still lay helpless in bed.

"I've been going over this area again," Blake said in a distracted way. "I'd ask you to assist, but I know you must not feel like working yet, especially down in this airless place."

"As a matter of fact, I do." Her statement wasn't entirely a lie. She had awakened this morning with a restored sense of well-being. She had suffered little after-effects from the fall. In fact, the swelling had gone down so much around her ankle she had even decided to abandon the bulky wrapping the doctor had insisted that she wear.

Her answer caused a crease to form between his eyes. "If you insist on working, you could start sketching the opposite side of this wall."

"If you don't mind, I'd rather resume my own work" Ardis drew out supplies she had stored in Jane's desk drawer. Trying not to think about Blake, she attempted to immerse herself in the long rows of hieroglyphics she had started to translate earlier.

Regardless of her concentration, Ardis was still aware of Blake, his glances toward her, the quick, skillful way he sketched.

After a while, one of his guarded looks toward her failed to shift back to his sketchbook. "You must have seen something yesterday that would give some clue to who pushed you," he said, "some indication of size, hair-color, clothing."

"As I told you before, Blake, I saw absolutely nothing." Even as she spoke, an image, vague in the haze, appeared ever so briefly, flitting, as it had in reality, behind a shield of stone. "Actually, just before this happened, I did see a figure on the rocks not far away, but I'm not certain he's the one who pushed me." She spoke uncertainly. "I thought it was Ramus."

"Ramus is very loyal to his own. You as Jane's friend would qualify as a protectorate."

"Unless he mistook me for Faye." There, she had said it outright.

Blake's reaction, just as she had expected, was firm and stanch in support of Ramus. He did not, however, claim that Ramus was incapable of such a murderous act. "Ramus, under no circumstance, would have made such a stupid misjudgment," Blake said. "He's not a fool."

"It would have been a natural mistake. Faye and I are near the same size, and the way we were both dressed ..."

"I see you do not know Ramus," Blake interrupted. "He is a man who would most certainly accomplish whatever he set out to do. Because Faye is unharmed, you can be sure Ramus had not planned to harm her." His tone became softer as he went on. "After thinking it over, Ramus probably considered Faye just some scatter-brained girl, one he decided to ignore."

"I hope that is true."

"What about Faye herself?" Blake asked. "To me she is more to be suspected than Ramus."

"Once you told me she had no reason to be involved in any of this."

"I could have been wrong," he said.

"You're forgetting, it was Faye who heard my cry and called out to you."

"We all heard you at the same time," Blake corrected.

"The list of suspects is very small," Ardis said, finishing the drawing she had started. "The only ones nearby were Ramus, Faye, Thomas—Laurence Tolliver, who went back down—Nihisi, and ... "

"and me," Blake finished.

Ardis overlooked Blake's inclusion of himself and went on quickly. "Of course someone else, unnoticed, could have trailed along in secret."

"Matthammed, you mean. Impossible. He is aghast at any sort of violence. He wouldn't harm anyone or anything."

"You can't always tell. Often I've thought I really understood someone only to find I didn't know that person at all."

Ardis was thinking of her sister, still astounded that both Lisa and Mike had carefully concealed their marriage plans from her.

"I'm going to talk to each of them again just as soon as I can," Blake said. "Right now I've questioned everyone but Faye and Thomas."

For a long while they worked in silence. Ardis painstakingly recorded and sketched each minute detail of the endless stream of hieroglyphics that seemed to cover every bare inch of space upon the thick blocks of stone. Ardis recognized among them the recurring painted likenesses of Hathor and Horus, Osiris and Amon.

When they took a break, Blake showed her the section he had been working on, a frieze of life-sized figures of gods and men. The closest figure depicted a man dressed in kilt-like garment. Ardis knew by the scepter and ankh he held that the likeness was a representation of Amon, the god Queen Hatshepsut had faithfully worshipped. A bent and crippled figure bowed low before him, holding in his upraised hands an offering in a smooth, golden vessel, which the god accepted with a placid smile.

Blake translated the surrounding hieroglyphics, "I, Harmose, most worthy of trust. Accept, oh great Amon, the offering of your humble servant."

"Who was Harmose?" Ardis wondered.

"I've come across the name in this tomb before," Blake said. "So I did some research. It appears Senmut had a loyal servant, an elderly and crippled man by that name." He paused a moment, then said, "I have a theory. Senmut's name appears on the tomb, but nowhere upon the sarcophagus. No name does. I have this feeling that it was Harmose, his loyal servant, and not Senmut, who was actually to be buried here."

"But why would a servant be buried in a tomb bearing someone else's name?"

"As you had observed, the curse is written differently on the papyrus than on the tomb. The word *rest* was replaced with *duty*. Perhaps Harmose was laid to rest here as a guardian of some sort of treasure, one that belonged to Senmut. When we transcribe every part of this tomb, we may know."

"Blake, take a look at this." Ardis' excited cry broke into his words.

The heavy shadow of the statue of Senmut fell directly upon the painted vessel, the offering. Ardis leaned forward, bending to inspect the bowl-like object, noticing its uneven texture, the way the handle seemed to protrude ever so slightly from the wall.

Ardis turned to find Blake close beside her. He, too, looked to where the faint image of a distinctly feline shape curved in bas-relief around the edge of the proffered vessel.

"There's another one here, on the other side." Ardis indicated a second, identical symbol emerging from the stone and meeting the other one face to face along the side of the vessel. They were positioned in the exact way they had been on both the papyrus and the obelisk.

Ardis drew in her breath. Had Jane also discovered these symbols and figured out the connection between them? Is that why she had summoned Ardis out to the tomb that day so they could speak in private?

A vision of Nihisi's demonstration at Deir el-Bahari caused Ardis to impulsively reach out and press both symbols simultaneously, as she had done with the obelisk.

Triggered by her motion, the handle of the painted vessel moved. As if spring-loaded, the wall of stone shifted slightly back and a small opening appeared.

"We've found it!" Ardis cried. "Another chamber!"

Blake, too stunned to speak, gazed at her. Ardis, caught up in the marvel of the moment, could hardly believe her eyes.

Blake reached for her hand and held it tightly. Together they peered into the darkness exposed by a gaping hole just large enough for a man to crawl through.

Blake led the way through the opening. "It looks more like some kind of tunnel or passageway than a chamber," he reported. The air's musty, but breathable," he added, "so the passage must not be air-tight."

Ardis, unable to contain her excitement, said, "Then it should be safe to explore. Let's go in now."

She had expected Blake to share her enthusiasm. Instead, she noticed a strange reluctance in his manner. "There may be trap doors, hidden spikes. We don't know what we'll encounter. It could be extremely dangerous," he said.

Ardis, not waiting for further argument, hastened to find lights—a flashlight for each of them and a huge drop-cord for the floodlight already in the tomb.

"You wait here," Blake said. "I want to go in first."

"Be careful."

Blake, taking with him a long-handled shovel to check the area before he moved into it, slipped cautiously inside. Ardis waited breathlessly, half-expecting to hear the snap-like spring of a trap door or the crushing slam of falling boulders.

Time passed. No noises issued from the dark entrance.

"Blake, I'm coming in." Ardis struggled through the small opening and stopped just behind Blake. The glow of her flashlight cast weird shadows upon paintings along the dry, close sides of the passageway.

"It looks like a very long corridor, but I can't see much," Blake reported.

"I'll get the floodlight." Ardis returned to the main chamber and connected the length of drop-cord to the light Blake had been using beside the Senmut statue.

As she reentered, she knew Blake had been right. They were not in an adjoining chamber, but a tunnel-like shaft rising steeply for as far as she could see. It was just large enough to comfortably stand in. Ardis realized it must be similar to the shaft that had been discovered at Deir el-Bahari, the one that Nihisi said had led from the temple to a secret tomb some distance away. How far away ... and to where ... did this passage lead?

She stole a glance at Blake. Was he disappointed because they had discovered no chamber, only an empty tunnel? "Where do you think it will lead?"

"To the cliffs," Blake said. "It is common for tombs to have a second way in and out. The Egyptians believed such a passage was necessary for the *ba* and *ka* to escape."

The *ka*, Ardis knew, was a sort of spiritual double who inhabited the spirit world, while the *ba* was the equivalent of the soul, or spirit.

"I believe what we've found is one of these. They are often well-hidden, virtually impossible to find."

"Let's go to the end," Ardis said.

All along the narrow passage the walls were covered with hieroglyphics that matched those inside the original chamber. This told Ardis that the same Egyptians had built this passage, too, and it was not added at a later date.

They moved carefully along, Blake holding the floodlight. Ardis dropped back and played her flashlight upon the fascinating writing and decorations. The linear line of paintings on solid slabs changed abruptly. On both sides of the passageway five huge stones extended from the wall in bas-relief. In the direct center of each, deeply recessed into the rock, was a solitary decoration.

She studied the series on the left wall. The center recess of the first and second contained a scarab, the next one, a dog-like figure wearing Hathor's necklace. The two on the end portrayed boats, whose sides were elegantly curved upward.

On the right wall the five giant slabs of protruding stones were each decorated with an obelisk about the size of the one back in the safety deposit box at the hotel. The image had been carved deeply into the exact middle of the stone. Five obelisks, each enclosed in a square—the same number displayed on the border of the papyrus Blake had shown her.

Blake was now far ahead of her. She wondered if he had noticed the obelisks. Evidently he had not, or at least he had failed to make the connection she was making to the five obelisks on the papyrus.

"Blake."

He turned back to her, his form shadowy behind the glare of light. She started to share her thoughts about the obelisks with him, but abruptly changed her mind. "I just wanted you to wait for me," she found herself saying,

"We're almost out of cord," Blake said after they had walked a little further.

"I can see the end just up ahead."

Soon Blake had to set aside the floodlight. Using only the flashlights, they continued until they could go no farther; but they were faced with a solid slab of stone.

Stooping down, almost as if he had done this before, Blake played his light upon a spot where once more the identical frieze with the matching cheetah symbols appeared. "An easy exit, if one knows the secret," he said.

The door slid open just as it had from the main chamber. Ardis, blinking from the brilliant sunlight, followed Blake through the small doorway that opened to the side of a cliff. Ardis stood beneath a fan-shaped formation of rock. All around loomed boulders of the same color.

"We're on top of the cliff far above the tomb," Blake said. He stood on a ridge and pointed almost directly into the sun. "Qurna is somewhere over that way."

"How far could anyone drive up these cliffs?" Ardis asked.

"Not far. A good deal of strenuous walking is involved in reaching this point. Ramus and I have been here many times," Blake went on. "We've passed right by this very formation."

It was obvious to Ardis that whoever had murdered Jane had gone in and out of this passageway when stealing items from the tomb. The day Ardis had returned to retrieve the obelisk, the intruder must have been inside the main chamber. When Ardis had entered, he had slipped though the opening into the passage and stayed there, making those chanting, muffled sounds that had been intended to frighten her away. He could also have used this passage the day he had ransacked Jane's cabin.

"We're not the only ones who know about this passageway," Ardis said to Blake.

"You're right about that. But whoever is coming and going from the tomb still believes the biggest treasure is yet to be found."

Maybe and maybe not, Ardis thought with a sinking heart. Senmut's gold, if it ever had existed, could already have been discovered and removed by now.

"Whoever knows about this entrance is still coming here looking for another chamber," Blake insisted. "So far he hasn't found it."

"We have to keep him out. We must secure this at once," Ardis said.

"No," Blake answered with resolve. "If we close this up, we will never find out who murdered Jane. We can prevent him from entering here again, but by doing so we are sure to scare him completely away. He's already taken a fortune in artifacts, and he might decide to settle for that and leave Egypt. I think we should keep quiet and leave the passage open just as it is and keep our own vigil."

"That is far too risky."

"There is nothing left to steal, Ardis. And it's obvious he hasn't been able to find any other chamber. Why not use our knowledge of how he gets into the tomb to our advantage, to set a trap for him?"

What Blake said was sensible. Slowly she began to waver. "Should we inform Nihisi of this?" she asked finally.

"No need to involve him ... yet." Blake's dark eyes met Ardis'. "I have a feeling another chamber does actually exist. And I can't help but feel that, for the time being at least, the fewer people who know about our little discovery, the better."

Chapter 15

Ardis drew back the drapes. Below her the patio, massed with flowers and decorated tables and swarming with people, told her the barbecue was already in progress.

She saw Thomas leaving his room on the bottom floor, a room very near the pool. He paused, towel strung over lanky shoulders, and looked around as if searching for someone, maybe Ardis.

If only she could skip this function. Hours of pouring over hieroglyphics had given her an intense headache, and the long walk through the tomb's passage had caused her injured ankle to hurt again. Despite how she felt, she knew she must attend, for the event had been planned as a final honor to Nihisi Khet before he returned to Cairo.

Ardis cast a longing look toward the stack of papers she had left in disarray on the desk. As soon as she returned to the hotel room, she started to go over again every detail of her notes on the Senmut tomb. Ardis stared down at five obelisks enclosed by a square. She had sketched them from memory just as they had appeared on both the papyrus and the newly-discovered passageway. Obelisk is key, Jane had written. Surely their arrangement had some important significance.

Deep inside, Ardis still believed it possible that Senmut had succeeded in hiding the gold for the obelisks in the tomb, before he had been murdered by Thutmose III. Blake, too, appeared to believe that another chamber might exist, one yet untouched by thieves.

The next few days would be crucial. As soon as possible, Ardis intended to return to the newly-discovered passage and study the pattern of the obelisks in greater detail. Her major problem was whether or not to trust Blake. If she did not, her work alone would go much slower.

Ardis had all but forgotten her injury until on the way to the closet a painful throbbing demanded her immediate attention. Her ankle had swollen considerably. She should have taken the doctor's advice and kept it tightly bound. She would now pay for her neglect … She would have to wrap the ankle or go shoeless to the barbecue.

Ardis had sent most of her clothing, including her best slacks, out to be cleaned. Only a sports skirt and matching blouse remained in the closet. Soft coral brought out warm tones in her lightly tanned skin and ash-blonde hair. The effect in the mirror was pleasing except for the bulky tennis shoes, the only shoes she could coax over the thick wrapping. They detracted more than a little from any attempt at glamour. She didn't care; she only wanted to get the evening out of the way so that she could resume her work.

Out in the hallway she met Laurence Tolliver. Despite the heat he wore a light-weight suit jacket. "Going to the barbecue?" he inquired.

"Yes."

"People keep mistaking me for one of the professors," he said with a clipped, very British laugh. "It must be the suits. I don't quite feel dressed without them, even, I'm afraid, in this insufferable heat."

Changing the pace of his step to match her slow progress, Laurence walked with her down the corridor. He spoke casually, as if their serious talk in her room just after her accident had never been. "It's so very good to be here," he exclaimed. "Back in London I have one of those high-pressure jobs where I'm always being harassed by the public."

"You must be involved in politics," Ardis remarked.

Laurence gave another one of those very distinctive laughs, which caused deep crinkles around his gray eyes. She thought by the slight look of doubt that appeared in them that he had been considering telling her about his real occupation—that he worked for British security—but he did not speak.

Without the smile he looked different. His mouth appeared weak and drooped. Lines of stress trailed downward across his cheeks and cut deep ridges on either side of his face. This gave him an air of worldliness or weariness, an air of disillusionment that might be acquired by a person dealing with crime day after day.

She decided to ask him outright. "What is your job?"

"Tonight I have none." He carefully side-stepped her question. "For the time being I'm just another one of Egypt's many tourists. As I've mentioned to you before, studying Egypt's history has always been a great hobby of mine."

They regarded each other as the elevator descended. Was she reading meaning into his words, or was he again subtly reminding her that his real purpose in being here was to investigate?

"I'm going down pool-side," he said when they reached the main floor, "to relax a bit."

Ardis detoured into the lobby, took a seat on the wicker couch, and readjusted the ugly, white wrapping that rose from ankle to just below her kneecap. Everyone must have gone out to the patio. Even BenSobel's desk was vacant. Ardis remained seated in the hopes that she might encounter Blake as he arrived at the hotel.

Not Blake, but Nihisi Khet, appeared at the dining room door. He lingered, as if enjoying a moment of privacy before facing eager professors and students that constantly vied for his attention. He spoke to her in a planned, automatic way. "I see you are back on your feet again. I'm glad your injuries weren't too serious."

"I'm all right. Luckily. I shudder whenever I think of rocks and cliffs."

Nihisi's frown sharpened."Everyone thinks what happened was an ordinary accident. What do you believe?"

"That I was deliberately pushed."

The news caused no change in his expression, but it called forth a fast rejoinder."If I were you, I would rethink my plans about continuing Jane's work."

"I'm going to stay,"she said."But I feel I've been kept in the dark about what's been going on." She paused, uneasy about pursuing this line with him."I know artifacts have been stolen from the site. What I haven't been told is how many or what they were."

Nihisi remained silent for so long she believed he had no intention of answering."Twenty items of extreme importance failed to reach the museum, a fact we were able to keep out of the news. That is a fortune in goods and a severe loss to our history."

"An ivory carving was among them."

"Yes. I was present at the opening of the tomb and noticed that one in particular."

"A cat of some kind,"Ardis spoke again.

"They were considered sacred by the Egyptians." He continued solemnly,"I've tried to keep this out of the papers, but we are working on it. Undercover."

Ardis' thoughts drifted to Laurence Tolliver.

"I am seriously considering the idea of abandoning Jane's original plans and, eventually, turning over the entire project to a committee."

"Please don't do that. Blake and I feel we are on the verge of discovering important information. Just give us a little more time."

Nihisi looked at her in his remote way. She felt as if he held control of a blade stronger than the one that slashed Jane's personal effects, one capable of shredding Jane Darvin's life-time dream. She held her breath and waited for the outcome.

The power was in his hands. She had no other alternative than to plead with him. "I must stay. It means so much to me. It would mean so much to Jane!"

"You are a very determined person. That is a quality I admire." His eyes moved from her face toward the noisy crowd beyond the double doors. "For now, then. But I will not be responsible … for whatever happens. If you stay, you are taking full control of your own fate."

Ardis remained in the lobby long after he had left. She wondered how much Nihisi really knew. Had Blake, despite swearing her to secrecy, told him about the hidden chamber?

Nihisi Khet puzzled her. She did not know whether he was self-seeking and corrupt or whether he was a very dutiful and forthright man. He certainly had not avoided speaking one truth—Ardis was risking her life in continuing Jane's work.

Out on the patio music floated lightly in the warm air, and Ardis could smell shish kebab sizzling upon huge, open grills.

She wound her way amid groups of strangers and spotted Thomas leisurely swimming the length of the pool. The water gleamed a deep blue from the painted cement and the decorative tile.

The moment he saw her, he swam easily toward her as she pulled one of the scattered metal chairs closer to a table.

She noticed his lean body. He seemed all legs and knees, as he climbed from the pool, dried off with a towel, and folded himself into the chair he had dragged forward beside her.

His gaze fell to the bandaged ankle. "I guess you won't be swimming tonight."

From the pool Ardis noticed Faye Morris in a very skimpy, red bikini cease swimming. She watched them with bold stare, as if tempted to join them. The sight of her reminded Ardis of their many unpleasant encounters. Ardis was relieved when, with a toss of damp, water-frizzled curls, she swam away.

"Swimming works up an appetite," Thomas said, patting his lean stomach. It looked as if it had never seen an extra pound. "I'm famished."

"Shall we see what's on the buffet?" Ardis started to rise.

"No. No, you just stay here. I'll bring you a bite to eat."

"You don't have to wait on me," she protested.

"I want to," he insisted. I'll be right back." He slipped a long shirt over his swim trunks and hurried over to the buffet. Ardis leaned back and allowed herself to relax. Beyond the pool area off to her right the Nile shimmering in the lowered sunlight. The breeze from the river felt refreshing after the heat of the day. She began to feel rested, momentarily removed from her worries.

Lulled by the music and the splashing movements of the swimmers, Ardis watched Faye Morris leave the pool and head for the buffet, almost as if she were following Thomas. In the bikini, high-cut to give the illusion of longer legs, she looked like a teen-aged girl. Ardis remembered seeing Thomas and Faye together several times at breakfast. She wondered if Faye was attracted to him.

Thomas came back with plates piled high with salad, barbecued meats, and fruit. He spread the banquet out on the white-clothed patio table. "What to drink?" he inquired.

"Lemonade is fine," Ardis said, "but you really don't have to wait on me. That's the point of this unsightly bandage. I can walk without pain."

"You just rest," Thomas said, flashing her a wink. "Tonight, you are getting the royal treatment."

"The princess in tennis shoes," Faye scoffed, setting down her plate at their table. "And having Thomas waiting on you. Maybe that's why you took that fall for me."

Ardis gave her a questioning look.

"It's no secret Ramus mistook you for me," she said. "It was me he intended to push over that cliff. Not that anyone will listen." As she spoke, she slipped a loose off the shoulder T-shirt over the bikini. Her pert little nose looked sunburned; her sprinkling of freckles seemed more predominant.

"We have no proof it was Ramus."

"He should be in jail for attempted murder!"

By the time Thomas returned with the drinks, Faye had calmed down.

"I hope this is lamb and not goat," she said petulantly, staring down at the meat on her plate.

"Don't spoil our appetites, love," Thomas laughed.

Undaunted, she began systematically picking grapes from her fruit salad and setting them aside. "I never eat grapes in a foreign country. Insecticide, you know."

"Faye lives on air," Thomas said.

"Air and spirits," she returned, signaling with that same flippancy to a dark-haired waiter. Ardis noticed how she flirted with him, fussing with her damp curls, as she ordered wine. Aside to Thomas she said with the authority of the experienced traveler, "Sterilized bottles. The wine's always safe."

Thomas chuckled. "I'll have to remember that."

"Safer than the waiters." Faye poised her hands in a gesture of generous tolerance. "Did you see the way he was flirting with his eyes? And the porters. They are even worse, coming into the room at odd hours, giving those bedroom looks. They know better than to try anything with me," she said. "Have you had trouble with the porters, Ardis?"

"No." Ardis wondered how much was real and how much Faye's imagination. The waiter accused of indiscretion had not seemed overly flirtatious.

"Must be those tennis shoes," Faye rejoined with a smirk, then continued, "Anyway, if you ask me, the whole lot of them should be reported to management."

"The only complaint I have with this hotel is the air conditioning," Thomas remarked, completely missing Faye's point. "The unit in my room keeps shutting off. Have you two had any trouble with yours?"

Thomas' air of detachment seemed to annoy Faye. It served to increase her eagerness to drive home the point of her own attractiveness. "The help at these places are all such sleezeballs. When I was in Cairo on assignment, one of the managers pinched me right in the hotel lobby. Can you believe that?"

"I can," Thomas joked. "I would do the same thing."

Faye was so completely self-absorbed that she saw herself as a perpetual heroine. Thomas met Ardis' gaze with an understanding smile. He, too, must wish Faye had chosen another table.

Ardis spotted Laurence Tolliver, plate in hand, wandering through the crowd. She waved to him and he smiled and headed to their table.

"No one but a bloody Englishman would wear a suit to a barbecue," Thomas remarked as Laurence seated himself between them.

At once they struck up a conversation about Thomas' restoration work at Karnak. Laurence Tolliver was impressively knowledgeable about the Karnak Temple.

Faye, as if resenting the gradual exclusion from their conversation, interrupted, saying with an air of confidence.

"Karnak is past history. What I'm interested in is history that is being recorded right now. Like my plans to expose Jane Darvin."

Not again, Ardis thought, an old, familiar sickness tightening her stomach. "I'd prefer talking about something else," she said.

"I bet you would," Faye retorted, then went on importantly. "I'm going to expose her for the fraud she really was. And other people," her eyes strayed to Nihisi Khet, now seated amid his companions, "will go down with her."

"Fraud?" Ardis challenged. "I can't allow you to say that! You are talking about one of the world's greatest Egyptologists." Ardis pushed back her chair. She thought of leaving the table, but Thomas' imploring glance caused her to remain.

"You see, I've figured out just what she'd been doing. She would set up bogus projects like this Senmut tomb thing that lasted thirty-odd years, spending precious government funds so she and her lovers could live in style."

Her words fell upon shocked silence.

"Ramus, in particular, who would have been a nobody without her," Faye continued.

"You are forgetting that Ramus is well-respected on his own right." As Ardis spoke, she wondered if the wine—Faye was now on her second glass—was making her a little tipsy.

"Ramus has been living for years off of Jane Darvin's faded glory. He hates me. He's out to get me because killing me is the only way he can stop my investigation!"

"Common sense should stop you," Ardis said bitterly, fully understanding why Ramus felt such passionate animosity toward her.

"And that Blake Lydon, the one who got the job as her assistant because he's the museum director's son," she continued in her all-important voice, "I think was in cahoots with Jane, part of the whole conspiracy. They are all up to something really sleazy. And I'm going to get to the bottom of it."

At the mention of Blake's name, the expression on Laurence Tolliver's face changed from patient disinterest to rapt attention. Obviously he, too, distrusted Blake. Ardis once more suspected that he was hot on the trail of missing artifacts; and that he had linked Blake to international crime, in this case concerning the black-marketing of Egyptian artifacts to and from England.

"Do you have any proof that links Lydon with stolen money or artifacts?" Laurence inquired.

"Not yet, but it's obvious that he's involved in illegal schemes. Perfect timing. All the real trouble started the minute Lydon arrived," Faye said, playing upon Laurence Tolliver's interest. "You hit the nail on the head, Ardis. Jane was intentionally poisoned, all right. And to cover it up, they give out all this hoopla about a curse."

Thomas' frown grew more and more evident. Suddenly he turned to Ardis. "If I were you, Ardis, I think I'd leave this project. Just to be on the safe side. Come work on the Karnak restorations with me. Then, if there is a scandal, at least you won't be caught in the middle of it."

Ardis tried to keep her answer light. "I'd feel like a traitor, deserting Queen Hatshepsut's cause to build up the work of her mortal enemy, Thutmose III."

Thomas smiled. "I don't think the old girl would care much. No one could hold a grudge for three thousand years. Or could they?"

"She might send old Senmut after you, Ardis," Faye said picking up on Thomas' slight sarcasm. In a pretentious way, she quoted the curse upon the tomb, "Death will devour he who disturbs the eternal rest of Senmut."

Faye, annoyed at Ardis for stealing Thomas' attention and trying to make Thomas jealous, added, "Blake Lydon, he is so *handsome*! If he wasn't associated with all this fraud, I'd be interested. He's always watching me with those big, soulful eyes." Faye studied Thomas, trying to gauge his reaction. "I might even regret sending him to jail."

"I wouldn't be tossing about accusations that have no basis in fact."Ardis said.

Ardis' attention turned to Matthammed, who was very noticeable in a gold-embroidered robe. He mingled in and out among the gathering groups. Occasionally, he would draw a prospective customer aside and whip out samples of his jewelry. From his happy look, Ardis concluded that he was doing good business.

With watchful glance, he sought the crowd for another customer. His smile brightened when he noticed Ardis.

"Oh, no, here comes that pest," Faye said, glaring at Ardis as if she were to blame for his appearance.

As Matthammed approached, his eyes, outlined with kohl, shone bright and dynamic in his hawk-like face. "I have your cartouche ready," Matthammed said. With an exaggerated motion, he produced Ardis' necklace from his black case.

"How do we know this is really gold?" Thomas took the necklace from him, weighing it in his hand. His expression was challenging, mocking; it reminded Ardis of a bully she had known in grade school. "I'll bet it is only gold-plate."

"No—solid gold. Eighteen karat, the purest kind," Matthammed insisted.

"You should buy from a reputable jeweler, Ardis."Without looking at the necklace, Faye commented, "These peddlers are always out to cheat us."

"You do not believe Matthammed?" He flashed them a haughty look, but one mixed with bewilderment.

Thomas drew a coin from his pocket. "This will tell if there is brass underneath." With a mischievous gleam in his eye, he made a motion as if to run the edge of the coin across the surface of the design.

"Fool! You will ruin it!"

Thomas and Faye laughed as Matthammed anxiously snatched the necklace away.

"We were only teasing you," Thomas said.

"He can't take a joke," Faye scoffed.

The glittering in Matthammed's eyes told Ardis that the jesting had not been well taken; he was deeply offended. She genuinely liked Matthammed, and she found herself embarrassed and ashamed of their cruel treatment of him.

"Please give the necklace to me." Ardis took the cartouche from Matthammed, noticing the careful, skillful way the small symbols had been carved and set into the metal. She slipped the necklace on over her head, pleased. It glowed warm and bright against the coral blouse. "It is beautiful," she said. "You are a very fine workman." As she drew out her traveler's checks, Matthammed smiled broadly, injury forgiven, as if profit suspended all insults.

Chapter 16

Shortly after Matthammed left, Faye nudged Thomas' arm. "See? Didn't I tell you Blake is always watching me?"

Blake, dressed in a white, woven shirt, stood alone. Behind him was the ever-darkening water of the Nile as it twisted in a snake-like pattern past the hotel. Even as Faye spoke, he began to walk steadily toward them. But it was Ardis, not Faye that he addressed. "I must have a word with you. Alone."

She rose and his hand gripped her arm in a forceful grasp as he ushered her through the crowd. Ardis looked back toward the table, seeing Thomas and Laurence Tolliver exchange concerned glances.

Blake solemnly led her away from the crowd. Steeling herself for the worst, she recalled his distant manner when he had told her about the missing papyrus. She asked, "What's wrong?"

"It is time we had a heart to heart talk."

Leaving the noise and bright lights behind them, they followed a well-worn path along the river. The noise and laughter grew fainter, and other sounds, the slight stirring of wind on water, sprang up around them. Neither of them spoke.

The bank was dotted with palm trees. Across the river fading by the waning light set mud-walled enclosures and patchworks of cultivated fields.

"Right from the first," Blake said sadly, "I shared your feelings about Jane's death." He fell silent again, and she waited for him to go on. "Jane's illness, the missing artifacts, how could anyone help but know they were linked? That is why I was so against your returning here. But you refused to listen. And now your life is in grave danger."

Ardis did not comment.

Blake stopped walking to face her. "Now that I've had time to think about it, I believe whoever pushed you at Deir el-Bahari planned it all in advance. They must have followed you and waited for an opportunity when no one was around. I've talked to them all now, but I still have nothing to go on."

"What did you find out?"

"Matthammed wasn't the only one who didn't reach the top. Laurence Tolliver said he rested a while on that rock and then started back down." Blake paused. "Do you know anything about him?"

Ardis, avoiding his gaze, replied, "He lives in London. He's here on vacation."

"Several times," Blake said, "I have been convinced that he's been following me." Blake continued to look at her, as if he were trying to judge how much she knew about Laurence Tolliver's activities … or his own.

"Probably you just have the same interests," she said. "It is natural you would find yourselves in the same places."

Blake, as if dissatisfied with her reply, waited a while before he spoke again. "Faye claims she was with Thomas the whole time. She also insists that whoever did this was not after you at all, but her. She says because you were dressed alike and your hat hid your hair, you were mistaken for her. Of course, she believes Ramus was to blame."

"What do you think?"

"I don't believe Ramus had anything to do with it," Blake said sincerely.

"That *accident* was planned for me, not Faye." Ardis stated with conviction. "It must concern my involvement in Jane's work."

"We are both deeply involved in Jane's project. Why would … this person be after you, instead of me?"

"Because I was publicly quoted as believing Jane was murdered." Ardis told him about the tea sent to her room in Cairo, sent as a clear warning. Whoever it is must feel that I am a threat, and that if I keep pursuing this idea of Jane's being poisoned, that I will eventually be able to identify him."

They continued to walk. The outline of trees and water faded into the darkness. Blake's manner had become more and more somber. "Of course you *are* pursuing this idea," he said, as if testing her response. "You are investigating."

Ardis hesitated. Blake seemed so worried about her. For the first time she was tempted to trust him, fully and completely.

He stopped walking again. "What are you working on? I know you received a call from Dr. Fahmy in Cairo. Are you attempting to trace the type of poison used?"

"I was, but I ran into a dead end." Ardis spoke reluctantly, "I believe that Jane's past is very much a factor in what is happening now." She glanced toward the water, her hair stirring in the soft wind. "I am trying to find Jane's child."

Her words threw Blake off-balance. "You can't believe this is some insane revenge on Jane for something that took place thirty-odd years ago? After all this time, it would hardly be a front-burner issue." He went on quickly, seeming, Ardis thought, overly anxious to convince her. "Just because one is abandoned by his mother, doesn't mean he has a murderous vendetta against her." •

"That depends on the person."

"It doesn't explain other activities like the missing arti-facts."

"They must be in some way connected. If I am able to find Jane's child, I will find the link to her death. I know it. And I'm going to continue to pursue it."

Even though she could not fully see Blake's eyes, they seemed to burn with some over-powering emotion. He worked to control himself.

"Someone is watching your every step, Ardis!" His voice suggested that he was only able to hint at what was going on. His words caused a chill to run through her. "You must at once drop all lines of investigation."

The dark encircling shadows increased her fear. Danger existed not only for herself, but for Blake. How deeply mired was he into all of these sordid events?

Total stillness, left in the wake of a gusty wind upon the nearby water, settled around her. She was aware of Blake's eyes, so fearfully intent. His hands gripped her shoulders, then one lifted to twine through her hair. "Don't go back to the tomb, Ardis. Leave everything to me."

Ardis might be getting too close to the truth, and that could be the real reason for Blake's concern. His wanting her out of the way might have something do with the chamber they had just discovered.

Nihisi and he might have already known of the chamber's existence. They could have found and transported rare items, including the missing gold, through the passageway. Maybe now they were afraid that Ardis, as Jane's replacement, would expose them as thieves and frauds.

Yet there still existed the possibility that the gold remained hidden within the tomb in some chamber they were unable to locate. In discovering the hidden passage today, Blake and she might be on the verge of finding the treasure, a treasure Blake and his co-conspirators did not intend to share.

She raised her chin to meet his dark gaze. "You are willing to take the risk. Why shouldn't I?"

"These people are not amateurs. They are cold-blooded killers."

The vehemence in his voice caused her to draw away from him and look back toward the distant lights of the barbecue.

Blake tried to bridge the terrible silence that once again separated them. He changed his tone and said, "Let's not go back, yet. Let's sit here a while."

He led her toward a stone wall near the water's edge. Ardis seated herself and woodenly stared out across the silvery water.

Blake lifted the golden pendant at her throat and in an attempt to cheer her, said, "I see Matthammed has made a sale."

Ardis noticed the well-sculptured firmness of his lips as he lifted the pendant and studied the symbols.

"Everyone says I paid too much for it," she remarked, trying to answer with a lightness of her own.

"Matthammed is an expert. One of the best jewelers in Luxor."

"He claims it is eighteen karat."

A trace of a smile touched Blake's lips. "Ten karat, maybe. Whatever the gold content, it has Matthammed's special touch. And worth any price, to add to your beauty."

Quietness, as after a storm, slowly changed to serenity. Ardis watched the scene in front of her, feeling an affinity for the strange surroundings, the age-old monuments of stone, the great Nile.

Blake, too, watched. She was aware of the clear-cut lines of his profile close beside her and saw his dark hair flow from his face in waves tousled by the gentle wind.

When he spoke, his deep voice seemed to possess the same intense undercurrents as the water. "It's been said that once you drink from the Nile, no other water will ever quench your thirst."

"Maybe that's true, but I wish Jane had never seen Egypt!"

"What about you? Do you wish you had never seen Egypt?"

His hand reached out for her, drew her close against his solid, muscular body. But instead of the romantic words she had expected, Blake tried again to warn her—this time pleadingly. "You don't know what you're facing here, Ardis. You must stop trying to uncover Jane's killer."

"I can't do that."

"Then I can't protect you."

"Why do you feel that you are responsible for me?"

The clouds above them had thinned and cleared. Blake's features shone brightly in the moonlight. The opaque depth of his eyes, black as night, held her captive. "Because I love you," he said.

Instead of a rush of happiness, Ardis felt an incredible sadness.

As if to overcome this feeling, Blake's lips caught hers with a passion that drove away the strong suspicion that she had fallen deeply in love with a guilty man. In that moment where logic was suspended, there was only marvel and excitement, as beautiful, as breathtaking as Egypt itself. As she fell under the spell of his kiss, she realized that it was Blake, not Egypt, which she never wanted to leave.

Thomas Garrett and Laurence Tolliver, still sitting exactly where Ardis had left them, ceased talking the moment Blake and she returned to the barbecue. Thomas strode quickly to meet them near the pool. He addressed Blake, his angular features set, his mouth pulled tight across his prominent teeth. "Mind if I have a word or two with Ardis?"

Blake glanced doubtfully at Ardis. "I'll be at the table," he said and quickly walked away, leaving Thomas and her alone.

"What did Blake want?" Thomas asked.

"We needed to discuss some matters concerning our work," Ardis said.

"You should be wary of him."

Ardis' gaze strayed to Thomas, then away from him and through the crowd. Blake had disappeared into the cluster of people that milled around the tables.

Nihisi Khet had joined Laurence Tolliver, taking the chair Thomas had vacated. Laurence, leaning forward, earnestly talked while Nihisi frowned and stared down at the table. Had Laurence spoken to Thomas with that same air of confidentiality, almost covertness? Surely, something Laurence had told him had prompted Thomas' sudden desire to warn her about Blake.

"It's beginning to dawn on me just how much trouble you're really in," Thomas said. "You've got to listen to me, Ardis. Finishing a job isn't worth risking your life."

"I promised Jane."

"If Jane were alive, she would understand. She would want you to think of yourself. Nihisi Khet is talking to Mr. Tolliver right now. This is the time to go over and tell him you want to leave the project, that you want to work with me at Karnak."

Ardis shook her head.

"After what happened at Deir el-Bahari, he can't expect you to stay on."

Thomas' words were cut short by Matthammed zigzagging toward them carrying a tray of drinks.

Thomas attempted to change back to his old easy manner. "What? Playing the waiter now, Matthammed?"

"I am a man of many talents. This is my special drink, a blend of exotic fruits. You must try it!"

Impatiently Thomas waved him away, saying, "Just set our drinks on the table. We'll be along shortly."

"I've observed that you don't partake of strong drink, Ardis," Matthammed said. "Yours will be the one with the pretty little umbrella."

Matthammed remained to exchange a few more quips with Thomas before he walked away. During that interval Ardis spotted Blake. He stood alone by the table Matthammed had just left. She felt incapable of moving her eyes from his and did not until she felt the pressure of Thomas' hand on her arm, demanding her attention.

"You must disassociate yourself completely from the Senmut project and from Blake Lydon." Thomas said with deep feeling.

"I know you are trying to help me, Thomas, but I am fully aware of what I'm up against. And I'm not going to abandon my job, no more than you would yours."

Both of Thomas' hands caught her shoulders as if he intended to shake her. "This is not an ordinary situation! You must do this to protect yourself. Why won't you listen?"

She slipped away from him.

"This whole thing is going to blow up in Lydon's face, and if you don't watch out, in yours too."

"Let's go back to the table."

During their talk, Blake had walked over to say something to Nihisi. Nihisi left immediately, and Blake seated himself beside Laurence. Laurence, looking ill at ease, started to make small talk with him. Blake's dark eyes gazed into Ardis' as Thomas and she came forward to join them.

"Matthammed left you some drinks," Laurence said with a smile. "Let me propose a toast."

Blake lifted both glasses and extended them to Ardis and Thomas.

Ardis, following Matthammed's instructions, selected the one with the little paper umbrella.

"To the Senmut project!" Laurence said, lifting his glass to the center of the table to click with other glasses that had been raised in acknowledgment.

Suddenly very thirsty, Ardis sipped the fruit punch, the color of dark, sweet grapes. Matthammed, who had been hovering around the edges of the table, hurried over. "How do you like my specialty?" he asked eagerly.

"It's different." Ardis forced a pleasant expression. She had supposed it would be sweet, but it had an unexpected sourness, a citrus flavor she definitely didn't like.

Faye Morris, who had sauntered forward to join the toast, came up to Ardis and said, "I was looking for you earlier. Where did you and Blake disappear to?"

"We took a walk along the Nile." Ardis touched the necklace at her throat. Blake's eyes, lighting a little, met hers across the table as she quoted his words, "It's been said that once you drink from the Nile, no other water will ever quench your thirst."

"If you drink from the Nile," Faye contradicted with raised eyebrow, "you'll get dysentery and a mouthful of parasites!"

Faye's comment, combined with the slightly bitter taste of the drink, caused Ardis to place aside her half-finished glass.

Ardis, aware of Thomas' concerned, almost accusing glances toward Blake and her, fell silent.

"Saw you talking to Mr. Khet," Thomas said to Tolliver. "If you're one of his confidants, how about convincing him that I need more funds for the Karnak project?"

"You're on your own there." Tolliver chuckled. "I've trouble enough convincing my boss that I could use a small advance."

Ardis was gripped by a sickness in the pit of her stomach. Even though she had loved the spicy barbecue, she should have known better than to have finished the entire portion Thomas had brought for her.

Hoping the flu-like symptoms would subside, Ardis tried to concentrate on the conversation. She was aware of Faye watching her boldly.

"What do you think, Ardis?"

Ardis looked toward Thomas, surprised that her mind had drifted so totally away from his words.

"All those looks she gives to Blake," Faye said with a bitter laugh, "that should give you some idea what she's thinking!"

With annoyance Ardis turned toward her. The sudden movement caused a spinning sensation, which distorted Faye's image.

"A joke," Faye said, holding up her hands as if in defense.

Voices swirled around Ardis like the mindless buzzing of insects.

The dizzy sensation was becoming worse. Ardis lifted a hand to her forehead and found it damp. Only Blake seemed to notice. He leaned forward to ask in a low, concerned voice, "What's wrong?"

Perhaps she hadn't completely recovered from her fall at Deir el-Bahari. "I'm just tired. It's been a long day. I believe I'll go on up to my room."

Ardis stumbled a little as she rose to her feet and was forced to clutch at the edge of the table to steady herself. Blake came around the table immediately to assist her. "I'll walk with you," he said.

"No, please stay. I'll be fine."

Blake's grip remained firmly on her arm, and she felt very grateful for his support.

Inside the Oasis he ushered her into the elevator, and after a long, perceptive gaze, said, "Might be the water. Most people avoid the water, but eat the fresh foods and salads and are exposed to the same results."

"I just ate something that doesn't agree with me. I'm not used to spicy food."

At the door to her room Blake detained her. "Are you sure you're all right? Why don't you let me stay with you for a while?"

"Go on back down to the party," Ardis insisted. "I think I can sleep. In the morning I'll be fine."

Blake drew her gently, protectively, into his arms. Feeling the beginning of a chill, Ardis rested her head against his shoulder, comforted for a moment by his nearness.

"My darling," he said, "you must take care of yourself!"

The air-conditioned room, such a change from the warm air outside, caused the chills to become more pronounced. Ardis didn't bother undressing. She fell across the bed, drawing the spread over her. Almost at once the bed began to reel. The discomfort in her stomach became a sharp pain.

Time passed slowly until finally the whirling motions stopped. Her face streamed with sweat … Her body had grown very cold. With each breath her heartbeat pounded in a rapid, uneven way that alarmed her. Her illness progressed with unrelenting swiftness that no amount of rest or quiet would cure. A fog of darkness blotted her vision. She must act quickly before she totally lost consciousness.

She must get help! Ardis turned her head. The phone beside her bed was only a blur. Ardis tried to lift her arm, to rise, but every nerve in her body seemed coiled and every muscle paralyzed.

The room lightened, blackened, lightened.

Ardis struggled to fight against waves of darkness. She forced her impossible-to-focus eyes to remain opened, and she stared at the black void around her. Forms began to take shape inside the darkness. Terrified, she tried to rise, but fell back against the bed. Shadowy figures drifted through the haze. Eerie faces undulated around her—Anubis, Osiris,

Egyptian gods of the dead. Menacing voices called to her from the depths of a tomb, disembodied voices that seemed to be threatening her from the Egyptian underworld.

Then Blake was standing before her. He wore a collar necklace fashioned of tiny golden beads closely strung together. His bare chest and strong muscles gleamed above a kilt-like garment that was knotted around his waist.

"Blake?" Ardis realized this must be a dream of some kind, a hallucination. Even though he looked like Blake, it couldn't be him. Blake would never be dressed like that! She struggled again to rise.

Without making a sound, a graceful woman floated slowly from the shadows, slipped her arm through the man's, and stood proudly beside him. Her head was covered with a stylized headdress, intricately detailed in imitation of thick strands of hair. The great size of the head-covering caused the bones of the woman's face to appear small and delicate, but her eyes, large and black, dominated all else.

Ardis shrank away.

"Don't be afraid," the woman said. "I am Queen Hatshepsut. And this is the great and mighty Senmut!"

Behind them another figure was emerging … a figure Ardis vaguely recognized. His elongated face with its rodent-like eyes glowered with hatred. His raised hand clutched a long, jagged blade, a dagger.

"It's Thutmose!" Ardis heard herself scream, but her voice seemed to come from far away. "He's going to kill you!"

At the same instant of her warning, the blade struck the man. He staggered closer to Ardis. She could see the sudden widening of his large dark eyes, tragic with pain and surprise. He wasn't Senmut! He was Blake! She held him in her arms trying to protect him. In the background heartless faces watched— Nihisi, Ramus, Matthammed. Blake was dying because of her, *for* her, just as Senmut had died for Queen Hatshepsut!

"Blake, no!" she cried out. She tried to draw him closer to save him from the conspirators, but Blake and all of the others faded into the blackness. Only Thutmose remained, frozen in place, evil and threatening. Ardis realized with a start that she was staring at the gift Thomas had given her, the statue of Thutmose III upon her nightstand.

What was happening to her? In fear and confusion, Ardis again struggled to move, to reach the phone. A deathly stillness pervaded the room. The hallucinations had stopped. Thank God!

Through a fog of darkness a familiar voice called to her, "Ardis!"

The form shimmered as if it consisted only of lights. Was the queen appearing again? The willowy shape paused and a lift of her chin revealed her aquiline features.

"Jane!" Ardis gasped.

"You must be very careful."

"Jane, I'm going to fail you. I will never be able to finish your work."

"You will, Ardis. I am counting on you. The obelisk is the key. You will find Senmut's gold. You must if I am to fulfill my destiny."

Ardis knew that Jane wasn't really in the room with her. Jane was dead; but the over-powering presence was so like reality that when the sparkling outline disintegrated before her eyes, she cried out, "Jane! Jane, please don't go!"

Ardis, shaking uncontrollably, felt the wild, erratic pounding of her heart. Like a drum it beat in the silence, frightening her. Strong chills racked her body, and her throat burned with a terrible thirst.

The drink ... the one with the umbrella! When Ardis' mind cleared enough to grasp the truth, her fear deepened into panic. The illness, the hallucinations—someone had poisoned her tonight, exactly the same way they had poisoned Jane Darvin!

Chapter 17

Ardis stared up at the blank white ceiling. How long had she been here? She had trouble concentrating, remembering. She vaguely recalled grabbing her purse and jacket and stumbling down to the lobby desk in the middle of the night, of summoning a startled BenSobel, of being transported to the hospital.

Nausea gripped Ardis. For a while the intense sickness would subside, then it would return like the impact of a strong ocean wave. Each recurrence left her weak and shaken.

With horror, she realized she was lying in the same room where they had taken Jane after finding her unconscious in the tomb. Ardis' gaze kept returning to the empty bed just across from her own where Jane had lain.

In a small, dingy hospital in Luxor, Egypt—is that where she would die? Ardis' thoughts flitted back home to Chicago. The only family she had left was her sister. Ardis longed to see her one last time, to tell Lisa it was OK that she had married Mike, that Ardis wished her every happiness.

She must have drifted off, for when she woke again, daylight had begun to fill the room and she could hear voices in the corridor. She recognized Nihisi Khet's.

"From what you say, Ardis is experiencing the same symptoms as Jane."

"There are many causes for such symptoms." The prompt reply was spoken calmly. "Bad food or water, flu, even fatigue or heat exhaustion could ... "

"Jane is dead," Nihisi Khet reminded the doctor.

"I assure you, Miss Cole's condition is not that serious."

"I'll just talk to her. Alone, if you don't mind." Nihisi closed the door between the doctor and him and stepped close to Ardis' bed. Standing very straight, he gazed down at her, his frown sharp, his stare judgmental. His stern image began to blur, and Ardis felt the queasiness returning. Was this the last face Jane had seen before she died?

"How are you feeling?" No hint of caring—why was he here? Ardis thought of Blake and wondered how he, as a child, had reacted to such coldness.

"I'm glad you stopped by," she managed to say. "I need to talk to you." With great effort she pulled herself up. She opened the drawer of the small stand beside the bed and took out her purse, which the nurse had stored there.

Nihisi watched her remove the ripped picture of Jane's baby.

Ardis placed the photograph in front of him on the stand. "I want to know if this is Blake," she said.

Nihisi glanced at the picture. "No. I mean I don't know. How could anyone tell in the condition it's in? Where did you get it?"

Ardis felt the presence of the chilling wall he could rise at will between himself and the world—a wall she guessed few, if any, had ever fully bridged. "I found this picture in Jane's cabin the day it was ransacked. I'm convinced it has a special importance, that it can be linked to what is going on here today."

Nihisi took the parts of the photograph and placed them close together. "You mean you think this baby, Jane's baby, grew up and has returned here?"

Curtly he handed the picture back to her. "Blake is not Jane's son."

Ardis remained silent.

"Blake will be thirty-two in August," he said. "A year too old to be Jane's child."

"What happened to Jane's baby? Do you know?"

"Jane's husband, Neil Darvin, never quite … came up to Jane's standards. They were on the verge of separation when Jane found out she was pregnant. Because of her pregnancy, they tried to reconcile and they left Egypt together. I don't know where they went, but I assumed they had gone back to New York City."

"You weren't in contact with Jane after she left Egypt?"

"No. She told me she would keep in touch, but she did not send any address. One day, two years later, she walked into the museum, alone. I assumed the baby had died at birth, but I see by this picture, I was wrong."

"Do you know Blake's natural parents?"

Ardis expected a rude dismissal. Instead, Nihisi seemed to withdraw even further behind that safe wall that separated them.

Finally, he spoke. "I have a great respect for the truth. In my entire lifetime, I have told very few lies."

Or was Nihisi so accustomed to lying he had become a master at it? Ardis, feeling weak, lay back against the pillows, seeing Nihisi's thin frame in a wash of rising sunlight.

"After Blake grew up, he wanted to find his birth parents. Regretfully, I did not tell him what I am about to tell you."

"What did you tell him?"

"That I had traced them. That they had been killed in a car accident in the states."

"But you do know who his parents are."

"I knew the mother. No one knows who Blake's real father is; I doubt even if his mother knows. She was one of Jane's American students. A very young, irresponsible girl. from an extremely wealthy family who dominated her and who, I'm sure, she feared. Her father was a foreign ambassador. She gave birth to Blake in Cairo, abandoned him in an orphanage, and fled back to the U.S."

"What happened to her after that?"

"She is alive and well, the mother of two more sons."

"But she's never tried to contact Blake?"

"Once, I called her, but she hung up the phone." Iciness crept into his voice. "She did not want him. Lami and I did. I raised Blake and that makes him my son, not hers. She does not want to see him; his showing up would be an embarrassment to her. Even if she felt differently, after all these years, she has no right at all to ever see him again."

"You could have left that decision up to Blake," Ardis said wearily.

"So I could have. So I should have." Nihisi turned back to her and said decisively. "You can tell him everything I've told you, if you like."

"No, that is none of my business. Whether or not you tell Blake is up to you."

"I have not had many people in my life to care for," Nihisi said, his voice distant and without sentiment. "I haven't told Blake who his real mother is, because I do not want to lose him."

Nihisi headed directly to the door. "I'm glad you're feeling better," he said without even glancing back toward where she lay. He stopped, his hand on the knob. "What I came here to tell you," he added coldly, "is that I am dismissing you from the project. Effective today."

The astounding news, the last thing she had expected from him, hit her like a vicious kick.

Ardis brought an arm up to cover her face. She felt much too ill to present any argument or to plead with him. Not that it would do any good. She knew beyond any doubt that when Nihisi Khet made up his mind, nothing would ever sway him.

Clearly, Nihisi had decided. She would immediately be denied access to the Senmut tomb. That meant that Ardis had failed, failed Jane's lifetime work, but much worse than that, she had failed to find Jane's killer.

Dr. Sardi, looking old and frail, entered her room late that afternoon. Leaning heavily on his spindly arms, he eased himself into a chair beside her bed. Ardis, propped against pillows, waited tensely for him to speak.

"I see no reason for you to remain at the hospital. You are no longer in any danger."

"Whatever you gave me worked," she answered. "I'm beginning to feel better every hour, only a little weak."

"You are very lucky," he said. "I could not determine with any accuracy just what caused your sudden illness."

"Just like Jane's," she answered.

She thought of how she had become ill at the barbecue shortly after sipping the drink Matthammed had brought her. Clearly, her drink had been laced with some deadly chemical. She thought of the many people who had had access to her drink—Matthammed, Blake, Nihisi, Faye, Thomas, Laurence—Any of them could have been standing by the bar where the drinks were being mixed. But only two had motives. Nihisi Khet … and Blake.

"Someone must have given me the exact poison they gave her," she said.

"So you insisted many times last night," he said. "But you are the only one convinced that you have been poisoned." He paused, removed his glasses, and rubbed a heavily-veined hand across his eyes. "Bacteria in the food or many other factors, could have been the cause of your symptoms."

Ardis' heart sank. By now, like the drink Jane had taken at the hospital, there would not be any proof. If the fruit drink had been tampered with, the glass would have either disappeared or been carefully washed of all traces of its deadly contents. "Assuming that something was slipped into my drink at the barbecue, what kind of poison might cause these symptoms?"

When Dr. Sirdi seemed reluctant to answer, Ardis prompted, "I remember reading once about a certain deadly plant that can cause the exact symptoms—chills, rapid heartbeat, hallucinations. Belladonna, I think, was the name of it."

"Allowing that we are dealing with a poison, which I sincerely doubt, your symptoms would lead me to suspect some form of atropine," Dr. Sirdi allowed finally. "Atropine is an alkaloid," he explained, "obtained from a plant, possibly from the belladonna. Some call it the deadly nightshade, although it could be some other Solanaceane plant. You are correct in believing it can cause all of the symptoms both Jane and you described."

"Is this type of plant easy to find?"

"Not around here. In India, they grow wild. The entire belladonna plant is poisonous—the leaves, stalk, seeds, fruit, and even the root. In India, it is prevalent in criminal cases, but there have been very few such poisonings reported here in Egypt. Of course they could easily go undetected. The symptoms are similar to so many diseases." He hesitated. "A very deadly substance." He gave her a meaningful look. "In fact, if you were given much of that, it's highly unlikely that you would be here talking to me now."

Ardis changed positions in the bed to face him. As she did, she felt a rapid, unsteady pounding in her chest, just as she had the night before. For an instant she was gripped with fear. Someone was trying to kill her. If she didn't leave, they would succeed … just as they had succeeded in killing Jane. No one would ever know what happened to her, nor would they care. She would be just another "death by natural causes."

"Could it or some similar poison be administered a little at a time?"

"It's possible. Even a minute dose could make a person very ill."

Ardis considered his words. She was grateful she had not finished the entire glass of punch. "How much would it take for a fatal dose?"

"That's impossible to answer with any precision." Dr. Sardi's face, so lean and skull-like, became even more tight and serious. "It varies with the individual. Some people could take a moderately large dose with impunity. In other cases, a fairly small dosage could prove fatal."

"Then this poison, or something similar, could have been administered to Jane over a long period of time."

"Any answer I could give you would only be a guess. You have been working within the tomb just as she did. If we're dealing with poison at all, it is much more likely that we are dealing with old poisons, very rare ones, which were sealed within the tomb centuries ago."

Ardis thought about the passageway Blake and she had just discovered. Could she as well as Jane have come into contact with the same fungus or toxin? It could have been inhaled or somehow dusted on her skin or clothing. But would it be capable of producing a delayed reaction?

"Then why is no one else ill? Blake, Ramus, and many others work in the tomb as much as I do."

"I have no idea … different people have different immunities. If your symptoms recur, you should avoid all contact with the tomb and be admitted for a battery of tests."

"In the meantime, could you run a tox test for atropine?"

After a moment's hesitation, he said, "I have already sent blood samples to the lab. I will request special testing if that will put your mind at ease. Of course, it will take some time to get the results."

Rising from the armless chair seemed slow and painful for him. "Just in case this was a reaction to something you ate or drank last night, I would advise that you be very careful and sensible. In addition to the medicine I prescribed, drink lots of fluids and try to get plenty of rest."

Weakness and weariness blended with a growing sense of desperation as Ardis returned to her hotel. Jane's killer was watching her and waiting, as he had with Jane, for the next opportunity to strike. Ardis was no closer to discovering Senmut's gold and no closer to finding Jane's killer. Even her attempts to identify Jane's child had once more reached a dead end. Her prying had resulted in losing Nihisi's support and getting her barred, this time permanently, from the Senmut project. Without Nihisi's authorization to enter the tomb site, her plans to study the unusual pattern of the obelisks seemed hopelessly blocked.

The sudden ringing of the phone interrupted her gloomy thoughts. Dispiritedly, she answered, "Ardis Cole."

"Ardis? You sound as if something's wrong."

As Ardis recognized the voice of Dan Hall, her father's old friend, her spirits lifted. Explaining to him would only cause him to worry and would do no good. "Nothing, Dan. I'm quite all right."

"I've just uncovered information about Jane's child that should be of interest."

Gripping the phone tighter, Ardis remained tensely silent.

"You were right all along. Jane did have a baby."

"Did you locate Jane's ex-husband, Neil Darvin?"

"No luck there."

"Then how were you able to trace her child?"

"I haven't gotten that far with it, Ardis. I haven't actually located anyone." His pause increased her anxiousness. "A long-time associate of Jane's told me that Jane and her husband didn't return to the States after leaving Egypt. Instead, they lived for a while in Paris, France. Records from a hospital there indicate a live birth. A boy."

Ardis' thoughts flitted to Faye. "I had been thinking the child might be a girl."

"I was surprised to find out that Jane and her husband split up shortly after the child's birth. I wasn't able to trace Neil Darvin's whereabouts after Paris. At least not in the United States, Egypt, Brazil, or any of the places he was known to have lived." Dan paused again. "I have a feeling he may be deceased."

"And the child?"

"No further record of him, either. I doubt we'll be able to locate him after all this time, but I'll keep trying." Dan's next words took Ardis totally by surprise. "But I thought you'd like to know just for the record ... the name on the birth certificate is Thomas Darvin."

Ardis couldn't keep the astonishment from her voice. "*Thomas* Darvin?"

"Thomas Oliver Darvin. Correct. I hope I've been of some assistance. And I hope you are all right, Ardis. I still have the feeling that something's wrong."

"No need to worry about me. And thank you, Dan. This may turn out to be of the utmost importance."

Ardis dropped the receiver into place, jolted by what he had told her. Until she had talked with Nihisi, she had sincerely believed that Blake was Jane's son. The only other possibility had been that Faye Morris was her daughter. Now that these theories had both fallen in ruin, her thoughts turned completely to Thomas Garrett.

Perhaps because there was so little resemblance between Thomas and Jane, Ardis had never once considered the idea that Thomas might be Jane's son. And yet he was about the right age. The British accent, too, had thrown her off track. She had assumed Thomas was British; however it was altogether possible he had been born somewhere else. Thomas might have grown up in England or moved there as an adult to complete his studies. If Thomas' father and he had lived abroad, it might be difficult for Dan to find any record of them.

Ardis crossed to the window and parted the drapes. Thomas didn't seem an embittered person eaten away with hatred. An additional motive must have brought him to Luxor and caused him to conceal his real identity. Or had he taken an assumed name in order to meet his mother without her knowing him? He could have, after all these years, wanted to meet her face to face. If that were the case, he might be innocent.

But what about the slashed baby shirt and the angry destruction of Jane's work? That was surely a valid sign of some personal vendetta. Ardis quickly rejected this idea. She had known all along that the vandalism of the cabin would be tied in with Jane's child … but that didn't necessarily mean that the person who had ransacked the cabin was a thief and a murderer.

She stared down at Thomas' room on the ground floor near the pool. She had glimpsed Thomas entering the hotel lobby when she had arrived a short time ago. She recalled his boyish look as he had smiled and waved. How could she really suspect him of furious, unchecked vengeance?

Her question was followed by a strong image of Thomas handing her the drink containing the poison. And fear, real fear, stole over her.

She leaned closer to get a better view of Thomas' room and of the window, which had been left carelessly open. That meant he could still be in the building and would return soon. But when Ardis had passed Thomas in the lobby, he had not lingered, as he ordinarily would have, to stop and chat. His mission must have taken him from the hotel. If so, she had time to slip into his room while he was gone. Surely, she would find a clue among his personal effects. Perhaps some letter or photograph, some proof that would identify Thomas Garrett beyond a doubt as Thomas Darvin.

This opportunity did not allow for careful thought or planning. She had one chance, this one! She had no other choice than to take it. She exited the hotel by way of the side stairs and emerged in the enclosed courtyard near the pool.

The merciless afternoon sun had driven the hotel's visitors inside. As she crossed to Thomas' room, Ardis glanced furtively over her shoulder. In the intense mid-day heat, the pool was deserted and not a soul lounged on the sun-drenched chairs of the patio.

Only when she had reached the window did she have second thoughts. What if one of the hotel staff saw her sneaking into his room? What if Thomas returned and caught her inside? She had no time to wrestle with such misgivings. If she were to accomplish her goal, she must hurry.

Ardis looked back a final time. Heavy drapes, protection from the sun, were drawn across most of the nearby windows. No one stood at the back doorway. Ardis pushed Thomas' window further open and agilely climbed inside.

A stifling heat had settled over the room. This addition to the hotel was not connected to central air. The window had been left open, because Thomas had moved the air-conditioning unit to the floor near the bed. He had probably been trying to fix it himself.

Ardis took a quick look around to orient herself. The identical pattern of foam-green spread and drapes along with the same arrangement of desk, chair, and bed made it almost seem as if Ardis were back in her own room. A half-open book and glasses rested upon the nightstand. Near the telephone lay a neat stack of papers. Shifting quickly through them, Ardis saw that they were notes and sketches concerning Thomas' recent work on the Karnak restoration.

Feeling like a burglar, she began opening desk drawers. The top one held only hotel stationery. The contents of the desk, like the room, were oddly barren and impersonal, empty of photos or correspondence with friends or family.

Increasing the speed of her search, Ardis lifted from the desktop a silver watch she had seen Thomas wear many times. She read the engraved message upon the back, "To my son Thomas on his graduation." No initials or surname, nothing to prove or disprove her suspicion. Feeling frustrated, she returned it to its exact position.

Surely there must be something in this room that would give a clue to Thomas' true identity!

A quick inspection of the nearby dresser turned up only carefully folded shirts, socks, and underwear. Ardis hastily went through the small closet. Jackets and trousers hung neatly upon hangers; below was an extra pair of shoes and a large brown suitcase. Ardis lifted the suitcase. It felt light, empty. She opened it up just to check and then snapped the lock in place again.

In the bathroom the sight of Thomas' personal items— comb, toothbrush, and toothpaste— carefully arranged on the vanity magnified her feeling of intrusion. Ardis hesitated, her hand on a carry-on sized zippered duffel bag that set nearby. It had been her intention to go only through the desk drawers where she was certain she would discover some letter or personal link to Jane, not to snoop shamelessly into Thomas' personal belongings. Impulsively, Ardis unzipped the bag, almost the last place left to look, and peered inside.

Ordinary supplies were neatly arranged, a razor, shaving cream, hand lotion. Near the bottom, her hand brushed against something wrapped in a towel. Ardis drew out the bulky object and unwound the layer of cloth. Within lay what appeared to be a bottle of men's after-shave still in the box. Ardis frowned as she tested the weight of it. It seemed extraordinarily compact.

Perhaps she had found some gift or souvenir Thomas had carefully wrapped to keep from being broken in his travels. She unfolded it slowly, then gave a little gasp. She held in her hand an item familiar from Jane's sketches! What she was looking at was invaluable, not merely some replica purchased at a local shop. The carved cheetah, regal and stylized, displayed exquisite workmanship. Intricate embellishment swirled in a free-flowing, circular manner. The ivory, smooth and slick to her touch, had yellowed and browned with age.

Instead of triumph, Ardis felt a terrible sinking of her heart. She had not wanted Thomas to be guilty, yet she knew beyond any doubt that what she had found was the missing ivory cheetah that had been stolen from the tomb!

She had come here expecting to find proof that Thomas was Jane's son. What she held in her hands was indisputable evidence that Thomas was a robber and a murderer!

Voices sounded from the hallway just outside the door. She heard Thomas' easy drawl, "I've looked all over this hotel for you. My air-conditioner has quit again."

BenSobel's voice drifted to her. "I'll send someone to look at it."

"Don't take too long, old boy. I don't want to die of heat stroke."

No place to hide! Ardis looked around frantically … She should have run from the room while BenSobel had been in the hallway to help her. Now her only chance was to leave through the window, before Thomas could open the door. Please, please, keep on talking, she thought.

Ardis reached the window just as the door swung open. Thomas, his expression a mixture of surprise and alarm, stood motionless in the doorway. He stepped in and closed the door behind him, still standing against it. "Is it a product of the heat, or is there a lovely lady in my room?"

Ardis, her heart pounding, could not supply an answer.

With a sinister lack of motion, Thomas remained blocking the door. His eyes hardened and lost their glint of humor. They shifted to the ivory cheetah she still clutched in her hand.

His voice sounded low and deadly, "Just what are you doing here?"

"I came to find out who you really are," Ardis said. Escape impossible now, she moved slightly from the window. Her hand tightened on the ivory cheetah. She was aware of its smoothness, its weight.

"I've found out you are not Thomas Garrett. You are Thomas Darvin, Jane Darvin's son."

"So you did." Bitterness, dark and ugly, crept into Thomas' face. He gave a short laugh. "Jane Darvin, world famous archaeologist! For years I've followed her career, listened to stories about her success. I've despised her!" He took a step toward Ardis. Beneath his calm veneer burned a terrible fury fueled by hurt and rejection. "Did she ever tell you how she abandoned me when I was barely old enough to walk?"

"How I hated her!" Thomas' familiar features transformed and became the face of some ominous stranger. His narrowed brooding eyes, his lips drawn back over slightly protruding teeth, reminded her of Thutmose III as he had appeared in her hallucination.

That day when she had met him at the Temple of Karnak, Thomas had talked with great hostility about rights and heritage. Ardis should have known, then, the depth of his feelings. Now she fully realized that Thomas had been speaking of himself and Jane.

"You have misjudged Jane," she said. "If she let you go, it was because of circumstances beyond her control." Ardis wanted to say more, to explain how Jane had never stopped caring, how on her deathbed she had called for him, her "baby." But the fierceness of his expression stopped her.

"She never wanted me."

"Even if that were true, there is no justification for what you've done."

"What I've done?" he repeated, his features distorted. He seemed lost in his own world of seething resentment. "What she did to *me*, you mean. All these years she never once tried to see or contact me. I had to call for an appointment to meet her … my own mother." He took another step closer to Ardis. His lips formed a taut and cynical smile. "Do you think she would have even recognized me, her only child?"

In the stillness that followed an image arose in Ardis' mind of Jane's cabin. She saw Thomas ripping Jane's papers, slashing the baby shirt, and hammering with such brutal force the award that symbolized her accomplishments. A shiver of fear ran though her. "So you came here seeking revenge?"

His gaze moved to the ivory cheetah. "That … and so much more."

"You managed somehow to steal items from the tomb." Ardis felt shock, like a jolt of electricity, pass through her. Thomas was a tomb robber and a murderer. He had killed his own mother, and he had tried to kill her. This time he would be successful and no one would ever even suspect him!

Unless … he was under surveillance. That day at Karnak, Laurence Tolliver, the British investigator, could have been watching Thomas and not her.

This might not be the first of Thomas' robberies. Tolliver must have trailed Thomas from England, following some lead that linked him with international smuggling. Thomas had thrown suspicion on Blake, so Ardis would assume that Blake was the one being investigated and not him.

"I found the hidden passage right away," Thomas announced, "and followed it to the opening in the cliffs. That gave me easy access into the tomb. But that," he pointed to the ivory cheetah, "that … is nothing but a mere trinket. It is the *gold* I am going to find!"

Thomas had been present the day Matthammed had shown her the secret room in his shop. He had stolen the papyrus, and through its clues he would eventually discover another chamber in the Senmut tomb.

"So you have the papyrus. How did you even know of its existence?" she asked.

"I grew up knowing about the papyrus. You're forgetting, my father and Jane searched for Senmut's tomb way before I was born—the elusive tomb they couldn't find. When I read in the papers that Jane had returned to Egypt and about her discovery of the tomb, I came here to claim my legacy." He gave a dry laugh. "The gold does exist!" His lips tightened with a rage he no longer suppressed. "The papyrus is real, not a fake, not a sham like everything else in my life has been!"

"You must turn the papyrus over to the Egyptian authorities," Ardis said, trying to sound calm.

"I can't do that," he replied almost sadly. "I can't let you leave this room, either, Ardis." Thomas had reached the edge of the bed. He lifted the end of the mattress. Ardis knew before she saw the gleam of silver that he had a gun. He pointed the small, snub-nosed weapon at her. "Give me the cheetah. It belongs to me."

In this room, far back from the main part of the hotel, no one would hear her screaming. If the shot were heard at all, it would never be identified as gunfire. Thomas would dispose of her body and get away with another murder.

Unless … BenSobel returned to look at the air conditioner. Her heart raced at the prospect. She must keep Thomas talking. It was her only hope of survival!

"Turn yourself in, Thomas. You'll never be happy after what you've done, not even if you do find the gold."

"Then you believe it exists, too?"

"Yes, I was searching for it myself."

"Together we could find it. I wish you were on my side, Ardis. I really do care about you. Is there any way … any way we can work together?"

"No."

With steely composure he lifted the gun barrel.

She had cared about Thomas, too. Almost worse than her fear was the numbing shock of deception, of friendship betrayed. The heat of the room caused beads of moisture to dampen Ardis' forehead.

If he intended to fire the gun, why didn't he? Sweat trickled in streams down Thomas' face. "Why did you have to come in here?" he asked. "Why did you have to try to find out my identity?"

She wanted to tell him that it was not too late, that he could turn himself in. But it was too late. A part of her still struggled to deny the grim, horrid reality of it all. Not Thomas … it couldn't be. But it had happened. Thomas had killed the best friend Ardis had ever had. Thomas had murdered Jane.

Ardis edged toward the phone on the nightstand. "I'm going to call BenSobel. He will notify the police." She turned her back on him, tensing for the shot that was sure to follow.

Ardis hesitated. She had set down the ivory cheetah, but she did not lift the phone. Her hand poised motionless; her bravery was suddenly gone.

She looked back at him. Jane's son's angular face tensed. His lips tightened across his teeth as he watched her. His was the gaze of a desperate animal, trapped and dangerous. She had underestimated him! Thomas had killed before. He had been responsible for the death of his own mother. He was going to pull the trigger!

"You are being investigated right now," she told him. "No use killing again." Through a blur of fear her eyes held to his. The gun was still pointed at her, but Ardis read in Thomas' face a moment of indecision. An all-consuming, obsessive bitterness had driven him to commit a terrible crime, a crime of hate. But Thomas had once considered Ardis a friend, perhaps even more than a friend.

Then just as quickly as it had appeared, the doubts vanished from his face. Ardis recoiled. All traces of the man with the quick wit and the easy smile were gone now. Yet she still had faith in the person she thought she had known, the person that must in some way still exist. Despite what he had done, she did not believe the Thomas she knew could really shoot her in cold blood.

She would have to risk her life on that chance. The phone was within easy reach of her hand. She lifted the receiver and pressed the button to summon the main desk. BenSobel's voice sounded, "Essa BenSobel speaking. May I help you?"

The gun in Thomas' hand trembled as much as Ardis' voice as she replied, "You must come at once to Thomas Garrett's room. But before you do, summon the police!"

Thomas still had time to shoot her and to flee. Ardis, hardly daring to breathe, waited. For a long moment they stared at each other as if suspended in time. Slowly, ever so slowly, the gun in Thomas' hand lowered.

"I'm sorry, Ardis. So sorry." A look of total regret, of infinite sadness, filled his eyes. "I could never really have hurt you. I never intended to harm you … or anyone."

The total dismay in his voice made her almost pity him. His shoulders shook as he placed the weapon on the desk. He pushed the gun away as if it were suddenly appalling to him and covered his face in his hands. "This has gone too far. I'm glad it's all over."

Chapter 18

That night Ardis dreamed of obelisks—obelisks recessed in the huge squares fashioned in bas-relief upon the passage wall, five obelisks that formed a distinct pattern, an elusive clue she could not quite decipher. Through dream-hazed sleep Jane's voice floated above her, clear and certain, "The obelisk is the key."

In the pre-dawn stillness Ardis awoke, the dream still lingering. Even though she managed to shake free of it, the strange idea that she and Blake had somehow overlooked the obvious remained. Jane's miniature obelisk must serve in some way as an *actual* key, a physical means to open some hidden chamber within the passageway!

Dawn was breaking as Ardis rose and dressed. She had found Jane's killer. Now she owed it to Jane's memory to return once more to the tomb and attempt one last time to find the hidden chamber and the gold.

Under BenSobel's watchful eye, she picked up the obelisk from the safety deposit box and left the hotel. She felt increasingly anxious to test the theory that would either prove her right or force her once and for all to accept defeat.

As she crossed to the West Bank of the Nile, she gazed out across the water and thought of Thomas. He was being held by the police for the theft of the ivory cheetah, but a search of his room had failed to uncover the other stolen artifacts or the missing papyrus. Despite intensive questioning, he had not confessed to Jane's murder.

He had killed his own mother! The thought filled Ardis with revulsion. At the same time she felt haunted by the sad, regretful look in Thomas' eyes as he was handcuffed and led away. Part of her couldn't help pitying him; the part of her that still could not quite believe Thomas had been responsible for Jane's slow, agonizing death.

There was no use going to the main gate where she was certain to be denied access. She would head directly to the cliff entrance known to only Blake and to her.

Still having the keys to the compound, Ardis acquired a Jeep and headed directly to the cliff entrance she and Blake had discovered.

Ardis passed Qurna, shimmering like a mirage in the hazy morning light. Outside the little village, she pulled to a stop and studied the terrain. Jagged cliffs were lit like burnished gold by the slant of the rising sun. Far in the distance she could see the bare outline of fan-shaped rock that would guide her directly to the passage entrance.

She left the main road, taking a trail that rose sharply upward. Outcroppings of jagged stone soon began to impede her progress. The Jeep's wheels thumped against ruts and rocks, until at last she abandoned the vehicle and continued her journey on foot.

Lifting her pack containing water, a flashlight, and the stone obelisk, Ardis began to climb up the buff-colored rocks that towered just behind Senmut's tomb. No breeze stirred around her. Although the sun had just fully appeared, heat already emanated from the rocks and sand. The pack she carried grew heavier with each step.

Her lips were parched. Halfway up the slope, she stopped to take a drink from her canteen. She paused to catch her breath and gazed out at the miles of barren land. The total emptiness of the desert landscape gave her a feeling of isolation, as if she were the only person left on earth.

With renewed energy, Ardis made the strenuous climb up to the fan-like rock formation. Directly beneath this ledge lay the entrance, almost undetectable even to her. To her relief, she saw that Blake had not yet taken any steps to block the opening.

She easily located the hidden symbols, as Thomas must have done. The hidden wall of stone slid back allowing entrance into the oppressive atmosphere of the passageway sunk deep into the heart of the cliff.

Before entering, she hesitated, unnerved by the absolute stillness. The small flashlight was no match for the inky darkness. Its light created long, blue-black shadows along the wall. Risking discovery, she would first have to enter the main chamber and find a better light.

Ardis worked the hidden catch leading into the main chamber. Once inside, she paused, thinking she heard a sound echo from deep within. Was someone in the tomb with her? For a moment she stood statue-still, listening. Hearing nothing but the sound of her own breathing, she moved cautiously forward on the lookout for guards that Blake might have posted there for security. But in the early morning, the tomb appeared empty.

Ardis quickly gathered a large, battery-powered light, which was stored in the tomb. With it she took some tools she might need. She tested the light, flickering it off and on, satisfied with the way it illuminated the darkness.

Ardis returned to the passageway and shone the stronger light upon the wall, upon the ghostly images of Hathor, Osiris, and Anubis. Ardis continued down the passage to where the five large stones stood out from the wall in bas-relief. Each contained the reverse image of the stone obelisk.

Ardis studied the images, and then she drew Jane's obelisk from her pack and compared it with the first recessed depression. It was an exact fit, a mirror image of the obelisk wrought in stone.

Ardis' heart pounded with excitement as she fit the stone into the depression. Once the obelisk was in place, she attempted to turn it like a lock in a key; but her efforts were met with stony resistance.

Disappointment filled her. She had been wrong. Still, Ardis continued. She fit the stone into the second recession, then the third. She heard a rasping, scraping sound as the middle stone moved slightly. She caught her breath. With all of her strength, Ardis turned the obelisk and pushed against the solidness of stone. The entire square panel opened, leaving a narrow clearing just wide enough for her to pass through.

Gripped with a breathless excitement, Ardis directed the light into the hidden chamber. First it glowed upon a dazzling, golden boat that lay upon the floor not far in front of her. No more than two feet in length, the skiff had rolling tips and exquisite, decorative sides. It pointed on course, as sure as a sailor's compass, frozen in time on its perpetual journey toward the land of Punt. Ardis let out her breath slowly. Did she dare go inside? Would the newly discovered chamber be filled with snares and traps or dusted with ancient poisons?

Almost as if she had no will to resist, Ardis left Jane's obelisk still lodged into the opening and moved cautiously through the parted slab.

The glow of the battery-operated floodlight shone palely upon the walls painted with fantastic murals. They were similar to the ones covering the walls of Deir el-Bahari, but these were untouched by vandals, unworn by the elements. Precious, detailed stories of Senmut's journey to Punt, as deep and rich in color as the day they had been painted, spoke to her through the barrier of time. Five ships sailed toward the Somali coast, Senmut led the expedition through the Puntite villages of domed grass huts. Carvings depicted the loading of ships with wood, myrrh, resin, ebony, ivory, and gold—great quantities of gold nuggets carried in overflowing baskets and sacks of gold dust carried like bags of grain.

Her gaze moved from the fascinating murals to the contents of the chamber itself—to the giant statue of Senmut's faithful servant, Harmose—guardian of treasures beyond imagination—treasures Senmut had brought back for Queen Hatshepsut from his wondrous expedition.

Jane had been right. Senmut had hidden a wealth of treasure within this humble tomb. Ardis could barely contain her amazement. She ventured deeper inside, feeling as Howard Carter must have felt when he had first entered the tomb of Tutankhamen.

Before her lay the find of the century! She wished Jane were with her to share the thrill of discovery—Jane and Blake. But Ardis was alone in the tomb, alone with a wealth of treasure no one else had been able to locate. With awe, her eyes scanned the magnificence of that hidden room—the wealth of leopard and panther skins, the chests of ebony and ivory, the gods and animals carved in gold and alabaster. Everywhere, precious treasure crowded, feasts for the eyes and the imagination. The wealth of a kingdom hidden, safe from the vengeance of Thutmose III.

Immersed in the discovery, Ardis lost all caution. She peered into chests and coffers, some open and overflowing with neck collars, rings, ear pendants, and scarabs of precious stone. She saw the image of a falcon, golden with obsidian eyes, then a brilliant blue hippopotamus, then tiny golden figurines. A life-size cheetah statue with staring eyes crouched in the darkness as if ready to spring from its hidden corner where it had rested undisturbed for over 3,000 years.

Had Queen Hatshepsut died before Senmut? Had she been murdered by Thutmose III? Could this place be Queen Hatshepsut's burial place? Ardis began to circle the chamber searching for a sarcophagus, but she found none. Still, the items in the chamber had been arranged carefully, lovingly, as if this were a very sacred place.

In the direct center of the chamber where the sarcophagus would have normally been, stood twin obelisks of stone about five feet in height, small-scale replicas of the originals at the Temple of Karnak. Ardis stepped toward the rock obelisks. More than anything else, she was drawn to them, fascinated by their plainness, their simple presence amid such treasure.

A dried and shriveled Myrrh tree with bound roots, a tree, that had never been planted, had been placed like an offering before the obelisk. The sight of them made the connection between the tomb and Punt complete. Blake had been right. Only Harmose, a humble servant, had been buried in Senmut's tomb. He had been buried in the main chamber to guard this treasure. This chamber was not a tomb at all; it was an underground shrine, a tribute to Senmut's great, undying love for his queen.

Ardis began to feel a part of some grand unfolding. She felt Senmut would not have objected to her discovery of this secret chamber. He had hidden the queen's treasures from Thutmose and his greed; he had buried them to keep them safe. In a museum, the beautiful objects would be protected and would remain an everlasting tribute to Queen Hatshepsut and to Senmut.

"Queen Hatshepsut's dreams have turned to stone." Ardis gazed in wonder at the twin obelisks. She felt a deep stirring of amazement as the words Senmut had written in the papyrus took on an entirely new meaning. Suddenly, Ardis knew that Senmut had not failed in his mission.

With an ever-increasing excitement, Ardis knelt by the nearest obelisk and began to examine the stone. Upon closer inspection she could see that the exterior was only a facade. Using the tools she had brought along, she very carefully removed a segment of one of the blocks that made up the base.

Ardis drew in her breath. Something gleamed beneath the covering of rock. With nervous, impatient hands she worked faster until a portion of stone was sufficiently removed to see beneath the obelisk.

Aiming the light directly into the opening, she leaned for closer observation. Her heart pounded loudly against her chest as she discovered among the row upon row of glimmering hieroglyphics the familiar cartouche of Queen Hatshepsut.

Here was the gold Senmut had brought back from Punt to sheath the giant obelisks at Karnak! Because of Thutmose's threat, Senmut was prevented from doing so, but he had found a way to keep the gold safe from Thutmose, a way of fulfilling his promise to his queen.

In his own way, Senmut had beaten Thutmose III. By melting down the gold, he had saved this fortune for his queen. Queen Hatshepsut's dreams had come true; Senmut had managed to fashion and hide away for her these two beautifully inscribed obelisks of solid gold!

Chapter 19

"I knew if anyone would find the gold," a pleasant voice said, "it would be you."

Laurence Tolliver had slipped through the opening into the chamber and had for a long time been keeping silent vigil. Shadows formed hollows under his eyes and beneath his cheekbones. The effect served to intensify his alert gaze and highlight the damp gray hair that curled in the intense heat.

"Did you come out with Nihisi Khet?" Ardis asked, her startled voice resounding in the small, airless enclosure.

"We've known about this passageway for a long time." Tolliver's eyes roamed over the treasures, taking in the slender golden skiff, the terra cotta vessels, the jewel boxes of gilded wood that had remained untouched by human hands for centuries. He carefully moved past them, knelt in front of the obelisk, and began to inspect the portion of gold Ardis had worked so hard to expose.

Thomas was in jail in Luxor. Quite naturally the inspector would be here at the crime scene. Still his sudden appearance left her shaken, probably because he had arrived at the tomb at the exact time she had discovered the chamber.

"Where is Nihisi?" she asked.

"Forever busy with his own pursuits."

His eyes fell to the golden skiff. "What craftsmanship! Look how this boat is decorated with such fine detail. With all our fancy machines and methods, we can't reproduce anything like this."

He began sorting through the masses of vases and statuettes, his enthusiasm growing. His manner surprised her, or maybe it was the look of greed on his face. Clearly he was more interested in the treasures than he was in the crimes that had been committed here.

Anyone, of course, would be overwhelmed by such a sight.

"What will happen to Thomas?" Ardis asked.

Continuing to look around, Tolliver answered with an air of disinterest. "He will be tried in Egypt for theft."

"Since Thomas killed an American citizen," Ardis said, "isn't it possible that he will be extradited to the United States?"

Tolliver spoke slowly, emphatically, "There is not enough evidence to convict him of murder."

For a moment Ardis was aghast. Thomas was going to get away with killing Jane! While they waited for the police in his room at the Oasis, he had looked so totally finished with his crimes, so regretful, as if he were glad to be caught and have it all over.

"Maybe he will confess," she said.

"That is very doubtful."

Tolliver lifted the lid of an intricately carved wooden box and drew out a jeweled necklace. Still holding the precious object, Tolliver looked around at her. The light fell directly upon him. His slight smile showed satisfaction that was emphasized by the strange glint in his eyes. He rose swiftly, his form caught in the direct beam of the floodlight. He had a stocky form, like Ramus'. It was very similar to the one she had so briefly glimpsed on the cliff at Deir el-Bahari.

The smile remained. The vision of him, as affable as ever, whirled unsteadily before her eyes as realization struck her—Laurence Tolliver was not a British investigator of stolen artifacts. He was a robber working with Thomas. He was a thief here to steal the treasures of the tomb.

Laurence Tolliver was Thomas' accomplice.

Faye had not been lying. Thomas and she had really stayed together that day at Deir el-Bahari; Laurence Tolliver had followed along on the climb after all. He had been the one who had pushed Ardis from the cliff. Tolliver had been seated at her table the night she was given the poison. This man, not Thomas, had been the one who had tried to murder her!

Knowing Ardis had the obelisk and might lead them to the papyrus they needed so badly, both Laurence Tolliver and Thomas had been following her that day at Karnak. When she had become suspicious of Tolliver, Thomas had deliberately caused her to believe that he was a police investigator. Tolliver had played that part well; he had totally convinced her he was working undercover.

His voice, sounding so agreeable, caused her to start. "Whose sarcophagus was out in the main chamber? Was it Senmut's?"

Trying to conceal her wariness from him, she answered, "Blake believes the sarcophagus is that of Harmose, one of Senmut's entrusted servants. Senmut was probably never entombed here. He would have wanted to be buried at Deir el-Bahari with his queen."

"That shows what a fool he was!" Tolliver said. "Senmut spent his whole life loving and serving Queen Hatshepsut. No doubt she loved no one but herself." Great bitterness sounded in his voice. "You can be sure the queen was only using Senmut to build herself up, to accomplish her own selfish, vain-glorious purposes!"

Tolliver moved to the second obelisk. He lifted the chisel she had used and began stripping away the false stone front. He worked with an immense skill, careful not to do any damage, almost as if archaeology had been his life's work.

When the first gleam of the precious metal caught his eye, he gave an appreciative chuckle. "Gold behind this one, too!" he said excitedly. "What a bonanza!" His tone became triumphant as he added, "What Jane would have given to see what I am seeing."

The familiar way he called Jane by her first name made a chill run though Ardis.

Ardis had been totally side-tracked by her desire to find Jane's child. She should, instead, have been tracing Jane's husband—Neil Darvin, who now stood before her.

Why hadn't she known all along? Clues to his identity had been in plain sight—a man in his late fifties, listening, following her. The first day she had met him, he had just left the Cairo hospital where he must have given Jane the fatal dose of poison.

Knowing Ardis would pursue an investigation into Jane's death, he had tried to frighten her away by sending the tea to her room in Cairo. The night of the banquet when Ardis had told Faye of her resolve to locate Jane's child, Laurence must have realized then that he must kill her, too. He couldn't risk her uncovering Thomas, for that would surely mean finding Thomas' father—Jane's husband, Jane's killer!

Trying to keep the horror from reflecting on her face, Ardis forced her gaze away from him. She pretended to focus her attention upon one of the precious golden vases, imprinted with the ankh, the symbol of life and immortality.

Even as she pretended to examine the item, an image of Laurence Tolliver, or rather Neil Darvin, silently watching her remained in her mind. Despite how civilized he appeared, he was a man filled with rage. How he must have hated Jane! She thought of how violently he had destroyed Jane's cabin, left her possessions ripped, slashed, broken.

The terrible silence that had settled over the chamber deepened. Ardis stared at him. The worldliness she had noticed in him before became magnified. It was expressed in his drooping eyes and the pitiless sag to his mouth.

Ardis glanced back to the open doorway. Even if she could reach the main chamber, it, too, would be isolated. No one would arrive at the tomb for several hours. By then she would be dead, and Laurence Tolliver would have closed the chamber and taken the obelisk, planning to return and remove the gold and the other treasures. Without the obelisk, no one would ever be able to get into the chamber; the gold would be secure until he returned to claim it.

No doubt he had done this sort of thing before. He had been the one doing the stealing at the time the first scandal broke concerning Jane's projects.

Trying to maintain an outward calmness, Ardis moved closer to the chamber doorway. Once there, she feigned great interest in the golden vessel inlaid with ivory and turquoise.

Ardis tried not to give any hint that she suspected him, that would only speed up his plan to kill her. "I've known that you work for the police for some time," she said with a forced casualness. "With Thomas' confession, I'd say your job here is complete. What a relief that it is all over!"

She must take him by surprise. Before he had finished his sentence, she lunged toward the small opening leading into the passageway. At the same time Tolliver sprang forward. Strong hands clawed at her, forcing her backward. She clung to the thick stone of the door, inching her hand further and further toward the recess that contained the obelisk. If she could free herself from his grip and slip through the entrance, she would twist the obelisk and the door would close locking him inside the tomb chamber.

Just as her fingers caught the obelisk, Tolliver gave her arm a violent wrench. With a gasp Ardis managed to yank her hand back inside, safe from the heavy door that clamped shut between the chamber and the passageway. Tolliver stared at the closed door, his eyes fixed and glassy with fear.

"Look what you've done!" He began a frantic search for a way to open the chamber. With growing anxiety he tried again and again to apply pressure to the recessed imprint of the obelisk. Yet he must know unless the obelisk was used as a key, those heavy stones would never spring apart.

"On either side, the obelisk must be used to open the chamber. With the obelisk on the other side of the door, we're trapped!" she said.

"There must be another way out!" With mounting horror he turned to face her. "How long will we have to wait here before we're discovered? Surely Lydon knows about this chamber!"

"No one knows about it."

The air around her seemed to have diminished with the tight closing of the chamber door. Only the glow of the floodlight illuminated the complete and utter darkness. Escape would be hopeless. She was locked in here to die with Jane's killer!

It took some time for Ardis to collect herself and to begin examining the wall. Using the light to guide her, she started a slow, methodical search. "I am afraid there is only one way out of this chamber," she said, her voice sounding muffled and distant.

She started around again. Her pace continued to increase as edges of panic threatened to overtake her.

Tolliver, who had also been searching for another way out, suddenly stopped. His voice rang out emptily. "No one will ever find us! I will die here in this tomb!"

His hand moved to his stomach as if he were becoming physically ill. His light jacket parted and revealed the butt of a small-caliber gun. The sight of it caused no increase in Ardis' fears. He wasn't going to kill her now. They were both fated to die together—a slow, insufferable death.

How long would it take? … How many days? How many nights? How many endless hours of agony?

Tolliver, as if in a stupor, stumbled through the maze of treasures. He sat down heavily on the base of the obelisk and rested his head back against the stone, hiding the gold he had searched for all of his life.

Determinedly, Ardis continued the useless motions of looking for a way out. Laurence remained deathly still. His eyes were closed and sweat streamed in trails down his face.

At first frenzied, Ardis' search eventually slowed. She could no longer judge time. Feeling the lack of air, a total exhaustion of her both body and spirit, she sank down beside the second obelisk, closing her eyes the way Laurence had.

"Why did you hate Jane so much?" she asked finally, gasping for breath.

"Jane and I could have found this tomb together. We knew if we ever located Senmut's tomb, we would find the gold. We used to study the papyrus, the one I have now. We were young dreamers, with our whole lives ahead of us. Then she abandoned me."

"No," Ardis said. "She caught you stealing from one of her projects."

"She made such a fuss over the few old statues I took," he said. Only the sound of his heavy breathing cut through the silence. At last he said, "One day I opened the paper, and there it was in the headlines—Jane had found our tomb. The moment I read about the find, I knew I had to come and claim the gold for myself."

"The gold doesn't belong to you. It belongs to Egypt."

"It belongs to me! Finding it was my life's work! My dream! When Jane left me, she stripped me of everything. I only wanted to get it back."

"Over thirty years ago when she discovered some missing items ..." His voice stopped, then deepened with irrational rage. "She actually turned me in to the police. Because I returned the artifacts, they quieted everything down and pressed no charges; but my career, my work, was ended, entirely destroyed."

"If you ask me, you were treated very generously."

As if he had not even heard her, he ran a hand across his face, along his mustache. His hand rose and he twined long fingers through his hair. "When Jane left me, I followed her to Paris where she had Thomas. I tried so hard to reconcile with her. I was the one who was generous. At the time I didn't even believe the baby belonged to me. It was much later when I found out that he did." He paused again, caught up in the old anger that still flared despite the years. "Even though we had this tie, this child, Jane would have nothing at all to do with me. So I hung around. I plotted a way to get even with her for ruining my life. I took what she wanted most," he said spitefully, "her baby. I kidnapped Thomas." He paused, sucking in his breath. "I established new identities for us in London as John and Thomas Innes. Despite the iron determination Jane was noted for, she was never able to trace us."

"But you told Thomas about her?"

"Yes."

Ardis shuddered. "You fed Thomas with hatred. You turned him against Jane. You convinced him that she was the evil one and not you."

"She was," he snapped back.

"You knew what Jane was really like," Ardis said. "She was so gentle, so wrapped up in her idealism."

"Wrapped up in herself, you mean!" he countered scornfully. "With never a single thought of me!" Tolliver stopped, then went on, pride mixing with his contempt. "I did my research well. I found a poisonous plant that would give symptoms similar to those experienced by other people who have worked in the tombs. Jane always loved tea." He emitted a short laugh. "I prepared for her a little tea out of the leaves of the belladonna and poured it into the drink she always carried."

Ardis shrank from his heartlessness, from his inability to face the pure evilness of what he had done.

"I wasn't the only one who hated her!" he said defensively. "When I showed Thomas the news article, he was more than willing to help me beat Jane to the treasure!"

"When I woke up in the hospital, I became suspicious that someone had tampered with my drink at the barbecue. At this very moment Dr Sirdi is running a tox screen, looking for evidence of atropine poisoning. That's going to link Thomas with an attempt on my life and Jane's murder. And you are planning to let him take the blame, while you run off with the gold," she said.

Poor Jane, even she must have had difficulty seeing and believing the self-serving greed that drove this man who once was her husband.

"Don't make it sound as if I don't care about him," he said petulantly. "I was careful to keep Thomas from being involved in murder. I didn't even tell him that I had killed Jane, and that I fully intended to get you out of the way." His voice trailed off. "But now I won't have to kill you. You are dead. And so am I."

In despair Tolliver's head rolled against the rough stone of the obelisk. Sweat trailed in uneven streams down his face. Wet, gray hair clung to his forehead.

At least a little of what he said rang of truth. They were fated to die here together. Terror gripped Ardis. In the profound silence she thought of Blake—the man she loved, the happy years they would never have together. How could she ever prepare herself for a slow death—starving, dying of thirst or from lack of oxygen—when she wanted so much to live?

They were doomed, or as Matthammed would say, "Cursed!" The curse of Senmut! Ardis closed her eyes against the sting of tears.

Ardis didn't know whether minutes or hours had passed. Once again time seemed fully lost, without any meaning at all. The short years Queen Hatshepsut had lived and the short years she herself had lived merged into a timeless void. As she thought of the great queen and of Jane Darvin, calmness filled her. She would do her best to face death with courage.

Tolliver—she still thought of him by that false name—had begun to cry. Hopeless sobs shook his heavy frame. She cast a glance at him, so pathetically weak and frightened. One thing was certain; Ardis would die in a much braver manner than would Neil Darvin.

Chapter 20

Ardis carefully poured one-half of the remaining water from her canteen to a cup and passed it to Tolliver.

She brought the canteen to her lips. She wanted to drink on and on, but the warm liquid soon quit flowing and left a horrible dryness in its wake. Her unquenchable thirst, along with the terrifying lack of air, renewed her sense of panic.

She rose, lifting the floodlight from the immense wooden coffer between them. Unlike Laurence Tolliver, she could not remain inactive. Yet she had gone over every inch of the wall surface. Ardis had found no sign of another doorway and no cheetah symbols which had been used to open the entrance from the main chamber into the passageway.

The floodlight cast sinister patterns of light across the wall, across the endless rows of pictures set in small squares. She allowed the light to focus upon two kneeling figures, a man and a woman, painted in amber and white. They faced the ram-headed god Arietes with his formidable blue face.

Ardis continued her exploration. The motif changed, portraying ominous lines of men, interrupted by the appearance of a boat, shaped like the statue of the golden skiff which lay nearby. Aboard stood three figurines; the center one represented Senmut, making the journey to Punt.

Tolliver's muffled voice reached her, "You caused all of this. It was your doing that got us locked in here!" His voice, no longer edged with fright, sounded toneless, as if he had become one of the ancient Egyptians so vividly pictured on the stones in front of her. "You know there's no way out. You've killed yourself and me!"

If she hadn't had more urgent and immediate fears, she would have been afraid of him, of the slight chanting tone to his voice. She thought of the way he had hidden himself in the passageway the day she had returned for the obelisk. Having worked in Egypt, no doubt he had learned some of the Arabic language and had used it in his attempt to scare her away from Senmut's tomb.

She glanced around at him. He no longer slumped; he sat tensely straight, still holding the cup she had given him. He looked like a statue in an evil pose like the one of Thutmose III. She did not say anything to him but went on with her search.

Ardis trained the light squarely on the painting of a bent, crippled form being presented to Osiris. Anubis with his jackal head supervised the weighing of the dead man's heart against the balance of his deeds. From his expression he had found the man worthy. This would be Senmut's faithful servant, Harmose, who Blake believed Senmut had entombed in the main chamber to guard the treasure.

A small cry of joy escaped Ardis' lips as her eyes lowered to tiny paintings, small animal faces, directly beneath Harmose near the floor of the chamber. Her heartbeat quickened. They were set in a series—cheetah symbols. Dropping to her hands and knees, Ardis wiped the rock clean with her bare hand. With stiff fingers she applied pressure to the first two. She waited. Nothing happened. Growing increasingly anxious, she tried again and again, pressing this one and that as if working the combination of a lock.

No door sprang open. The stillness and silence remained.

She worked on doggedly, but to no avail. The heat and the tomb dust had begun to affect her eyes made them dry and gritty. No moisture remained in her mouth. It was impossible to swallow.

Was it her imagination or had the light beside her grown visibly dimmer? No telling when the battery had last been recharged. How long would it be before the light would go out completely, adding to their agony, sinking them into blinding blackness?

With mounting fear, Ardis continued to work with the symbols, until she was convinced it was useless. She had put forth every effort. Nothing resulted from it because there was no door to open. Only one entrance existed for this chamber, and that one must be unlocked with the obelisk.

Previously the terror she felt had risen and subsided. This time it persisted.

She forced herself to rise and move away from the symbols. She would keep on trying to find a way out! She would not give up! "If we make enough noise," she said, "maybe Ramus or Blake might hear us."

Tolliver had not spoken for a very long time. She did not wait for him to comment. She began to call out and to pound the rock wall with a stone she had found near the obelisk. Her cries rose and fell, echoing against the thick walls. "Help! Help us!"

Surely Ramus or Blake would by now be working in the tomb. Blake might even be out in the passageway searching, as she had been, for another chamber. She shouted louder and continued to cry out, until her voice grew strained and hoarse.

Tolliver set aside the water, part of which he was saving for later. "No sound is going to penetrate these massive rocks. You're wasting your time."

The truth of his words set a tremor of fear throughout her body. She backed away from the wall, stumbling as she did against a jumble of artifacts. Small items of gold scattered across the floor. As she set down the light to pick them up, the room became engulfed in blackness.

"What happened?" Tolliver's voice rang out with alarm. "What did you do?"

Ardis grabbed the light with both hands. She disconnected and replaced the battery line. To her relief the light came back on again, although its glow was decidedly weaker than before.

"It will soon go out for good," Tolliver said, his words marked by a slight quaver. "Do you have any matches or a lighter?"

"No."

"Neither do I."

Fighting panic, Ardis returned to the solid base of the obelisk and sank down again. The vision remained in her mind of the scales of justice, but this time it was her heart that was being weighed, her own worthiness being determined. Did similar thoughts fill Tolliver's mind? If she allowed herself to continue this train of thought she would go mad!

The waning light gave the illusion of walls drawing toward her. She slumped back feeling the sharpness of the rock against her spine. At length she became acutely aware of the tomb complex and of the crippled Harmose, charged with the eternal duty of guarding Queen Hatshepsut's gold.

In the dismal silence she wondered if Tolliver's body and her own would ever be discovered, or if they would remain like the gold or like undiscovered mummies in the Theban hills— sealed away for endless centuries. If they ever were found, would archaeologists speculate about why they were here or think about the conflicts and desires of their lives that had led them to this place of death?

As she thought the word *death*, the light extinguished again. Ardis snatched it up, but this time it remained off. They were encased in absolute blackness.

"Give the light to me."

She could hear Tolliver's frantic motions beside her. He spoke words under his breath she could not understand, but no light came on. After a while, he groaned, then the chamber became appallingly soundless.

"Where are you?" She needed to hear a human voice. "Are you all right?"

She waited. Tolliver did not reply and she heard no movement at all in the ghastly void. Time passed—minutes, hours, she wasn't sure. She tried not to think about the days of intolerable confinement that lay ahead.

Ardis expected in time she would acquire an involuntary acceptance of the inevitable, an acceptance that would allow her thoughts to drift, to evade the horror of being trapped in this ancient tomb to die. But the opposite proved true. Without image or sound to give direction to her thoughts, they became surprisingly lucid.

She pictured Jane Darvin, so alive and vibrant. Jane hadn't deserved the endless lies told about her or a death by treachery. Ardis felt great contempt for the man locked in here to die with her.

The surge of anger renewed her spirit. She wasn't going to wait for death. She would fight to the last. She inched her way through blackness to the wall where she had been working with the symbols. Using her hand to guide her, she continued moving around the tomb. Perhaps she would be able to feel what she had not been able to see, some indication of a doorway.

Disoriented by the complete darkness, Ardis lost track of her location. Where was the entrance? Where was Tolliver? She called out to him, but again, he did not answer.

More unnerved than before, Ardis continued walking, her hands pressed against the stone wall. She stopped, puzzled by a faint vibration against her fingers. A noise, like a slight rumbling, broke through the stillness. A grating sound followed as if some object of great weight were being moved. Where was Tolliver? What was he doing?

Astounded, she distinguished a small beam of light barely able to break through the terrible blackness. Behind the narrow glow, a tall form towered in shadowy outline. Ardis, too startled to speak or to breathe, stared toward it. As in her hallucination, the shape and carriage of the man resembled Senmut. It was almost as if Senmut himself had come to life and emerged from some pitch-black recess!

With a relentless steadiness, the form moved deeper into the chamber. Ardis kept her eyes fastened on the obscure shape wavering weirdly in the ghost-like veil of light. Was it a phantom? An apparition appearing from the boiling point of her own fear? No, the man was real. Senmut's form merged into that of Blake's! Blake had discovered the obelisk out in the passageway and had unlocked the chamber!

Ardis' thoughts leaped to Tolliver. Even though she couldn't see him, she was aware of his swift movement. Like a predator catching the scent of food, Tolliver had sprung to life. Then all motion stopped. He had stalked forward, lying in wait somewhere near the golden skiff that lay between the obelisks and the doorway. Without a doubt, Ardis sensed what he intended—to kill Blake, their rescuer, and then her!

"Ardis!" Unaware of the danger, Blake continued to move toward her. She heard the joy and relief in his voice. "Thank God! How did you … "

Her despairing cry cut off his words, "Blake! Blake! Look out!"

Blake was close enough to her that the light gave a slight illumination to his features. She had no time to reach him or even to move before the shot exploded. The gunfire blasted, the booming of it resounding around her.

Blake had not expected to confront an armed opponent. Tolliver's ambush had taken him by complete surprise.

Ardis glimpsed Blake's startled eyes that in shock grew wider. He looked just as he had in her dream—stricken, features registering stunned surprise. Except, now, in real life, he staggered backward instead of toward her.

She heard a clatter as if he had fallen. At the same time the flashlight went out immersing them in absolute darkness.

A groan of pain escaped Ardis' lips. Tolliver had shot him! Blake was dead! Ardis' dream had been a forewarning. Blake had been fated to die, not because he was guilty of any crime but because he was trying to protect her. Because he loved her.

"Blake! Oh, no!"

Ardis, realizing the mistake of revealing her exact position, lurched to the left. Just as she did, a second shot sounded. It zinged inches from her. Particles of rock sprayed against her arm as the bullet struck against the stone wall.

Ardis frantically attempted to orient herself. Instead of her own safety, Ardis could think only of Blake, wounded, dying alone in the darkness. She could not bear the thought of losing him! She did not want to go on living without Blake!

Filled with outrage and not caring what became of her, Ardis dropped to the ground. She groped through the darkness, until her hands closed over the golden boat. Every sense became alert.

The shot gave away Tolliver's location. She could hear him shuffling through the blackness. He intended to kill her as he had killed Jane, as he had just shot Blake.

Ardis rose to a crouch holding the heavy golden skiff as a weapon. At any moment she expected to feel the impact of bullets against her body.

Tolliver was still trying to locate her, but she had the advantage of being certain of his exact position. She must act quickly. She leaped to her feet and blindly struck out at him. The blow smashed into him. She heard his curse. She was aware of his stumbling backward, of his sudden cry.

Silence fell again—more terrible than any before it.

"Blake!"

When the bullet had struck him, Blake had reeled and fallen somewhere near the entrance. Ardis groped blindly on hands and knees, but she could not find him. She stopped and listened intently. Thinking she detected the faint sound of breathing, she changed her course, moving off to the right. "Blake!"

She ran her hands across his face. As her left hand lowered to his chest, she drew it back in terror. Her fingers were moist with blood.

Blake couldn't die! She wouldn't let him!

Ardis groped for the flashlight. The small glow illuminated Blake's features then moved down to the blood that spread in an ever-widening circle just below his shoulder. She couldn't tell how badly he had been hurt.

Ardis aimed the light again at his face, wet with sweat. With a moan she pushed the black hair back from his forehead. As she did, his eyes opened.

"Blake! No, don't try to move. I'll get help!"

For an instant he looked dazed, as if he had no idea where he was or what had taken place. Then he struggled to a sitting position. His hand moved to his shoulder and he winced in pain.

"It's not serious," he stated bravely, as if to calm her. "Only a surface wound." He tensed suddenly. "Where is Tolliver?"

"I struck him. He's unconscious … somewhere." Once on his feet, Blake took the flashlight from her and shone it around the chamber. The beam settled on Tolliver where he lay at the foot of the obelisk.

They moved toward him. Blood reddened Tolliver's gray hair and trailed down across his face. Ardis' blow had caught him unaware. When he had stumbled backward, he must have struck his head against the rock obelisk.

"Blake, is he … "

Blake knelt beside Tolliver where he lay at the stone base. After a while he said, "He's alive." Blake lifted the gun from the floor beside Tolliver and with an effort he rose.

With the glow from the lowered light she could see Blake clearly. She heard herself say with trembling voice, "I have never been so frightened. I thought he had killed you!"

Blake's breath was quick and uneven with pain; but his eyes, the dark depth of his eyes, were wonderfully steady.

"I can't believe that you found me!"

"I had a long talk with Thomas," Blake said. "He admitted that he had an accomplice, although he refused to disclose his identity."

"Until they took him to jail, I don't think Thomas realized his father was a murderer." Ardis added with sadness, "Even then, I'm sure he planned to keep quiet even if it meant taking the blame himself."

"Though he refused to implicate Tolliver, he did tell me something that might have saved your life. He told me that if you continued to look for the gold, you would be in great danger."

"How did you know I was here?" Ardis asked.

"BenSobel told me that you had taken the obelisk. When you weren't at the hotel, I knew you must have gone out to the tomb. I searched everywhere. I should have seen the obelisk at once, but I didn't. I looked up and down the passageway a dozen times before I spotted it."

The rescue had happened with such speed. Ardis could hardly believe it had occurred at all. She stared wonderingly at Blake, as if suspending final judgment.

He returned her gaze, a look of relief overriding the pain and worry. Still Ardis didn't fully realize she was safe and that Blake was safe, until he had drawn her tightly into his arms.

In the dining room of the Oasis, Blake and Ardis sat at a quiet back table. From the window they could see the Nile, broad and deep, as it wound past the hotel. On the nearby bank a young man struggled with a crate of chickens; in the distance several people fished from a makeshift boat. The sun cast glimmering lights across the water, highlighting the tranquility of the early morning.

Blake had spent last night in the Luxor hospital. Yesterday's trauma seemed past and forgotten. If it hadn't been for the bulge from the bandage under his shirt just below his shoulder, Ardis would never have known that he had been shot.

"After I became aware of Laurence Tolliver following me," Blake said, "I attempted to check his identity. I tried to trace him to London where he said he lived, but the name kept coming up totally unknown." Blake paused. "I had never seen a picture of Jane's husband; but after Thomas confessed that he was not working alone, I finally made the connection— Laurence Tolliver was really Neil Darvin. I knew you believed Jane's killer was in custody. That left you in a very dangerous position. I knew I had to find you at once."

"I was convinced all along that Tolliver was an under-cover investigator."

"That is exactly what Thomas and he wanted you to believe."

"Thanks for saving my life, twice," Ardis said.

Blake reached for her hand. "I also have you to thank for saving mine," he answered. "It looks as if we will always be in debt to one another." A smile formed in his eyes and touched his lips. "Since that debt will take a long time to repay, we might just as well get married."

A thrill of happiness rushed over Ardis, but she had no time to respond. Nihisi Khet had entered the dining room and was briskly approaching their table.

"I'm leaving for Cairo this morning," he said. He turned to Ardis and spoke earnestly, "Before I go, I want you to understand why I dismissed you from the project. I saw the same thing happening to you that had happened to Jane."

"I realize that."

"I don't know whether to reprimand you for disobeying my official dismissal, or to applaud you for what you did for the museum … and for Egypt."

"I would prefer the applause," Ardis answered with a smile.

"Then be sure to be in Cairo on the 20th." Nihisi glanced from Ardis to Blake. "You, too, Blake. We're having a banquet in your honor in recognition of your work." Then he addressed Ardis again. "There is a special award I want you to receive, Ardis, in memory of Jane. I called the museum yesterday, and we're getting a replacement for the sphinx award Neil Darvin destroyed."

"I understand that you'll be receiving your own award, too," Blake said, his dark eyes sparkling, "a miniature golden obelisk, a small-scale replica of the ones found in the tomb."

"You deserve the honor as much as I do."

"Who knows," Nihisi cut in, "there might be two, like the real ones, one for each of you. Now, I must be going."

"May we take you to the airport?" Blake asked, rising.

"There's no need. Professor Mendon and delegates from the museum are waiting for me." Nihisi Khet reached into his breast pocket and took out a folded paper. He laid it on the table between them. "This is something that might interest you," he said. "It is in regard to what we were discussing last night—the name and address of your natural mother."

Abruptly, Nihisi started away.

"Father."

Nihisi drew to a slow stop and turned back.

"At one time I thought I needed this," Blake said, handing the paper back to Nihisi—unfolded. "But now, I know I don't. I already know who my parents are."

Puzzled and surprised, Nihisi Khet accepted the paper and without another word left the dining room.

After Nihisi had departed, Matthammed and Ramus appeared.

"I just saw Nihisi in the lobby," Matthammed said. "Would you believe, he was actually smiling? I hope that means he's not going to give us a hard time on our next project."

"If I know Nihisi," Ramus responded, "it means just the opposite. His smile is only temporary, because he's able to personally escort Queen Hatshepsut's golden obelisks to Cairo."

"The curse of Senmut has finally lifted," Matthammed said. "Senmut can rest now because the gold is safe."

"So is Jane's name in history," Ramus added.

"The entire world will be able to share in the wonder of the obelisks," Matthammed marveled.

"That is what Jane would have wanted," Ramus said, "not to mention Queen Hatshepsut. Their dreams have been realized."

"The dream of my life has come true, too," Blake announced. "Ardis and I are talking about marriage."

"Marriage?" Matthammed tossed the hood of his white robe further back on his head, his features lighting with great interest. "Did I ever tell you I specialize in wedding rings?" He indicated the black briefcase he carried by lifting it slightly. "Inscribed, if you like. Or plain. Eighteen karat gold."

Matthammed's sharp, black eyes darted from face to face. "But this is not a good day for me to close a deal. I am in much too generous a mood."

Smiling, Blake leaned across the table to Ardis. "Ardis, what do you think? Shall we buy our rings from Matthammed?"

Feeling a surge of great joy, Ardis gazed into Blake's dark eyes. "Only," she answered teasingly, "if Matthammed is willing to give us a very big discount."

The End

Turn the page for a preview of the
second exciting adventure of …

THE ARDIS COLE SERIES

Unmarked Grave

by

VICKIE
BRITTON
LORETTA
JACKSON

Rowe Publishing
and Design

Chapter One

"This is the place where I found the skull," Bruce McBrier said, pointing toward the narrow but deep river that wound through the valley toward the Firth of Tay. "It either washed ashore or was simply uncovered by the recent rains."

Ardis Cole, who had arrived in Scotland only this afternoon, suffered from an unusual lethargy, which she attributed to the long hours in flight from Chicago to Edinburgh. She lagged behind, stopping beside the suspension bridge that separated the main road from the grounds of Venwell Castle. Bruce, stocky figure with rumpled jacket and equally rumpled gray-blonde hair, moved eagerly ahead with surprising swiftness for his girth and years.

"I'm convinced," Bruce said, hair blowing in the wind as he turned back to face her, "that I have found the remains of our long missing ancestor, Sir William, who would have been the fourth Lord of Venwell. I'm certain the ancient piece of metal found embedded in the skull can be dated back to the 1500s." Bruce's look of enthusiasm mingled with a smug satisfaction. "I always knew that he had returned to this castle after the Battle of Flodden."

"Think of all the wars since then. What makes you so certain that the skull you've found is his?"

An excited light glowed in Bruce's eyes. "Because Sir William didn't die in battle as was commonly believed. Ardis, I've found a 16th century document that proves beyond all doubt that he did survive the war. Where else would he go but here, back to Venwell Castle?"

Bruce McBrier, who had many times visited her family when she was a child, had contacted Ardis only two days ago. "You are one of the finest archaeologists I know," his voice had boomed into the phone. "Only you can help me solve the mystery of Sir William!" Because of his insistence, Ardis had finally agreed, without, she thought now, her usual cautious preparations and totally without sufficient answers to her questions.

She had flown to Scotland mainly to try to free herself of the grief of losing Blake Lydon. It would soon be a year. Ardis twisted the beautifully crafted gold ring she wore on her forefinger adjoining her diamond—the wedding ring she had planned to give to Blake. Would she ever be able to forget, to become immersed in her work again, to go on as if the plane Blake was in had not gone down at sea never to be seen again?

A sense of extreme weariness washed over her. She brushed back her ash-blonde hair that the wind had tousled across her forehead and attempted to collect herself.

Bruce's gaze left her, wandered across the flowing water, and on to where glimpses of a distant castle could be seen through the trees. "Yes, Sir William Venwell returned home— only to be stricken down by one of those treacherous Lloyds."

"Is that the Lloyd's castle?" Ardis asked as she joined him at the edge of the water.

"Indeed it is. We are neighbors, but certainly not friends. Even back then, the Lloyds fought for England, backing Henry

VIII, while Sir William …" Bruce paused to chuckle, "rather against the family desires, took it upon himself to ride with James IV in defense of Scotland."

Bruce had left her side and was pacing up and down the shoreline. He stopped suddenly beside a tall pine tree and pointed to the ground, "I found the skull right there." Bruce, a twinkle in his lively blue eyes, exclaimed proudly, "We are on the verge of solving a centuries old murder!"

"Have you shown this find to anyone?" Ardis asked.

"No one outside the family. I've been keeping this relic of history in a special room under lock and key. Of course, eventually, I plan to turn the skull over to the local museum curator." He stopped again. "But this is my find and I want to be the one to authenticate it. That's where you come in, my lass. I know you can do a facial reconstruction from the skull, just as you did with those Mayan heads in Central America." He hesitated, then added hopefully, "We have an excellent bust of Sir William we can use to make a comparison."

"Hold on a minute, Bruce." A shadow of doubt creased Ardis' brow. "I can't work on a project like this without going through proper channels."

With a wave of his hand, he brushed away her words. "Wading through reams of red tape is out of the question. Besides I don't want any of this in the local papers, not until you have helped me prove the skull is Sir William's."

"A facial reconstruction might tell us if the person who died here bears a resemblance to Sir William, but it won't serve as positive proof."

"Timing is of the utmost importance," Bruce responded, again carefully side-stepping her words as if she had never even spoken. "News of this discovery must coincide with the release of my material on Venwell history. What interest the skull will create! Sales of my book will skyrocket. You know how fascinated everyone is by intrigue, betrayal—murder!"

Murder—the word lingered between them. A human life had met with violent death right at the spot where they stood. That fact hadn't seemed real to Ardis Cole until her gaze followed the sunken bank-line that fell from tangled weeds into brackish water.

"He does belong to us, you know," Bruce said almost in apology. "He <u>was</u> our hero, a Venwell. Aye." The slight Scottish burr crept into Bruce's voice. "Strong enough to resist even his own family and fight for what he believed was right!"

As they began walking back toward Venwell Castle, Bruce's ardor, which had been momentarily replaced by sadness, returned full force. "I'd show you the skull right now, but it's almost time for dinner. Morgan will soon return from Denning and will want to meet you."

Ardis had never met Morgan, Bruce's older brother, but Bruce's caustic comments about him made her almost dread the inevitable encounter. "He has a son and a daughter who live here too, doesn't he?"

"Only his daughter, Gwynne." Ardis thought she noted some embarrassed hesitation. "Morgan's son, Edan, is … away at present." Bruce went on quickly as if he wanted to avoid all further discussion of his nephew. "Gwynne has been anxious to meet you. I don't know where she went, but she's around somewhere. The girl is far to shut in here," he added. "Your visit will be good for her. She needs a friend, someone close to her own age to talk to."

They followed a narrow road, Bruce still in the lead, walking with his quick, sure stride. They rounded a sharp curve and passed through the wide open gate that was set between two gigantic stone pillars. The full view of Venwell Castle made Ardis feel as if she were passing through a portal of time into a century long past. The first sight of Venwell Castle, on their return from the airport, when Bruce stopped to open the gate, took her breath away. She felt the same sensation again.

A huge cylinder tower, very smooth and light gray in color loomed high above the front entrance. Ardis noted the ancient markings above the door, the family crest of crossed swords beneath a raging lion's head, under which in large, clear letters was etched, VENWELL.

When she had thought of the castle while on the airplane, she had expected it to be sprawling, rambling, but its hugeness consisted mainly of height, a magnificent, towering fortress, unlike anything she had ever seen.

Instead of guiding her to the entrance, Bruce led her off on a side path. "Let me take a moment and show you the garden," he said with pride. He took her past manicured hedges and tall rhododendron bushes laden with purple flowers into an open garden area alive with the brilliant colors of early summer.

In the center of the abundant garden set a stone fountain, as old as the castle itself, where water flowed freely down from a gargoyle-like, human face. In the shadow of this monstrosity, Bruce stopped walking and glanced toward her. "As I told you, I've been keeping the skull under lock and key." An odd expression appeared on his craggy face that Ardis could not quite interpret. He did not speak for a long time. "Strange things have been happening ever since I found Sir William's skull!"

"Don't tell me. It's a haunted skull," Ardis joked. "And Sir William is trying to get it back."

"Laugh if you want to," Bruce said, looking a little hurt. He leaned closer, lowering his voice to say confidentially, "But one night I was certain I heard noises coming from my study near the room where the skull is being kept."

Remembering Bruce's unshakeable faith in the paranormal, Ardis became serious.

"Venwell Castle is still filled with sorrow," Bruce said, "just as it was then, centuries ago. And new sorrows attract old sorrows."

An uneasy feeling began to possess Ardis. She glanced toward the fountain, her eyes locking on the gargoyle. His ugly head inclined forward, as if intent on listening to them.

With absolute sincerity, Bruce went on. "Sir William made an oath to always protect this castle. He swore he would return whenever it needed defending!"

"Why would it need defense now," Ardis asked cautiously, "in this day and age?"

"Morgan and I—as much as we hate to admit it—are getting on in years," Bruce replied. "Venwell, and the vast land and power that goes with it, is in danger of falling into the wrong hands."

"But Morgan has children," Ardis remarked, puzzled. "A son. And Gwynne, who still lives here."

Instead of offering further explanation, Bruce spoke with great earnestness, "It is just recently that I have begun to sense Sir William's presence. It is as if he has returned to help us avert some imminent danger."

"Ordinarily I would be afraid of ghosts," Ardis answered lightly, "but this Sir William seems very helpful."

"Make light of it, if you will," Bruce said. "But the secret to getting by successfully in this world is to never stop believing in spirits, in intervening powers, in miracles."

Bruce gave her one of those kindly smiles he could so easily assume. Besides the assistance she could give him, Ardis knew this old friend of her father's had summoned her to Scotland in part to help her get over her own personal tragedy. His next words convinced her of it. "I'm so glad you're here, Ardis. You will be renewed by a change of thought and scene. Shall we go inside now?"

"It's so pleasant here, Bruce," Ardis replied, wanting to be alone and think things over. "If you don't mind, I'll just stay in the garden for a while."

After Bruce left, Ardis seated herself on one of the wrought-iron chairs and gazed at the smooth, soaring outline of Venwell Castle. The sight of those thick, foreboding walls made her grateful for the peaceful, fragrant garden.

She watched the slow, preening motions of a peacock that wandered into the clearing. A soothing wind, carrying the salty scent of the North Sea, stirred through the branches of larch trees, sycamores, and Scots pine.

In the warming rays of the sun Ardis began to relax, feeling comfortable, even a little drowsy. She attempted to assess the situation. Bruce's enthusiasm had taken hold of his reason, but she believed she could find some way to convince him to turn the skull over to the local experts. Once the skull was properly examined, she might even be able to proceed with the facial reconstruction.

Still weary from the long plane ride, Ardis drew a deep breath and closed her eyes against the glare of late afternoon. Half dozing, she contemplated the possibility that Bruce could be right; the skull he had found might indeed belong to Sir William.

Old sorrows—new sorrows. What trouble was arising now to threaten Venwell Castle?

A chilling apprehension washed over Ardis. As if a shadow had fallen upon her, she sensed a presence. She thought perhaps Bruce had returned or sent his niece Gwynne to keep her company.

As Ardis' eyes opened, she glimpsed the figure of a man watching her through the trees. She had a blurred impression of green plaid through thick branches and slanting sunlight. The tartan made him look like someone who had stepped right out of the past, a warrior from another age dressed in kilt, ready for battle.

Ardis strained her eyes to see his features, but they remained indefinite, blended with the blotches of green foliage. She was aware only of eyes fastened upon her.

More startled than fearful, Ardis remained for a moment immobile. Was this apparition only a figment of her imagination, the product of jet-lag and the influence of Bruce's superstitious talk of Sir William's ghost?

Hearing the distinct rustling of branches caused her to rise, tense and alert. "Who's there?"

No one answered.

Ardis took a few steps forward. Her sudden movement must have taken the watcher by surprise. Before she could call out again, the form vanished.

To be continued …

CPSIA information can be obtained at www.ICGtesting.com
Printed in the USA
BVOW030335190412

287969BV00001B/263/P